FLIGHT OF THE TURNER

FLIGHT OF THE TURNER

SAMANTHA LEE HOWE

First published in the UK in 2026 by No Exit Press,
an imprint of Bedford Square Publishers Ltd,
London, UK

noexit.co.uk
@noexitpress

A Maxim Jakubowski book

ISBN
978-1-83501-336-6 (Paperback)
978-1-83501-337-3 (eBook)

2 4 6 8 10 9 7 5 3 1

Typeset in 10.8 on 13.5pt Garamond MT Pro
by Avocet Typeset, Bideford, Devon, EX39 2BP
Printed and bound in Great Britain by
CPI Group (UK) Ltd, Croydon CR0 4YY

The manufacturer's authorised representative in the EU for product safety is Easy Access System Europe, Mustamäe tee 50, 10621 Tallinn, Estonia
gpsr.requests@easproject.com

For Linzi

Prologue

London, September, 1946

JOAN PULLED OFF HER HEAVY GLOVES, STUFFING them into her coat pockets, before inserting the mortice key in the lock of the back door of the pub. It was five in the morning and she was weary. An autumn chill was nipping at her fingers, and dawn had barely peered through the darkness. It was dreary and unpleasant to be out this early but Joan had no choice. The pub cleaning job was the first of four she would do that day and Joan had to start early in order to make it through the next few gruelling hours.

She came into the kitchen, closing the door but finding little relief in the room, which was also cold. Even so, she removed her coat, hanging it up on the hook on the back of the door. She was cold, but she would soon work up a sweat and the bulky coat was restrictive when she was doing physical labour.

The small kitchen was in turmoil, with beer jugs and glasses stacked high and left unwashed. Joan sighed. The bar staff were supposed to wash up before they left at night but rarely ever did. She considered complaining to the day manager, but feared losing the job. The war hadn't been kind to her, and she had been left widowed, with three small mouths to feed, and no sign of the widow's pension she had been promised, which seemed to be tied up in red tape. She couldn't afford to lose even an hour of the work she did, which brought in just enough to make ends meet, but left nothing for emergencies.

Joan pushed away any irritation because it was pointless. There was nothing she could do. Her babies needed to be provided for, and it was the least she could do for all the bravery her stoic husband, John, had shown: he hadn't wanted to return to the western front on his last leave, it was almost as though he knew he would never return. Even now, Joan remembered the desperation of their last coupling – which had left her stranded with yet another mouth to feed. But little Betty gave her such delight, with the smile that so resembled her father's and the quiet acceptance in her young attitude that was so like Joan's.

Joan gave a smile thinking of little Betty, Stevie and Mary, all still tucked up in bed, with Joan's mum there to sort everything for them when they woke.

Joan filled a kettle and a large pan, putting them on the stove. She would need plenty of hot water if she was to get these glasses and jugs pristine and, of course, there would be the bar and tables which were often stained with sticky remnants of beer. While the water came to the boil, she began to tidy the kitchen. But as she drew closer to the door leading to the bar, she became aware of music coming from inside. She paused: it was unusual to hear the Wurlitzer playing when the place was closed. Joan shrugged, then turned back to the sink.

Not my business, she thought.

From the storage cupboard Joan pulled out the mop and bucket and picked up a carton of detergent before pushing open the door again between the kitchen and the space behind the bar.

Once the door was open, she could make out the song and the singer: *Surrender* by Perry Como was one of her favourite records. Joan paused and looked around the room, half expecting someone else to be there because the machine couldn't play on its own.

The bar area, however, was empty, as it should be at this time in the morning.

Joan went back in the kitchen and filled the bucket with the detergent and steaming hot water from the pan. She added a little cold water to the mix, enough to be able to put her hands in. The brass-covered bar surfaces would need a good clean, as would the tables around the room before she began to sweep and mop the floor. Nothing but the hottest, soapiest water could deal with that mess.

As she carried the bucket back into the bar, the song finished. There was silence but for the slight whirring of the machine as it stowed the record back in its bay, only to lift it again and place it back on the turnstile.

Joan placed down the bucket and came around the bar as Perry Como's voice echoed around the empty space. She reached the brightly lit machine – a dark-brown imposing gadget that held twenty-four discs – the latest thing the owner had installed and she suspected it was popular among the youngsters who frequented the pub. She had never paid much attention to the jukebox beyond polishing the glass and now she was at a loss as to how to turn it off.

She waited until the record finished before pulling the plug. She would have to leave a note for Rob, the manager, to say the thing was broken and explain what she had done. Although she wasn't sure he would be too happy with her decision, especially when she noticed the record hadn't returned completely to its bay.

Joan turned away, shrugging. 'Not my fault,' she said realising that Rob must have left it that way, even as he locked up for the night. He must have known it was stuck so why hadn't he done something about it?

Behind the bar, Joan took out a clean cloth from under the sink and dipped it in the bucket, wringing out the cloth before she began to clean the spills from the counter. Her hands stung with the hot water, years of hard graft had caused thick callouses to form on her palms and fingers, leaving them looking so much older than Joan's real age. But there was no time for vanity, survival, for her and the children was all she cared about, and maybe soon, with the widow's pension forthcoming, she would be able to ease off a little.

An hour later she was done in the main bar, she changed the water and made her way to the women's bathroom which would likely be an easier clean than the men's as it was little more than a single cubicle with a toilet in, but as she pressed down the handle, the door didn't budge. Joan pushed against it. This door was prone to swelling in the wet weather and it had been a damp month. She pressed her shoulder against the wood, giving every ounce of her slight weight until it shifted slightly.

Joan took a deep breath and tried one final push. The door gave; she fell forward into the cramped space.

A woman's body lay across the toilet, slumped against the wall.

'Oh good God!' Joan said, stepping back. Her shoe skidded slightly on the damp floor. She backed away, taking in what she saw, horrified by the sight, and not at all sure if the poor creature was alive or dead.

Turning and hurrying towards the front door to call for the local bobbies, Joan didn't even pause when she heard the jukebox firing up again and the sound of Perry Como filling the air. All she thought of was getting outside and raising the alarm.

She didn't see the figure behind her, a dark shadow emerging from the gentlemen's toilets, and only knew she wasn't alone when a hard object hit her in the back, followed by intense pain as the knife slid home.

A sharp shock. *Almost*, she thought, *like the bite of a snake*.

1

South Yorkshire, October, 1946

LADY MELINDA GREENWAY CAME INTO THE KITCHEN to find the cook, Mrs Weston, hard at work. Mel was soaked through from the unexpected downpour that had caught her and the gardener, Joseph, out on the lawn soon after they had finished deadheading the roses. The roses had survived so well that year because of this practice, and Mel was sure that with the continuing mild weather, they may yet get another bloom.

'Good heavens!' Mrs Weston said. 'Get to the fire before you catch your death!'

Unperturbed by a little rain, Mel smiled at the cook and took the offered towel, wiping her face and hair of the excess water.

'I wanted to talk about the dinner party,' Mel said.

'Everything is just as you asked for. A simple three-course dinner consisting of vegetable soup, a main of roast chicken breast in a pepper and cream sauce, and Daisy has just finished assembling the Victoria sponge cake. Mr Williams brought up some decent wines from the cellar and I think they are ready to be decanted in the dining room.'

'Perfect,' said Mel, her mind immediately organising all the items into a pattern for dinner which made her stomach growl slightly. 'But time is galloping on and I didn't expect to get wet today so I had better go and change. I confirmed how many would be attending?'

Mrs Weston nodded. 'The table is set for six. The bedrooms are made up for four guests. And I'll send Ruby and Toby to light the fires and warm the rooms shortly. It's chilly up there and the damp weather doesn't help.'

'You think of everything,' Mel said. 'I'm so grateful for you, especially with Mrs Felman in London with Laura and Jonathan.'

'When is his Lordship due back?' Mrs Weston asked. 'Only I thought it was soon.'

Mel's second cousin, Lord Jonathan Greenway and his wife, Lady Laura, were currently the custodians of Avonby, inheriting the title during the war after Mel's father, George, and her brother, Valentine, were killed in the blitz, along with Mel's mother, leaving her an orphan. They were all now away with the chauffeur Henry, and the housekeeper, Mrs Felman, at the Greenway London house.

'By all accounts the autumn season has been a lot of fun for them both. A proper introduction into society for their new status according to Jonathan's letters. It has especially been a triumph for Laura and they have decided to stay another week.'

Mrs Weston grew thoughtful, 'I'm glad you've reconnected with some old friends, but didn't you want to go with them? Do the balls and parties?'

'Oh no, none of that is for me. I'm much happier being at Avonby and it has been rather restful these last couple of months, especially after all that awful business with Ned and the poor wretch we found in the rose bed.'[1]

'Indeed,' Mrs Weston said, recalling the former farmhand's murder by his own uncle, and Mel's part in solving the case with Inspector Derrin Bradley. Life had returned to normal despite these awful events on the estate.

'Talking of Ned,' Mrs Weston said now, 'have you heard anything from Nancy?'

Mel smiled at the mention of their former scullery maid and fiancée of the late farmworker. 'She's settled into her new life well. It's quite something how she has taken to being a "woman of means" and running her own household in Sheffield.'

'Fancy Ned leaving a will like that. Taking care of the woman he

---

1 See *The Thorn in the Rose*

loved. It's so romantic!' said Daisy as she rounded the nook corner where the kitchen fireplace was positioned with an empty coal bucket in her hand.

'Is that fire stoked then?' Mrs Weston said. 'And stop eavesdropping girl and go and refill that bucket from the cellar.'

'Yes, Mrs Weston,' said Daisy and, with a nod in Mel's direction, she hurried off towards the cellar door to take care of the task.

'I'm happy for Nancy,' Mel said.

Mrs Weston nodded, before turning her attention back to the pan on the stove. She scooped out a spoonful of the warm vegetable soup and tasted it.

'A little more salt I think,' she said.

Mel picked an apple from the bowl in the centre of the huge kitchen table which served as both a communal eating place for the staff and an extra work surface when needed. Even now, the table held a pan of peeled potatoes and another with some green beans and carrots, ready to be made up for the main course. The fruit bowl was always kept full these days from the estate's own orchard which had now nicely recovered from the neglect of the war years and was yielding both cooking and eating apples. Therefore, Mel felt no guilt at biting into the apple and enjoying it as the first food she had eaten all day.

She experienced a twinge of nerves about the dinner. She hadn't asked Laura and Jonathan if she could have friends staying over, or host a small dinner party, but she didn't see why she shouldn't be able to when they were in London enjoying themselves and Mel, as always, was left running Avonby single handed. Not that she had any less of a workload when they were home, since Jonathan had all but abandoned any show of an effort where the estate was concerned. Mel did everything, and it was, she realised, just how she liked it. She loved Avonby and was proud of the estate and all the hard work she had put in to make it what it was today. Better in some ways than the pre-war days, because it was now a working farm, selling their own produce as well as using it to feed the estate.

She thought now of her old school friends. Clara Taylor-Smith, Eleanor Parkinson and her fiancé Charles Harris, not to mention

Michael Chase whom she hadn't seen for years because he moved to India with his parents when he was in his teens. Before the war, hanging out with Clara and Eleanor was comfortable, easy. She didn't know Charles of course, but she trusted Eleanor's taste in men as she was always the most sensible of the group and Mel couldn't imagine her choosing a future husband without due care and consideration.

The fifth guest was Inspector Derrin Bradley who she hadn't seen for a few weeks. He had been busy since they last spoke, after an argument had ensued that left them both wondering where their relationship was going. But her invitation to dinner had been accepted showing that Derrin was open to receiving an olive branch.

It was such a stupid argument, Mel thought now. She couldn't even recall how it started.

They had been discussing a case he was working on and something about her response had hit a raw nerve. After that Derrin had shut both her, and the conversation, down. They'd always been fiery, Mel knew that, but he'd always valued her opinion during the war and Mel didn't understand why that changed. Perhaps it was an ego thing, or maybe because he didn't want to put her in harm's way again. Either way, since then, they hadn't seen each other, though Derrin had called the house phone a couple of times showing he was willing to talk. It was a shame that on both occasions she had been out of the estate and missed the calls and her returned phone calls had found him unavailable also.

Ships that pass in the night, she thought now recalling Henry Wadsworth Longfellow's poem 'The Theologian's Tale', which appeared in *Tales of a Wayside Inn*, a well-thumbed copy of which was in Avonby's library. The metaphor was not lost on Mel as she and Derrin failed so often to negotiate common ground in any normal capacity, but somehow managed to come together during adversity. Mel wanted to change this pattern and whatever happened between them, be they friends or lovers, she did not want 'them' to be just *nothing*. Better they be enemies than that.

But we're not enemies, she thought, even though she wasn't sure what they were.

'I had better go and change,' Mel said aloud to no one in particular, but Mrs Weston nodded and Daisy, returning with a full bucket of coal, gave her a smile in acknowledgement.

Mel left the kitchen, going upstairs via the servants' staircase as she often did. It was, after all, the most convenient and discreet way of traversing the huge manor house.

Now on the second floor Mel passed her former bedroom, the old seamstress's room in which her cousin's wife, Laura, had placed her when she first arrived at Avonby in December 1945. So much had happened in those ten months, but only recently Jonathan had offered her a change of room and Mel had taken the switch because of the sheer practicality of having her own ensuite bathroom. She had smiled when Jonathan had shown her the new room. Having her own bathroom was a luxury that she hadn't expected.

Her new room was in the North Wing and further away from the stairs, But Mel loved the privacy this afforded, though she still felt some fondness for her former room because it had offered some security for the first time since she had been demobbed and unable to find work. For this reason, she had left the room with some regret.

As the staff of Avonby had helped her move her few possessions into the bigger room, Mel had seen Laura lurking at the end of the corridor and she knew she was peeved. She had done so much along the way to maintain Mel's precarious position in the household, but Jonathan's decision changed her status and Mel was firmly ensconced as a valued member of the family by the move.

Even so, Mel's relationship with Laura remained tense. Mel had made many attempts to befriend and win her over, but Laura was always distant and reserved. No matter how hard Mel tried, Laura never met her in the middle at any point, so Mel decided that she had to look outside of the household for some female friendship.

She had been considering how to do that, perhaps even to get more involved in the local parish, when she received the letter from Clara and Eleanor. They had communicated several more times, had a few phone calls and expressed a wish to meet up. With Jonathan and Laura away, it was the perfect opportunity to have a reunion dinner party.

Mel opened the door of her new room and glanced around. Jonathan had arranged for it to be decorated before he told her this would be hers. The walls were painted a pale blue and Mel had a big dressing table in solid oak with a huge mirror that had two side pieces of mirrored glass hinged to either side so that she could see her face from all angles. Despite this Mel rarely spent much time in front of the mirror and only occasionally used cosmetics, of which she did at least now have a few.

There was a tall and wide oak wardrobe that matched the dressing table and a chest of drawers in the room. Although the wardrobe was still quite empty, Mel had more clothing than she'd had even two months earlier as Jonathan's generosity now stretched to a clothing allowance. Mel didn't take any of this for granted, however, as she knew it was all part and parcel of being a member of the Greenway family and image to Jonathan — and especially Laura — was everything. They couldn't be seen to neglect this poor relation now that things were improving overall because of her help. Thanks to Mel, Avonby's farm was flourishing. There was a bounty of fresh produce that was now seasonally sold at the market and even sent out further afield to Sheffield and Manchester. Construction had started on a new, bigger greenhouse to house the growth of even more. Lettuce, tomatoes, carrots, green beans and cucumbers were already in production and they were growing way more than Avonby's occupants could eat. This, Mel knew, would increase tenfold when the new structure was completed, and it meant that some produce could be grown year-round instead of just at certain times of year as a result.

This was all possible because Jonathan had listened to Mel. She had pointed out that if Avonby was to survive, they had to diversify and do more. Mel, as the overseer, kept a tight rein on production and they had even hired some more full-time workers to help their aged gardener, Joseph, and his wife, Rosa, in their endeavours now that they needed a more commercial yield. Post war, homegrown fresh products were even more in demand and Joseph's experience was needed to guide the younger, fitter, team. Fortunately, the old retainer loved to share his knowledge and was proving to be a very nurturing mentor for their new employees and Mel wasn't worried at all that he might be overdoing things, in fact, Joseph was showing a great deal of enthusiasm and energy for the task which had given him something of a new lease of life.

Mel stripped away her work clothes and went into the bathroom to wash, after which she began to prepare for the evening. Wrapped in a towel she sat down at her dressing table and ran a comb through her rapidly drying hair. Then she put a few curlers in to regain control, before applying a modicum of rouge to give her cheeks a warmer glow and her lips a little blush.

It wasn't a very formal affair, but Mel suspected that her guests, travelling all the way from London, would probably make some effort. Especially Clara and Eleanor who were always so fashionable before the war. At the very least the men would be in tuxedos and the women, evening dresses. With this in mind, Mel pulled out a sophisticated blue satin dress from her wardrobe and lay it on her new double bed. Would this be the thing to wear? She wasn't sure, not having done much in the line of socialising of late. But the dress was lovely, simple and elegant as she was not one for frills and flounces. *Yes.* It would be perfect and she would feel comfortable too.

Even in the north wing the distant echo of the doorbell ringing reached Mel. With a twinge of apprehension, Mel realised that the first of her guests had arrived. She had left instructions to show them to their rooms in the guest suites over in the south wing and knew that this would be actioned by Mr Williams, the butler, and the footman, Toby.

She took a deep breath, catching sight of herself in the mirror. Had she changed so much since they last saw her? Not that much physically, she realised, with the hard work on the farm keeping her figure from expanding, she still had that youthful look. But what of the others? She hadn't seen either of her friends since the night of the blitz when her parents and brother had died and she met Derrin for the first time.

How the world continues to turn and somehow we come full circle, she thought.

Despite her nerves, Mel continued getting ready, knowing that everything else was being taken care of by the very capable, and well-trained, employees of Avonby Hall.

2

'This is lovely,' said Eleanor as she came into the grand hallway of Avonby Hall.

'Indeed,' said Charles.

'I'll show you to your rooms Miss Parkinson and Mr Harris,' Williams said. 'Please follow me.'

'And my chauffeur?' Charles said.

'No problem, sir, we have a room ready for him in the servant's quarters,' Williams said.

'Very good,' Charles said nodding his approval.

Mr Williams and Toby took the small overnight cases and their garment bags and led the two guests up the main staircase.

'Is anyone else here?' Eleanor asked.

'Miss Taylor-Smith is already here, but Mr Chase hasn't arrived yet,' Williams said.

'Very good. Thank you,' said Eleanor.

'Here's your room, Miss Parkinson,' Williams said opening the door. 'Mr Harris is just across the hall and the bathroom is the second door on the left.'

Williams placed her case down on a blanket at the bottom of the huge bed, then left to take Charles to his room, closing the door behind him.

Left alone, Eleanor looked around. The room was beautifully furnished with a modern dressing table and matching chest of drawers and wardrobe. Her feet sank into the luxurious carpet, and there was a smell of fresh paint still lingering, as though the decorator had left just moments before her arrival.

On a small table by the window was a bowl of fresh apples and a jug of fresh water with a crystal tumbler. She noticed an envelope propped up against the fruit bowl and walked towards the window.

She picked up the envelope and opened it, pulling out a piece of paper that smelt of fresh lavender. The note had the most beautiful handwriting, which she recognised as Mel's. Eleanor had always envied Mel's penmanship which she took in first before reading the words.

Dear Eleanor,
Welcome to Avonby. I'm looking forward to seeing you.
Drinks will be at six. Dinner served at seven.
Mel

She read the short note a few times, before returning it to the envelope. There was little formality in the short letter showing how much Mel had changed since they last met.

The bed was covered in a luxurious throw of blue velvet and plump cushions. It promised comfort and looked inviting. Eleanor was tired from the journey and was tempted to take a lie down, but she knew Charles would want her to be ready on time so instead she opened her case and began to pull out the two dresses she had brought with her. One was a calf length black satin dress with a drop waist and the other a more traditional full-length empire line in peach chiffon. Both formal – but which was more impressive? What did one wear at a dinner party in a place like this? Thank heavens she had suggested Charles bring a morning suit and a tuxedo. Even now, she wasn't sure which it should be in this situation and formalities had changed so much in the last few years, sometimes more relaxed, and others far less so, it was hard to know.

Worried, she decided to go and speak to Charles to make sure she made the right decision. She was always worried about *faux pas*, and Charles always knew the right thing to do in any given situation. As she opened the door to her room, she found herself face to face with a man she didn't recognise.

'Eleanor!' he said immediately.

'*Michael?*'

'You haven't changed a bit old girl,' he said.

Eleanor laughed, feeling awkward and somewhat nervous as Michael certainly had changed, she could barely recognise the gangly teenage boy he had once been in this sophisticated man, with his modern haircut and expensive suit. He gave her a smile and then Eleanor saw a glimmer of her former friend and smiled back.

'Have you just arrived?'

'Yes,' Michael said. 'I thought I'd freshen up before changing.'

'Can I ask, would it be morning suit or tuxedo?' Eleanor said. 'I'm not sure how formal Mel is these days.'

'Tux,' Michael said. 'If in doubt.'

'Thank you! I'll see you downstairs at six,' Eleanor said.

Michael left in search of the bathroom and Eleanor headed across the corridor to find Charles's room to make sure he agreed that this was the right attire.

* * *

Mel was in the hallway ready to greet everyone when Eleanor and Charles made their way downstairs. She looked up, seeing the handsome couple, Charles in a tuxedo and Eleanor in the black, long-sleeved satin dress, which showed she still had an interest in modern fashion.

She always was stylish, Mel thought. She was relieved at her own choice of dress, which wasn't at all below par.

The couple reached the bottom of the stairs and there was a little awkwardness until Eleanor hurried forward and embraced Mel. Mel squeezed her back and at the same time wondered if this was the first time they had ever hugged each other. It wasn't a thing one did pre-war, but formalities had changed and Mel was glad of it. It was nice to be held, and it got rid of any discomfort they might have felt otherwise.

'And this is my fiancé Charles,' Eleanor said.

'It's great to meet you,' Mel said, shaking Charles's hand.

'Strong grip,' Charles observed and, embarrassed, Mel let go of his fingers.

'And here's Clara and… *Michael?*' Mel said looking back up the stairs.

The doorbell rang and Mel knew then that the final guest, her former wartime colleague, Inspector Derrin Bradley, had arrived and the evening could begin in earnest. She experienced a flutter in her stomach as Williams went to answer the door and she led everyone into the drawing room where Toby waited with a tray full of cocktails.

'Martini anyone?' she asked.

Michael was the first to reach the tray and he began to pass out the drinks to the ladies, before he and Charles finally took theirs.

'Excuse me for a moment,' Mel said. 'Please make yourselves comfortable.'

She went back into the hallway, just as Derrin, now relieved of his coat and hat, was walking towards her.

'I'm really glad you came,' she said.

'I've been meaning to catch up with you. You look beautiful,' he said.

'Thank you,' she said with a little smile. 'You look very handsome. Tuxedo suits you.'

Derrin took her hand and kissed her fingers, then his eyes skipped away from hers as they caught sight of someone standing at the drawing-room door.

'And who is this?' asked Clara.

'I had better make all the introductions,' said Mel turning around. 'Derrin this is Clara, Clara this is former First Lieutenant, now Inspector, Derrin Bradley.'

Derrin shook hands with Clara who gave him a flirty smile.

'Do go in and get a drink, I need to just confer with Mr Williams,' Mel said. 'I won't be a moment.'

Williams was looking awkward and loitering by the dining room door.

'Is something wrong?' she asked.

'We've had to make up two extra beds in the servants' quarters, Miss Taylor-Smith brought a maid with her and Mr Harris and Miss Parkinson came with a chauffeur. I've put the maid in with Daisy for now, but she wasn't happy with having to share with one of the house servants and protested her displeasure.'

'Ah. Clara didn't mention her maid and I wasn't expecting a chauffeur as I thought they were all coming by train and then taxi,' Mel said.

'Mr Chase did,' Williams confirmed. 'But Mr Harris seemed very attached to his driver and his Rolls-Royce.'

'Mmmm. Well, thank you for sorting the problems for now. Let me know if there is anything further. Can you make sure they are given refreshments?'

'Yes Lady Melinda,' said Williams.

3

Introductions made, and cocktails consumed, the group was ushered into the dining room for dinner. The large formal room was resplendent with Avonby's best china and crystal and highly polished silver candelabras positioned in the centre of the table with lit candles illuminating the room and creating the perfect mood.

Mr Williams and Toby have done Avonby proud, Mel thought.

Wine glasses were generously filled by Williams and Toby as they moved around the table. Ruby brought out warm, fresh bread rolls and salty butter and each guest had a bowl of Mrs Weston's delicious soup placed before them. Mel noticed that no one reached for extra salt as the broth was perfectly seasoned. She ate hers with slow dignity, mindful not to mop up her plate with her bread – leaving the barracks firmly behind her.

'Michael has spent the last few years in India,' Mel said to kick start the conversation between courses.

'How long were you there?' asked Charles.

'About fourteen years. My father was a brigadier and was posted over there,' he said.

'I remember,' said Clara. 'We were all sad when you left.'

'Indeed. We were inseparable at the time,' Michael said.

'We'd have been the original *Famous Five* if we had a dog between us,' Eleanor laughed.

A general titter ran around the table, dampened down by the entrance of Williams and Toby with the main course.

'I didn't really want to go to India,' Michael said, while Williams and Toby served chicken, vegetables and gravy. 'Even so, I enjoyed my time there. It's very different from the way we live in England.'

'Hotter, for a start, I shouldn't wonder!' said Charles.

Michael smiled. 'Very much so. But you get used to it. I was referring to the less formal behaviour of colonials though. Except for my father who was a stickler for propriety.'

'To parents and propriety,' Charles said raising his glass.

Eleanor reached for Michael's hand, feeling awkward. 'I'm sorry Michael… About your father.'

'Well, it's brought me home, so please don't be. And if this reunion is anything to go by, then I'm quite pleased now about being here.'

'Mel's parents…' Eleanor looked awkward by the conversation.

'Mine were killed in the blitz,' Mel said. 'But then there are always silver linings. That's the night I met Derrin.'

'Oh! You're the lieutenant that rescued Mel from the wreckage!' Clara said.

'Oh no,' Derrin said. 'No one would ever need to rescue Mel.'

'And that,' said Michael, 'is definitely worth raising a glass to!'

Questions abounded around the table as Mel's friends were curious about the past few years and her wartime activities.

'You'd never believe that this "delicate flower" could brain a man twice her size with a wrench,' Derrin said.

They were still subject to the Official Secrets Act, and Mel observed how Derrin, his tongue loosened by the wine, was enjoying telling the tale of one of their escapades without giving any names or real detail. He was more relaxed than she had been and it made her happy to see him enjoy such congenial company.

'No!' said Clara but her eyes gleamed with interest and a new respect for Mel.

'Me? *Delicate*?' laughed Mel.

The table erupted in mirth along with more tales from Clara and Eleanor about Mel's childhood exploits.

'Do you remember when she sent the milkman's son packing when he tried to kiss her?' Eleanor said to Michael. 'You wanted to punch him on the nose but Mel said, "don't worry, I know exactly how to deal with his sort". And she took care of him.'

Micheal shook his head neither agreeing with nor denying the story.

'What did you do?' Derrin asked.

Mel gave him a demure look. 'I'm sure you can guess.'

Clara began to giggle, 'You gave him "a kick in the crunchies", didn't you, Mel?'

The table erupted in a raucous bout of laughter that made Mel feel, for the first time since she left the army, that she was able to say exactly what she wanted and there would be no judging. She was among friends. She relaxed into her chair, all sign of formality gone.

She found Derrin's amused gaze on her from across the table and felt a slight flush colouring her cheeks at the scrutiny and the slight gleam in his eyes. At the time, neither Clara or Eleanor had understood what 'the crunchies' were but the terminology had still brought them all to fits of laughter for what it obviously implied.

'You were a bit of a Tomboy, then?' Charles asked. 'Hard to imagine now as you're so ladylike.'

Mel guffawed at the thought of being 'ladylike'.

'Well, we all grow into ourselves eventually,' Michael said.

'Yes indeed,' said Mel, grateful for his comments. 'And look at you now. I hardly recognised you. I'm very glad you reached out when you came back to England though.'

'Why did you come back?' Derrin asked.

'Changes in the country's government. The next year, I believe, will see the full evacuation of all British patriots,' Michael said.

'Mmm. Yes of course, Admiral Lord Louis Mountbatten is the Viceroy of India…' Charles mentioned. 'I heard about his position in this.'

'That's right,' said Michael. 'My father believed he will be the person to resolve the issues the British Government has in giving India what it needs – independence. But I do not want to bore any of you with foreign politics.'

The conversation switched when the beautifully iced Victoria sponge cake was brought in and despite protestations of watching their figures, both Clara and the very lean Eleanor had a piece and enjoyed it. They were feeling comfortable around their old friends and the anxiety of suspected awkwardness and formality had left. To Mel it felt as if the years between seeing them had never happened. Was it really that awful night at Susan's house when they'd been celebrating Mel's nineteenth birthday that she saw them last? Michael much longer of course. But the only difference was that he was less natural and open than he used to be. She had always seen him as perhaps her closest friend before he had left for India, but now their maturity and different life experiences created a crevice that was perhaps too deep and too wide to traverse. Plus, as a man now, and not a boy, their friendship couldn't be as simple as it once was. Though Mel regretted this, as friendship with him was something she would enjoy again.

'You never mentioned,' Derrin said, 'when or how you got in touch with Michael?'

'It was a complete coincidence. I bumped into Clara at the train station. She told me you were having a reunion. And here we all are!' Michael said.

'You were very welcome to join us Michael,' Mel said. 'We miss Susan… who couldn't make it, but with the gang, mostly, back together, the world does appear to be coming right again.'

There were murmurs of agreement around the table and Mel caught Derrin's eye. He had gone quiet, stopped drinking and appeared a little sullen compared to his earlier joviality. She forced her face to remain passive but his change in mood did give her pause for concern. What was it that had upset him?

'Shall we all go in the study for brandy?' Mel suggested.

'Oh, thank heavens you didn't suggest the men retiring to the study and ladies staying here,' Michael said. 'That's something no one does in India and it has been such a bore since I got back. I mean, the ladies are the greatest fun at most gatherings.'

'If my cousins were home, I'm afraid that might be the case here too. But as you see, formality isn't my strong suit.'

* * *

'That will be all tonight,' Mel said to Mr Williams as the guests settled into the study sofas, crystal glasses in their hands.

'Very good Lady Melinda,' Williams said.

When the butler left Clara said, 'It's very strange hearing you referred to as "Lady Melinda".'

'I know. I ask them all to call me Mel but it's hard to change the years of old-fashioned habits that have been ingrained through service to the Greenways.'

'Even so, Avonby suits you, Mel,' Eleanor said. 'You seem very at home.'

'I am. I love it here. Love taking care of the land. Love the house. It is, after all, my ancestral home, even though I never thought I'd live in it.'

'Didn't you?' asked Clara. 'Only I thought your father was next in line?'

Mel nodded. 'He was, yes. But my brother Valentine would have inherited from him, not me. A family custom, leaving everything to the next eligible male, which is why Jonathan now holds the title.'

'That's an incredible piece,' Michael said changing the subject. 'Turner?'

The group's attention was drawn to the painting above the fireplace.

'You know your art, Michael. And yes, it is a Turner. Jonathan loves that painting. It does have something. The ship. The storm. The atmosphere… He looks at it for hours sometimes.'

'Well, I know nothing about art,' said Charles. 'But this brandy is superb! I don't suppose your cousin has any cigars?'

'On the desk,' Mel said. 'Help yourself.'

'Any more wine, Mel? I'll confess I have no tolerance for hard liquor,' Eleanor said.

Mel stood up. 'Of course. I'll fetch some from the cellar.'

'I'll come with you,' Derrin said.

They left the study and made their way down to the kitchen via the servants' stairs. At the bottom of the steps, they heard voices in the kitchen, and through the slightly ajar door Mel saw Mrs Weston slicing up the remains of the Victoria sponge, before handing it out to Williams, Toby, Ruby and Daisy. She then noticed the two new faces sitting opposite from them. One was a man in his early forties, with a very serious expression and a younger, tiny girl, who was smiling widely at Toby who was oblivious to her obvious interest in him. She knew that these were the maid and chauffeur that Williams had told her about, and was glad to see them being taken care of. The maid appeared to be getting on with everyone, though she spoke very quietly, and appeared to be quite shy.

Mel and Derrin didn't interrupt the small group. Instead, Mel picked up a bunch of keys from a hook beside the boot room door and taking them with her she pushed open the unlocked cellar door. At the top of the stairs, she flicked on the light switch. The cellar staircase illuminated with stark electric light coming from bare bulbs hanging from the ceiling. Closing the door behind them, Mel and Derrin went down into the harshly lit cavern.

'You seem to know your way around every part of this house,' Derrin observed.

'There is not a corner in Avonby that I haven't explored,' she said.

'You meant it when you said you love it here, didn't you?'

'Yes. I did. I do.'

'I'm glad you're happy Mel,' Derrin said.

At the bottom of the stairs, Mel pushed open another door. They passed through the coal store and to the wine cellar door, which Mel now unlocked with the key. The door opened onto a wide room which was lined with wine shelves – covered with excellent wines and some bottles of French cognac.

Mel began to examine the bottles, carefully selecting a few. Derrin took any she chose and gathered them in his arms.

'Thank you. We'll get some fresh glasses from the cabinet in the dining room,' she said. 'There's also a corkscrew in the drawer in there.'

'I'm not sure we need this many bottles, though,' said Derrin.

Mel laughed. 'It's nice to have a choice. I suspect Charles and

Michael have some knowledge of fine wines and I would like them to be happy with what I present.'

'Your friends are fun,' Derrin said.

'I wasn't sure how the evening would pan out. It could have been awkward. Thank you for coming. I wanted to…'

'There's no need,' Derrin said. 'We were both in the wrong. It is time we stopped being at loggerheads all the time. And, I know I can be an arse at times.'

Mel laughed, 'We both can be.'

She grew thoughtful.

'It seems we are always fighting, unless we have a mystery to solve. Why is that?'

Derrin shook his head. 'I'm not sure. Mel…'

A sound came from the coal store behind them and Derrin fell silent. Mel listened as she heard the subtle movement of the coal pile.

'It'll be someone getting coal for the fires,' Mel said but her voice dropped to a quieter pitch, as though she didn't want whoever it was to discover them there.

Derrin nodded.

'We'll talk when everyone goes to bed, if you are willing to stay that long?' Mel said.

'Of course. I want things to be right between us,' Derrin said.

They made their way out of the cellar on the heels of the person who had been in the coal store. A large piece of coal rolled from the top of the pile, coming to a stop at the bottom.

They heard the door at the top of the stairs open, the light switched off and the door closed.

'Damn!' said Derrin as they were plummeted into darkness.

Mel shuffled across the floor, her foot kicking a piece of coal as she went, and felt around the wall at the bottom of the staircase. Very soon the light was back on.

'This sort of thing happens a lot, so we put another switch in down here.'

'Sensible,' Derrin said.

Back in the study, after much deliberation of which bottle to open, Mel filled Eleanor, Clara and Michael's wine glasses.

'What about you?' Mel asked Charles, but he shook his head.

'Still savouring this delicious brandy,' Charles said.

Once cigars were smoked, the group decanted back into the drawing room to play bridge. Mel left the empty wine bottle on the mantelpiece with a plan to dispose of it in the morning, and brought the remaining, as yet unopened, bottles into the drawing room with them.

After an intense card game, in which she learnt that Eleanor, Clara and Charles were very competitive, the electric lamps in the room cut out and the room was tipped into a semi-darkness, only illuminated by the fire still burning in the hearth.

Eleanor yelped in surprise.

'A power cut?' Clara said.

'Strange,' Mel said. 'That's never happened before.' She took some candles and matches from the cabinet drawer and lit them. 'I need to go check the meter. It's probably a fuse in the distribution board.'

'Oh, shouldn't you call someone for that?' Eleanor said.

'No. It's okay. I can fix it.'

'Probably best we all call it a night anyway,' Michael suggested. 'I don't know about the rest of you, but I'm a little worn now. And it is late.'

Mel glanced at the clock on the mantle it was almost midnight. Late, but it could have been later.

* * *

As the others were left to find their way, candles in hand, back to their rooms, Mel and Derrin went to the electricity meter under the stairs.

Passing her candle to Derrin, Mel opened the fuse box.

'The fuses look fine,' Mel said.

'Maybe it is a power cut,' Derrin said.

'I thought those days were behind us.'

'Could be an issue at the power station,' Derrin said. 'Is Avonby connected to Templeborough or has it been transferred over to Mexborough?'

'I think they transferred us soon after the Mexborough station opened, before my time here, though so I'm not certain,' Mel said.

'Mmm. Mexborough may have an outage,' Derrin said.

'I think I need that brandy,' Mel said. 'And our talk now everyone has gone to bed.'

Holding the candle, Mel led the way through the now quiet house. The only sound was the steady ticking of the grandfather clock in the hallway – which had just struck midnight – and the sounds the old house made when it was cooling down in the night. All familiar noises to Mel and she was at home walking the halls with nothing but a candle to light the way. She often traversed Avonby's corridors in the dark or by candlelight to avoid waking anyone when she couldn't sleep.

They reached the study door and found it ajar. Mel paused. She was sure she had closed the door after the party had moved back to the drawing room.

She put her hand on the dark oak and pushed the door open wide. As they entered, the candlelight cast a dull glow into the room which Mel found soothing. She placed the candelabra down on the desk by the brandy decanter and promptly poured generous amounts into the two remaining clean crystal glasses on the tray. She picked them up and turned to Derrin, handing him one of the glasses.

The fire in the hearth gave off a healthy glow and Mel made her way towards one of the chairs that flanked the fireplace. She sat down, and was about to take a sip of her drink when she glanced up at the painting. Mel placed her untouched glass down on the table.

'Derrin,' she said.

'What is it?'

'The Turner is gone.'

4

ᴅᴇʀʀɪɴ ʀᴀɪsᴇᴅ ᴛʜᴇ ᴄᴀɴᴅᴇʟᴀʙʀᴀ ᴀɴᴅ ᴡɪᴛʜ ᴛʜᴇ glow of the candlelight they could see the mantle and the frame above more clearly. The picture had been cut roughly around the edges leaving the frame still in place, with a few tufts of the canvas in one of the corners. The bottle Mel had left on the mantle had been tipped over and the rim was smashed, along with a glass that had been left there, obviously done in the middle of the theft which could only have happened within the last twenty minutes or so.

'We need to lock down the house, immediately!' Derrin said.

'We can't do that. It would be holding people against their will.'

'Are you prepared to risk them getting away?' Derrin said.

Mel hesitated. Derrin was a police inspector, he had the authority, even if she didn't. She couldn't see any other option than what he was suggesting.

'No. Jonathan would be devasted and… I really don't know what my position here will be if the painting isn't found. It's valuable. Perhaps priceless because it is impossible to replace.'

'All right,' Derrin said. 'Then you agree, we have to move quickly?'

'What do you want to do first?'

'I'll go and fetch Mr Williams, and make sure he locks all external doors downstairs. We'll check all windows and doors to see if they've been tampered with. When I get back, we'll secure the rest of the house.'

'How do you know the culprit hasn't already fled?' Mel said.

'My guess is they hoped to do that while we all slept,' Derrin said. 'To leave now would expose them to us immediately.'

'I can't argue with that reasoning,' Mel said.

'As to the power going off… what's your thoughts on that score?' Derrin asked.

'It was likely to be a coincidence as there was no sign of deliberate sabotage,' Mel said. 'But even so, it may have spurred the thief to act sooner once they realised our fun was curtailed and everyone was going to bed.'

Derrin left the study to fetch Williams, and Mel looked around the room for further clues. The windows were all locked, something she knew Williams would have done while they were at dinner. Only Mel, Williams and Mrs Feltman had keys to those windows and she was sure Mrs Feltman's were either with her in London or locked inside her office downstairs.

She glanced at the wall around the frame and studied the frame itself. There were no obvious fingerprints which meant the thief knew what they were doing and had most likely worn gloves. So, nothing the police could get from the frame itself.

Williams and Derrin came into the study. Williams looked flustered and somewhat untidy, as though he'd thrown his clothing on in a hurry, which Mel suspected he had since the servants had retired hours ago.

'We're fully locked up downstairs and all staff are accounted for,' he said.

'What about the maid and the chauffeur?'

'The girl went to help her mistress undress when the lights went off,' Williams said.

'I sent Toby and Daisy to round up everyone else,' Derrin said. 'And the chauffeur is in the hallway now with Ruby and Mrs Weston.'

'The front door is locked?' Mel asked.

'Yes. And no one but me and you have the key,' Williams said, confirming what Mel already knew.

'Get our guests down here,' Mel said. 'The inspector and I are going to lock up the entire house. No one gets out until we find the painting.'

Williams went off to make sure that the guests were all brought to the hallway.

Shortly after he left, Daisy and Toby arrived with Clara, Eleanor and the young maid.

'Everyone, come into the study,' Derrin said. 'I want everyone who was in the house in the same room.'

'But…' said Toby.

'No buts. *Everyone*,' Derrin said.

'Lady Melinda,' Daisy said, 'Are we suspects?'

Mel was about to say 'no' but Derrin cut across her.

'Until that painting is found, everyone is a suspect,' Derrin said.

Daisy's mouth shaped a shocked 'O' but she said nothing more as Williams appeared with Charles and Micheal and they were all ushered back into the study.

Now that everyone was accounted for, guests and staff alike were told to sit down and make themselves comfortable. The room was full of candles which the various occupants had brought with them and these added a great deal of light to the study and the obviously empty picture frame.

'I'll stay here,' Derrin said. 'Take Mr Williams and make sure every door and window in the entire house is secure.'

Mel nodded. She picked up her original candelabra and led Williams from the room.

Starting from the bottom of the house they worked their way through every room, locking windows and double bolting all outside doors until they reached the top of the house and made sure that the attic door was locked and secured. The lock was somewhat rusted and so Mel knew it hadn't been used in a long time, certainly not that day. And so, they didn't attempt to open it as there was no point.

Back downstairs, Derrin took Williams's keys from him.

'You'll stay here too, Mr Williams,' Derrin said. 'I'm going to lock the study door and Lady Mel and I, with Toby, are going to search the rooms.'

A spew of protests came out of the mouths of Mel's guests.

'Surely you don't think we are responsible…' Eleanor said. 'We're your guests!'

'Yes and you are strangers in this house,' Derrin said, so that Mel wouldn't have to. 'Everyone is a suspect until that painting is found and returned to its proper place.'

'This is outrageous,' said Charles. 'I must insist…'

'Oh, sit down old bean,' said Michael. 'The sooner we let them search, the sooner we can all go to bed. I'm flaked and so are the ladies.'

With that Michael sank down into one of the chairs by the fire and curled up into the side headrest and promptly closed his eyes.

Mel was quiet for a moment and then she nodded to Derrin and asked Toby to follow them.

As she locked the study door, Toby said, 'You don't think it's one of us, do you, Lady Melinda?'

'I hope it isn't one of our own. That would be awful. For now, we just have to do what Inspector Bradley says and search the house hoping we find the painting.'

'Top or bottom?' Derrin said.

'Let's start in the servants' quarters, that way we can quickly rule them out and they can go about their business,' Mel said.

'You can look in my room any time, Lady Mel,' Toby said.

'We'll start there then,' said Derrin.

They all hurried down the stairs and the detailed search began with Toby's room and followed on to all the others. Including Mrs Felton's office which had been locked since the housekeeper went away with Lady Laura and Lord Jonathan.

'But just in case the culprit had access,' said Derrin. 'We have to rule it out.'

After Toby's room was cleared, as well as Daisy's, Mrs Westons, and Mr Williams's room, they were left with Ruby's.

Before entering the room, Mel took a breath. She hoped she wouldn't find anything in the room because Ruby had only just rejoined the family's service following her flight from the former butler Aidan Peters. Peters was currently in gaol awaiting trial for the murder of both his wife and Avonby's farmhand Ned, as well as an attempt on Mel's life and the head gardener Joseph. Peters had terrorised Ruby into leaving Avonby, but with the help of the estate chauffeur, Henry, she had been hiding from the man, fearful for her life. To find anything negative now about Ruby might not only jeopardise her position as a witness but would be devastating to the family. It would make it far more difficult for them to place their trust in a new servant going forward. It was hard enough to find good staff as it was.

Mel pushed the door open and they entered Ruby's room. It was a small room with a single bed. This had been slept in, but the covers were neatly pulled back into place. There was a jug beside the bed with a single rose in a little water. Mel glanced at Toby and even in the dull candlelight noticed a small blush fill his young cheeks. So, he and Ruby were potentially involved? Or perhaps Toby had hopes of being?

'Wait outside,' Mel suggested.

Derrin glanced at Toby getting the message immediately that Mel was trying to convey. He shouldn't be in the girl's room under the circumstances.

They searched through Ruby's meagre possessions, she had a few Sunday clothes, but mostly the small wardrobe contained just uniforms. There was a bible on her dressing table, and another small book. Ruby, it seemed, liked to read Jane Austen and inside the copy of *Emma* was a pressed flower bookmark which indicated that she was almost at the end of the novel.

Mel placed the book back down on the dressing table. She wondered if Ruby had read all of Austen's novels.

Finding nothing else of any importance in the room, Derrin and Mel left and found an embarrassed Toby waiting outside.

'It's my fault. Please don't sack Ruby!'

'Whatever do you mean?' Mel said.

'The book. I borrow them for her. But we always put them back when she's read them,' Toby said.

'I can't begrudge anyone a book to read, Toby. Let's say no more about it. It's not a problem.'

Derrin said nothing as he followed Mel and Toby to the next room. Within a short time, they had cleared all the servants' rooms and even the visiting maid and chauffeur's belongings showed nothing to be suspicious of.

The ground floor rooms were combed with no luck. Then Mel, Derrin and Toby went up to the first floor and slowly worked their way through the many bedrooms, some of which were quicker to clear than others. But they found a routine of what and where to check first and were soon speeding up their search which included all the visiting guests' bedrooms. Mel even insisted that Derrin and Toby check her room. There was no sign of the Turner and Mel was losing hope that they would get it back.

'What are we to do?' asked Mel.

'I'll call the station,' Derrin said and then he went to the phone which was positioned near the front door and picked up the receiver.

'The line's dead,' he said.

'Do you think it's the power outage?' Mel asked.

'If the power's out everywhere, then the exchange won't be working either,' Derrin said.

'I suppose you could go to the station,' Mel said. 'Fetch some help?'

'I'm not leaving you alone here until we've found the culprit,' Derrin said. 'They could be dangerous if they feel desperate enough.'

Mel gave a small smile. Normally she would be angered by his tone but she knew it was coming from a good place and after all they had been through at Avonby, another crime to solve wasn't as welcome a distraction as she might have thought.

'I feel responsible,' said Mel. 'I opened the house to veritable strangers. And now Jonathan's prized painting is gone. Even so, I hate to think it is one of them. Is my judgement so poor these days?'

'You can't blame yourself, Jonathan can hardly talk with friends like Lord Stanley,' Derrin said.

'Lord Stanley wasn't a thief, he was just a cad,' said Mel. 'But yes, not a great example of good judgement in Jonathan's case either.'

Mel fell quiet. Her mind flicking briefly back to Lord Stanley's attempts at seducing her. She wondered now if Derrin bringing him up meant he was a little jealous. It showed he still held a grudge if nothing else. Such emotion of course would be wasted as Stanley was long out of the equation and had never been of interest to Mel in the first place. Though she suspected he was just the first in a line of men that Lady Laura would encourage in her direction, to rid Avonby of a pesky relative that she had never wanted living with them. Mel suppressed these awful thoughts, realising they were mean as she had no proof that Laura felt that way about her. She reassured herself that she had been useful and had freed Jonathan from the estate duties that he just hadn't enjoyed.

'Should we at least let our staff out now that they have been cleared?' Mel said bringing her mind back to the problem at hand.

'I suppose so. But I think I need to interview your visitors and learn much more about them than the social side.'

The three of them reached the study and Mel put the key in the door and turned the lock. Within seconds the door was pulled open and an irate Charles Harris was facing them.

'How dare you leave us locked up like animals!' he said, his face ruddy with anger and frustration.

'Please step back inside Mr Harris,' Derrin said.

Charles looked as though he would become apoplectic any second but Eleanor reached him, placing her hand on his arm. 'Darling it is all right; the door is unlocked now. All is well and soon this misunderstanding will be cleared up.'

Her words had a calming effect and Charles deflated and stepped back. Derrin and Mel came back into the room, at which point, Mel took in where everyone had chosen to sit, considering what it meant. Her eyes fell on the Avonby employees who were all huddled together in the furthest corner, ostracised from the former guests, turned suspects.

'Mrs Weston. Ruby. Daisy. Mr Williams and of course, Toby. You are all free to go about your business,' Mel said. 'I recommend you retire and get some rest.'

'Thank you Lady Mel,' said Mrs Weston. 'We can make some cocoa for everyone first. It's been a trying hour while you were gone.'

Mrs Weston glanced at Charles and Eleanor who were talking now in whispered tones in the corner of the room.

'Thought he was going to explode,' Ruby whispered to Mel as she passed.

Mel looked at Charles and frowned.

'Cocoa would be good, Mrs Weston,' Mel said.

The servants left the room but before departing Mr Williams said, 'I'm happy to be on hand, Lady Melinda.'

Mel nodded her thanks and Williams took up post just outside the study.

'I think I need to interview each of you,' Derrin said. 'There is a gap between Mel and me checking the electricity meter and you all dispersing supposedly to your rooms for the night. During that time, this painting was cut from the frame, taken and hidden. It must be somewhere in the house and, since there is no sign of any forced entry from outside, one of you must have taken it. And unless that person is willing to step forward now, then you'll be stuck here until we find the thief.'

'Well really!' Clara said. 'We're guests in this house, how you could possibly accuse us of theft! It is outrageous.'

'And that, my dear Clara, is exactly what a thief might say,' said Mel. 'Sit down. All of you. Inspector Bradley is right. One of you took the Turner. We need to know where it is and why you did it.'

'But what if it's not someone here?' Eleanor said. 'It could have been an intruder! I hardly think one of us…'

'The house it locked up as a matter of course every evening. There is no sign of forced entry and therefore we have no reason to believe there has been an intruder, or that anyone outside of this room is involved,' Mel explained. 'I don't suppose one of you will own up, as the inspector suggested, and end this charade?'

Mel looked around the room and, as they sank onto the sofas and chairs they had previously all occupied, she noted Eleanor's shocked silence, Charles's seething anger, Clara's frustration and Michael's somewhat bored indifference. Except for Charles, who she had only just met, Mel had once seen the group as friends but had to view them all in a different light. They were suspects, even though to think of them this way didn't sit well with her. Now, she steeled herself and was becoming guarded.

In her observation of the occupants of the room, Mel studied Charles's chauffeur and Clara's maid, whose names she was yet to learn. They were both uncommonly reserved. The maid was standing with her arms folded defensively across her chest and the chauffeur couldn't meet Mel's eyes, preferring to keep his gaze on the floor the whole time. She analysed their demeanours, storing it in the back of her mind for further scrutiny because instinct told her it was important. And, from now on, she intended to pay a great deal of attention to everything anyone said or did.

Mel's former friends stared back at her and even in the dim light of the candles each of them could see the firm determination in her face. Her expression had changed from warmth and friendship to a cold detachment. It was as though none of them knew her at all, which was what she was thinking about them.

'Can't we talk about all this in the morning?' Eleanor sighed. 'Charles and I have had quite enough for tonight.'

'I'm afraid not. You might as well get comfortable. Because none of you are leaving here until we get to the truth,' Derrin said. Then he looked at Mel for her agreement.

'You can't really believe any of us are behind this?' Clara said. 'We're your friends!'

'If you are my friends, then you'll help me tonight, not hinder this investigation.'

'But… you're talking to us like we're criminals,' Charles protested.

'You see, here's the thing,' Derrin said. 'Mel doesn't know *you* Mr Harris. She doesn't *know* any of you. She hasn't seen her friends for years, so how can she? From what I understand it was Eleanor and Clara, and later Michael, who reached out to reconnect with her, not the other way around. Then, you Mr Harris, were added to this impromptu reunion.'

'That's right,' Eleanor said. 'Clara and I jointly wrote to Mel. Charles came along for the fun of it. In fact, I had to work on him to agree to visit. Something both he and I are deeply regretting right now. So, Inspector, if you are implying my fiancé is some kind of… burglar. Then I must point this out: he didn't know Mel and had no real interest in being here, except for my sake.'

'That may be true,' Derrin said. 'But why did you and Clara reach out in the first place? From my perspective, that was a little sudden, considering none of you tried to find her during the war.'

Mel glanced at Derrin. Although she would never have voiced it quite this way, she agreed that their letter had come as a great surprise to her, and at a time when she had begun to feel isolated and in need of friendship. But Derrin was always astute, and in view of what had happened, Mel was certain now that this whole heist had been planned by one or more of them, long before that letter was ever sent.

Mel almost sank into a reverie of the last time she had seen her friends. But the thought of revisiting that terrible night, and the events following her nineteenth birthday celebrations, brought a slight tremor to her body. She folded her hands together behind her back to hide the slight reaction. Stressful events always brought back the grief and shock of that night and many other terrible moments that had occurred during the war. Mel had no intention of showing how affected she was by the evening's events though, and she took a calm breath and brought her attention back to the present, pushing back the flash of awful memory that exploded like the doodlebug that had landed right outside her former London home, killing her parents and brother in the blast.

'We thought it would be nice to meet up again. For old times' sake,' Eleanor said.

Mel was jolted back to herself, forcing her mind to focus on the words being spoken in the present and not the memory of horrors past.

'That's right. We had all been such good friends once. I thought we could recapture that,' Clara said.

As Mel listened to her former friends speak, instinct told her they were holding something back. They weren't exactly lying, but what was said wasn't totally the truth either. One of them had another motive for reaching out to Mel, and the other guessed or knew what it was but was keeping the secret. Separating them might be a way of learning the truth.

'Eleanor. Please come with me and Inspector Bradley,' Mel said.

'Why?'

'We want to talk to you in private,' Derrin said.

'Anything you ask her you can say in front of me. So I will come too,' Charles said.

'You'll get your turn, Mr Harris. But we'll start with Miss Parkinson,' Derrin said. 'On her own.'

Derrin had taken to addressing everyone formally, including Mel, showing that the time for friendship was gone, and the police inspector was now at work. It added gravitas to the request for the private interviews, which they could have refused.

'I must insist!' Charles said. 'I'm her fiancé.'

Mel frowned at Charles' pushy behaviour. He was showing a side of himself that had not surfaced previously.

'And I said you won't be there,' Derrin said again.

'Come on. We'll do the interviews in the drawing room. The rest of you are to stay here,' Mel confirmed, backing Derrin up.

As they led Eleanor from the room and the door closed and was locked again, they heard a loud eruption from Charles.

'Please don't lock him inside!' Eleanor said. 'He can't bear it.'

Derrin looked into Eleanor's eyes, looking for any sign of guile. He exchanged a look with Mel and she nodded. Charles was more than likely a sufferer of Combat Stress Reaction which those in the military referred to as CSR, something that Mel understood more than most. She shrugged, and then unlocked the door.

'Charles, perhaps you should wait out here with Mr Williams?' she said.

Grateful, Charles hurried to the door. Then as meek and mild as he could possibly be, he took a seat in the expansive hallway. Mel noticed the slight tremor of his hand as he tried to hold it still in his lap. Her thoughts on his potential trauma appeared to be confirmed, but even so there was a nagging doubt over his intense behaviour that wouldn't leave her.

'Thank you,' said Eleanor. 'I'll tell you anything you want to know.'

Just then, Daisy and Ruby arrived with two trays holding mugs of cocoa. Derrin and Mel took one each, one was given to Mr Williams, and another each to Charles and Eleanor. After that, Derrin led the way into the drawing room, leaving Ruby and Daisy to take the drinks into the study to the others.

She gave Mr Williams a nod, which he understood right away to mean he was to guard Charles. Williams's inconspicuous wink let her know that he was very much going to keep an eye on the volatile guest, which reassured her as she followed Derrin and Eleanor to the drawing room.

5

'S IT DOWN,' DERRIN SAID AS HE CLOSED the door.

Eleanor sat at the table where they had previously been playing bridge, her hand went to the pack of cards that was still on the top. She stroked the elegant printed design on the back of the pile and then removed her hand and rested it with her other hand on her lap.

Mel thought this an odd thing to do and thought she knew what it meant. It told her, that like all other people during the war, Bridge had been a game to take their mind off the horrors outside their front door and what was happening in the world. Strategically too, the game was very interesting. Whilst playing earlier that evening, Mel had noticed how Eleanor and Clara were something of a tag team, working together so that one of them would win. Mel hadn't taken part in the game, she had excused herself instead and sat talking to Derrin while the women had played against Michael and Charles, winning with a great deal of delight until the lights went out. This was an occurrence that none of them could be blamed for at any rate as they had all been present.

'How long have you known Charles?' Derrin asked.

'A couple of years. We've been engaged for almost a year. Our wedding is in two weeks,' Eleanor said.

Mel asked where they had met, a question that might have come up during the evening anyway but somehow hadn't.

'My father was working for the M.O.D.,' Eleanor said. 'I wasn't going to mention it because he got your father's job when he…'

Mel blinked but otherwise didn't react to Eleanor's revelation.

'Anyway, they had an officer's dinner. I was invited along with Mother and Father, and Charles was there with his parents. He was home on medical discharge but had been on the Eastern front… He was not… *is not*… in a very good place, even now, because of his time there. The claustrophobia, I think, is a symptom.'

'Did he tell you what he saw, what happened there?' asked Derrin.

Eleanor shook her head.

'He's a proud man. He deals with it like all soldiers do. And I'll never ask him to relive it. That would be cruel and *perverse.*'

A small shudder wracked through Eleanor as she spoke of Charles's Combat Stress Reaction. Her behaviour was odd in context, and Mel banked her reaction to review and consider later. Could it be that Eleanor was merely cold? But no, the drawing room was still glowing with the heat from the fire that hadn't quite burnt down because they had been adding to it so late, and the weather was mild for the time of year, so the house wasn't fighting against the outside cold to stay warm as it often did in the winter months.

Mel moved away from Derrin and Eleanor. Her hands trembled as she pushed them down into her the folds of her dress. She ran her hand over the bunch of keys on the chain in her right pocket, her fingers lightly touching the rough edges of some, and smoother, flatter surfaces of others. The stroking of the keys reminded her that she belonged to Avonby now, and the past, with its awful ordeals, of which this night had frequently reminded her, was gone. She was safe, despite the theft of the Turner. No one had died at least!

Mel grew calmer. She became aware of Derrin looking at her. Their eyes met and she gave him a look which she hoped would reassure him that she was fine, despite the fact that Charles's war-induced suffering was all too close to Mel's own struggles.

'Well, what we really do want to understand, is why you and Clara contacted me so out of the blue. Not that I wasn't pleased… it is just that you never tried at all after the blitz. So why now?' Mel said, deflecting from her brief anxiety.

Derrin gave a nod, and Mel knew she had asked the right question, but that also he had understood she was in control.

'We were sorry about your loss,' Eleanor said. 'But… the truth is… it was awkward. What could we say to make it better? And anyway, you pretty much disappeared on us straight after it.'

'You still haven't answered the question. Why now?' Derrin said.

'Well. It wasn't something I had thought of doing, but Clara said Susan had found out where you were. We all started talking about you, and expressed how much we had missed you. Then it was just so obvious that the right thing to do was reach out.'

* * *

Six weeks earlier

The opening of the door in the tea room was signalled by the sharp ringing of the small bell attached to the frame above it. Clara looked up and saw Eleanor coming in. She waved.

'You got our favourite spot,' Eleanor said coming over.

'No thanks to you. You were supposed to get here early this time. Not me. Just as well I was ahead of schedule,' Clara said. 'Why are you late?'

'Breakfast with Charles's family went on rather longer than I expected. His mother wanted to talk wedding plans again. And it is exciting for her. I get that. So, it was difficult to extricate oneself.'

Clara studied Eleanor. She was dressed as always with impeccable taste. A lovely day dress of lilac covered by a short purple jacket which she wore unbuttoned.

'I'm pleased for you of course about the wedding. But we've talked of nothing else for months. Now, I have some news of my own.' Clara paused for effect.

'Well spit it out, I have a dress fitting in an hour,' Eleanor said. 'And can you order a fresh pot of tea? This one is rather stewed.'

Clara gave the waitress a nod and the woman hurried over and took the offending pot away, returning shortly with a new brew and two fresh cups and saucers on a tray.

'We have some fresh scones and clotted cream if you ladies would like some?' the waitress said.

'Yes please,' Clara said.

'Oh, not for me,' said Eleanor. 'I'm never going to fit in my wedding dress at this rate.'

The waitress gave the very lean Eleanor a sideways look and nodded to Clara. 'Right you are then.'

'Well, what's your news?' Eleanor said pouring herself the first cup from the pot long before it had time to steep and Clara balked a little at the almost clear fluid that hit the milk in Eleanor's cup without affecting the colour at all. She then added two spoons of sugar and stirred.

The waitress returned with Clara's scone and condiments and placed them down in the centre of the table, perhaps expecting the two women to share it, and not taking the overly slim Eleanor at her word.

'Susan found Melinda Greenway.'

'Found her? Was she lost?' Eleanor scoffed. 'But really? I thought she had run away to the army or something after her parents and brother died.'

'You really can be very heartless you know? She did join the army. But now, she's got a title. *Lady* Melinda Greenway in fact,' Clara said.

'Mel? A *lady*? Well, I never thought that would happen. I mean she had said they were related to *the* Greenways but… well *poor* relation was what we all thought, wasn't it?'

'I didn't have any thoughts on it at all at the time. She was just Mel to me, and our friend. Anyway, she doesn't have the full benefits. Just the title and an allowance from what I gather. The whole lot went to some distant cousin.'

'*Which* cousin?'

'I don't know, Richard or John or something,' Clara said.

'She had a cousin Jonathan, I remember *him*. So, he inherited the title and estate? *Interesting*.'

'That's right! *Jonathan*! Mel is living on the estate now. They took her in, wasn't that good of them? I mean, her signing up like that after… well it was a bit of an overreaction and embarrassing too for the family I should expect.'

'*They*?' Eleanor asked but she appeared to have lost interest while she sipped her tea and winced. 'Still too strong.'

Clara hid a grimace.

'I'll ask for more water,' Clara said.

'No, it doesn't matter, I have to go soon.'

'Jonathan is married, which is a shame or it might well have been a different story for Mel.'

'What do you mean? They are cousins, they couldn't marry.'

'Very *distant* cousins. Barely related to be honest. But it doesn't matter as there is a wife, Lady Laura,' Clara said.

Eleanor put down the cup.

'So, what if Mel's a lady, her cousin got married and gained a title? It doesn't affect our lives, does it?'

'What's the matter with you today?' Clara said. 'You're so grumpy. I thought you would enjoy the gossip.'

Clara paused and looked closely at Eleanor who was uncharacteristically fidgety.

'Was it really horrible at the breakfast with Charles's parents?' she asked.

'Yes. They are dreadful people. Always talking about money. It's vulgar. I hope we don't have to see very much of them after the wedding. Thankfully, Charles is nothing like either of them.'

'I'm sorry to hear that. But it is why I'm never bothering to get married. I shall enjoy my spinsterhood with no in-laws or husbands to please.'

Eleanor laughed at this, pulled out of herself by one of Clara's humorous and sweeping statements which she always found amusing because she knew they were the exact opposite to what Clara wanted in life. They were, she thought, a defence mechanism for her failure to meet anyone who had shown any interest in her. Oddly, she could see Clara married and with several children, but she just hadn't met anyone suitable yet.

'You'll find someone,' Eleanor said, and Clara's face dropped.

'I appreciate you saying that. Anyway, back to Mel. I sent her a letter. I put it from both of us.'

'Why did you do that?' Eleanor asked.

'I don't know. It just seemed right to include you. I would have asked, but you were away in Europe for weeks. Anyway, she's replied.'

'Really?' Eleanor said, more interested.

'I'm thinking it would be nice to catch up with her. We were such great friends all of us, once.'

'I know. Well, you were more friends than I was, and Michael of course. But I did like Mel.'

'Wouldn't it be lovely to visit her then?' Clara said.

'Visit? You've only just started talking to her. What are you *up to* Clara?'

'Nothing.'

'Oh come on. I don't believe that for a second,' Eleanor said.

'Well… I'd love to get a look at Avonby. I believe its spectacular.'

'Ah. Now I know what you're doing. You're looking for a man of means, aren't you? And Mel may know someone, a fresh face, not from around here?' Eleanor gave a short laugh. 'Okay. Count me in and let's see where rekindling this friendship leads.'

'Thank you! I hoped you would say that,' Clara said. 'Now, can you pay for the tea and scone, as I'm a little short this month after buying a gown for your wedding.'

Eleanor shook her head. 'You're incorrigible.'

'I know. But what would you do without me?'

6

'Y OU'RE SAYING IT WAS CLARA'S IDEA TO visit?' Derrin said. 'I don't want to gossip but she was rather impressed that Mel had a title now. And wanted to see where you lived. I agreed to come to support her. And of course, I wanted to see you again, Mel! Then realised it might be nice for Charles too. To take him out of himself a little. London doesn't make him happy these days.'

Despite her best efforts to keep it neutral, Eleanor's face twitched for a brief second revealing her feelings. Mel noted it, storing it away for the moment when it would make more sense.

'What about Charles's finances?' Derrin asked.

'It's rather rude to ask such things,' Eleanor said. 'Very vulgar.'

'Inspector Bradley isn't asking to be nosy. Charles's financial circumstances could rule him out,' Mel pointed out. 'The painting is very valuable.'

'Charles has no need of a painting! His father owns a factory that made munitions for the war effort. He's the only man I know that managed to make war profitable. The man's rolling in it and makes sure everyone knows! Charles has a magnificent allowance. Besides, you saw how little interest he had when the picture was discussed. He was only interested in the French brandy. But Michael, however, knew exactly what it was, didn't he? Isn't it possible he also knew it was worth a lot?'

Mel studied Eleanor in search of guile. She felt she was telling the truth about the visit being Clara's idea, though the way she had switched from that subject to the leap about Michael's interest in art was clearly an attempt to take the heat off herself and Charles, which showed she wasn't exactly trustworthy or a good friend to either Clara or Michael.

You're not getting off that easy, Mel thought.

Mel and Derrin questioned Eleanor further about Charles and Clara. In the end they learnt very little more as Eleanor stuck to her story.

'We'll speak to Charles now,' Derrin said. 'Before you get an opportunity to get your story straight.'

'Well really!' Eleanor said. 'I've no idea what you're implying. I've told you the truth.'

While Derrin took Eleanor from the room, Mel's thoughts went to the other guests. Her once very close friends now felt like strangers. Unlike Eleanor, Mel's game of choice was always chess and she saw the people as pieces on her metaphorical board, poised and ready to move and be part of a game whose ending she didn't yet know.

Much had been said by Eleanor about Clara and about Michael, but what did Mel know about Eleanor and her fiancé, Charles? Not much, if the truth be known. They were completely blank to her and had lived lives so different from hers over the last few years that it was hard to reconnect. The Eleanor she once knew had never been so prissy and although she knew little of Charles, she already understood that he was arrogant and self-important.

A man like that wouldn't take kindly to being cross-examined by a woman, Mel thought, recalling others of his ilk from her past.

Mel took a seat near the window: Derrin would understand she intended to take on the role of observer – as she often had in the many years during the war when they had worked together – and the reason why.

* * *

London, 1943

It had taken two years for Mel and Derrin to track down the source of one of their previous cases. This wartime thug and black marketeer had been known for more than pushing illegally obtained booze and nylons. His name was Eric Stafford, and he had avoided being conscripted by providing a medical letter that claimed he had a heart murmur. Derrin believed the doctor who provided it had been coerced, because Stafford was a fit and strong thirty-three-year-old at the time and was known for running an extortion racket in London's underworld before the war started. Under normal circumstances, Stafford would have been on the Met's radar, but there had been so many changes since the war started that meant manpower was at an all-time low. When the police weren't guarding munitions factories, officers were deployed to find deserters. So, it meant that police officers on the beat were thin on the ground. For that reason, there was a lot of petty crime that went unchecked unless it led in other directions. There were also men like Stafford, who continued to run their gangs and who controlled the streets of London, feared, hated and, in no small way, respected by others of their ilk.

Derrin was aware of Stafford, and had suspected all along that he was also a spy for hire.

'Men like Stafford will do anything for money. Patriotism can be bought, as can their morals,' Derrin had explained during their briefing. 'He's dangerous for many reasons, but especially because we believe he is a traitor.'

'So why am I only just hearing about him now?' Mel had asked.

'As with most things, this was a need-to-know basis. But, you've seen him many times. I'm sure of it. And with your memory and attention to detail Mel, I'm certain when you spot him again, you'll make those connections. In fact, I'm relying on it.'

Mel hadn't let Derrin's confidence go to her head. He never said anything to flatter, it was more factual. She had spent the last few years honing the skills that had, at first, come naturally to her. Now she used them for the ministry of defence's benefit. During that time, Mel and Derrin had brought many criminals and traitors to justice. The job was reward enough, and Mel was glad to keep her mind sharp because it made her feel as though she was doing everything she could to support her country and to make the death of her family mean something.

That night, they had planned to meet an informant of Derrin's, but Mel's role was to be in the background and observe. They had arrived at the speakeasy separately. This club, like many before it, had sprung up overnight.

Mel took some of the girls from her barracks as cover. None of them knew of Mel's clandestine operations: they were just six women looking for drinks and laughter because Mel's secondment to the secret services, and her work with Derrin, was top secret.

As the evening wore on, the women got louder and were enjoying themselves. For every pleasure taken during those hard years was appreciated on extreme levels with an almost hysterical delight. They lived hard and partied harder.

By then, Mel had become an expert at pretending to drink, appearing tipsy, when, in fact, only water had passed her lips. Her friends however, free from the barracks for a night, had been on the real stuff. Several dirty martinis passed between them, as had many young soldiers, home on leave and looking for fun. The soldiers had jived with the best of them, holding the girls a little too close, but Mel kept her distance, observing her friends, knowing she would take care of them if things got out of hand and the soldiers were too full on.

Halfway through the night, Derrin came in wearing civvies. He was a young and handsome man that might well be questioned for his motives for not going to war when he appeared so vigorous. Derrin, as Mel knew, was fighting for the war in a way that could make the difference between their Allied forces' success or failure. The strategies behind the war were just as crucial as the ones on the front line. And, as they had learnt all along, there were spies everywhere, even on British soil. A war front line that was harder to find, and more challenging to win.

Once he was in the right place, Mel had become even more alert, but she never directly looked in Derrin's direction, taking everything in via peripheral vision.

Scanning the room, Mel had noticed Stafford. She hadn't seen a picture of him but she still recognised him, as Derrin had thought she would.

Like a film reel playing on the big screen, Mel's mind flicked through memories and images making sense of it in a matter of moments. Yes, she had seen him many times before and those times flashed back in her mind like a movie unfolding behind her eyes. *In the market place talking to one of the vegetable stall owners. On the high street coming out of the back room of the butcher's shop.* She had even seen him a few years ago in a similar setting. *Oh yes*, the night she and Derrin had taken their relationship from colleagues to lovers. That had been a very eventful twenty-four hours. Mel had shuddered at the memory, which was forever associated with the first time she had used a gun, shooting another criminal and saving Derrin's life, which somehow overshadowed the fact that it was also the first time they had made love. Did Derrin know that Stafford had been there? *He must have*, Mel thought.

Mel pulled all the pieces of that night together and she began to make connections between Eric Stafford and the criminal she had shot. He had been alive but injured and unconscious when Derrin had hurried Mel away from the scene before the Military Police arrived to raid the place. She never asked what happened to the man, assuming they had taken him in for questioning, like so many others Derrin and Mel apprehended.

Back in the moment, Mel realised that Stafford was talking to one of her friends. It made Mel look at the woman differently. Georgie was older than Mel, and they had been in the same troop since they both enlisted. They were colleagues more than friends as Georgie tended to sway towards the more gregarious group of women and was known to be a bit 'free' with her favours. Not that Mel judged her on that score, it was just that they had very different personalities and didn't bond. Mel had found herself studying Stafford and Georgie, wondering for the first time about the woman's past beyond the tale of grief she had told the girls on the first night in the barracks and then never mentioned again. Georgie, was, she had told them, a war widow and the double tragedy that she was also childless. She had enlisted because she 'had nothing else to live for'.

At that moment, Mel wondered how Georgie knew Stafford, because it was clear they hadn't just met.

Georgie's head had turned in Mel's direction as though she was aware she was being watched. Mel moved her eyes to look elsewhere and put a dreamy, half-drunk smile on her face, swaying slightly to the music as though she were lost in thought. When Georgie turned away again, Mel's eyes returned to studying her and her companion as they continued to talk together, not in any flirty way, but in a serious discussion.

Stafford frequently glanced towards the bar and the soldiers who were drinking shots interspersed with beer. The soldiers were becoming more raucous by the minute, but Mel hadn't thought that this would be a concern for Stafford. He tilted his head now towards one of them before saying something to Georgie. Georgie nodded and she moved away from Stafford, making her way across the room to the soldier.

The soldier in question was off to the side and slightly distant from the rowdy group, yet he glanced over to his friends, smiling with a tweak of indulgence. Mel had noticed that this soldier hadn't been drinking at all. He had been the 'designated sober' of the group and Mel wondered if this was a thing for all of them when they went out on the town. He had a glass of cordial in front of him and it was obvious he wasn't making any attempt to pretend to be drunk as he watched his troop having a good time.

Georgie made her way past the drunk soldiers and squeezed into a space at the bar. It was then that Mel realised Georgie had not been really drinking or partying either: she was perfectly sober. She gave the solo sober soldier a flirty smile and leaned in to talk to him, that was when Mel saw her slip something into his drink. It was a pill of some sort, or perhaps a powder – hard to tell at that distance – but the glass clouded for a split second and then cleared.

The soldier shook his head as Georgie pulled back and she feigned a sad face at his polite refusal for whatever offer she had made to him. Georgie ordered herself a drink and glanced around as though looking for another person to talk to.

Mel sipped her fake martini and wandered over to the dance floor in pretence of watching the other girls dancing, but really to get closer to Derrin. She didn't look in his direction but eventually ended up close enough so that he would see her out of the corner of his eye. Derrin turned and stumbled into Mel, spilling the contents of her mock-drink.

'Sorry,' Derrin had said, handing her his handkerchief.

'Mickey at the bar,' Mel said while pretending to mop the mess from her dress.

Derrin tilted his head towards the bar and pointed to Mel's now empty glass.

To the casual eye this exchange looked like nothing more than him apologising and offering to buy her another drink, but during this conversation Mel told Derrin what she had seen and her suspicions about Georgie and Stafford working together.

They went over to the bar, stopping near the soldier, who was sipping from the glass as they arrived.

'What can I get you?' asked the barman.

'Another martini for the lady. Make it a special,' Derrin said.

The barman, already in Derrin and Mel's pocket, knew exactly what this meant and brought Mel a martini glass filled with water, and sporting a single green olive on a stick.

'Thanks,' Mel said as he placed it on the bar in front of her. She didn't pick it up however, as she waited for Derrin to pay.

Meanwhile, the soldier sitting by the bar was now feeling the effects of his spiked drink and was swaying on the barstool.

'Hey,' said Derrin, catching the man just in time to prevent him from tumbling to the floor.

'What's up?' said Georgie appearing as if from nowhere, yet Mel had been aware of her hovering all the time watching the soldier.

'This guy's had too much to drink,' said Derrin.

'Can you help us get him outside for some air?' Mel said.

'Sure,' Georgie said.

She had cast a worried look in the direction of Stafford but Mel pretended not to notice and she let Georgie and Derrin help the soldier off the stool. Mel walked behind them, aware that Stafford was following, and he wasn't alone. But the soldier was just an ordinary private and she couldn't understand what Stafford wanted with him. With Georgie also there, Mel was unable to warn Derrin of the men following them in case she overheard and realised they were onto them. Derrin was sure to have a plan, might even have expected this when he suggested they take the soldier outside.

As they reached the door of the club, Derrin glanced back over his shoulder and met Mel's eyes in the process. Derrin winked. Mel understood and reached inside her dress pocket for the hidden pistol. Derrin had noticed the men behind them, of course.

Georgie looked back: she didn't notice the gun Mel was holding down by her side but she frowned when she saw Stafford and his stooge following as though this was a surprise to her.

'It's so kind of you to help this poor drunk lad, Georgie,' Mel said moving closer to her.

A van drove up just as Derrin, Georgie and Mel came out onto the pavement with the soldier who was all but unconscious now. The back of the van opened and two men got out leaving the doors open. They eyed up Georgie and looked past her to see Stafford and his companion coming out.

Mel didn't make any comment, but she slowly ferreted the gun away in a hidden panel inside the pocket of her flowing skirt, easily accessible but unseen.

'You look like you need some 'elp with this kid,' said Stafford.

'Oh yeah. 'E's 'ad a few too many,' Derrin said, mimicking the local accent perfectly and dropping all his refined tones so that no one could tell he was not only an officer, but of a far better class than those attending the club. 'Fanks, ladies, these fellas'll 'elp now.'

Georgie let Stafford's thug take the arm of the soldier and she ducked back inside the club without a word. Mel didn't leave, however, because she knew that Derrin couldn't take four of them alone.

'You be on your way, Miss,' said Stafford. 'I can take it from 'ere.'

'Well,' said Mel. 'I would, but this fella said he'd buy me a drink.'

Mel's hand slipped inside her pocket and wrapped once more around the handle of the pistol.

One of the men from the van stepped forward and took over the side that Derrin was holding, doing what Mel had hoped which meant that two of them now had their hands full wrangling the unconscious lad. It evened the odds and the situation now became two against two. She knew that she and Derrin could take out Stafford and his brute before they had a chance to react.

Derrin stepped away, but Mel saw his hand subtly move to the small of his back where she knew he had a gun holstered out of sight.

She pulled her gun free again and they both turned at the same time, Mel on Stafford and Derrin on the other henchman.

'So where exactly do you think you're going with this young private, Mr Stafford?' Mel said.

Stafford was shocked and reached for his pocket.

'I wouldn't do that if I were you,' said Derrin.

Then several men appeared from their hiding places: doorways, behind parked cars, another from inside the club.

'I think I have the edge,' said Stafford. 'Put your guns down or the girl gets it first.'

They saw they were outnumbered, but neither of them lowered their guns.

'Get 'im in the van,' said Stafford and the two thugs holding the private dragged his prone body towards the van.

Stafford turned his attention back to Derrin and Mel.

'You,' he said to Mel. 'You're going to be insurance. Get in the van.'

'No,' said Mel. Then she fired her gun straight into Stafford's face.

The man fell sideways and his men erupted into chaos. Derrin and Mel dived aside, ducking behind the van as bullets sprayed the side, narrowly missing them, the private and the other two ruffians that were holding him. The thugs dropped the private down onto the ground, reaching inside pockets for their own weapons, but were stopped short by the sound of police sirens driving towards them. The hoodlums scattered in various directions as the siren sound intensified and grew nearer.

Mel and Derrin came out of their hiding place in time to see the private crawling along the road, in the line of the oncoming police cars. They both ran towards him, picked him off the ground and pulled him back onto the pavement just as the first car halted in front of them.

'This kid needs a doctor,' Derrin said. 'Someone spiked his drink.'

'What about this fellow?' said one of the officers pointing to Stafford. 'Looks like he got shot.'

Mel ducked down and checked Stafford's pulse. 'He's still alive,' she said. 'Guess he needs an ambulance and handcuffs. He was trying to kidnap the young private.'

7

Bᴿɪɴɢɪɴɢ Cʜᴀʀʟᴇs ɪɴᴛᴏ ᴛʜᴇ ᴅʀᴀᴡɪɴɢ ʀᴏᴏᴍ, Dᴇʀʀɪɴ found Mel sitting by the window. They exchanged a look and Derrin took the lead, knowing that she was taking a passive role.

Charles was told to sit at the bridge table. From this seat, Mel had a clear view of his full face and could judge his reactions to Derrin's questions. Reading people was a strong talent that she'd always had.

As she watched Charles take his seat, Mel's hand trembled so she held it with her other in her lap, forcing herself to sit still. Her mind went back to Stafford and that fateful night once more. The past often reached out for her, but thankfully, threats of that nature had been few and far between, and their tasks more about gaining information. Mel had suspected it was because Derrin kept her away from some of the more dangerous situations at the time. Though he would never admit it for fear of offending her, or maybe because his urge to protect her wasn't needed; Mel reacted on instinct when threatened even now, and she often wondered what she would do if she had a pistol to hand on a daily basis. It had been easy to shoot Stafford, he was a lowlife, but afterwards Mel had been shocked by her reflex action to shoot to kill. And although she didn't kill him — he had moved too fast and the bullet just grazed the side of his head and badly damaged his ear — she hadn't been upset by the possibility, just at her ability to respond with violence. She was imperfect, flawed, damaged, even, by the experiences she'd had. But wasn't everyone in Britain, to a certain degree?

Now, she kept her distance from Charles and let Derrin lead the interview. It was the best way since her heart was so invested in what was happening at Avonby and Jonathan's missing painting. She knew she would never forgive herself if it was gone for good. She mulled over her emotions and frustration at the theft of the Turner. It was so insulting that someone she had invited into their home in good faith would behave this way. It put a big question mark around who she could trust going forward. Derrin, she knew, was the only person in the world she did trust and even that was problematic given their on-off relationship.

'Mr Harris, I wonder if you'd indulge me,' Derrin said now, 'in telling me more about yourself and your relationship with Eleanor Parkinson.'

Charles looked vaguely irritated, but he sat back in his seat. He pulled out his cigarette case from his jacket pocket. Taking out a cigarette, he put it between his lips, then retrieved a nickel-coloured lighter from his pocket.

'What do you want to know?' he asked, lighting up and then taking a long drag from the cigarette. He puffed smoke into the air and then seemed to relax, as though the nicotine was just what he needed.

Derrin began with a series of questions, and the answers corroborated Eleanor's story of how and when they met at a military ball. All of this was legitimate, but where Derrin was really going with the questioning Mel wasn't sure, until he twisted it towards Charles's past.

'Life before Eleanor?' Charles said. 'I'm not sure I had one. She's a great girl. Someone I thought I'd never meet or would want to be around me.'

'Why would you think that?' Derrin asked.

'Oh, I enlisted, but was honourably discharged due to health reasons. And girls do judge a chap on those things, you know.'

'What health reasons?' Derrin asked.

'You see... even you are. You *have* to know why,' Charles took a long drag from the cigarette again before answering. 'I have a disorder. Scoliosis in the spine. I couldn't do the training properly or carry the required weight of backpack and rifle. Even so, they were so short-handed, I was taken on. Then they sent me to the Eastern front. But the scoliosis limits my ability to do a lot of things. I was given some dispensation as an officer and didn't have to go over the trench tops, but…'

Charles paused as though the memory was almost too painful to continue.

'There was an explosion, near our bunker, the whole thing caved in on top of me. I'd had the sense to dive under my bunk; it supported some of the weight of the soil. I was able to breath, but couldn't move. I was buried beneath it for two days before they dug me out. A healthier, stronger man would have been able to dig himself out. But I couldn't. It left me with… issues. Things I couldn't get beyond. I was sent back to England. Discharged on medical grounds. As I've already said.'

Charles looked at Derrin and seeing the blank expression by return took it as scepticism. He stood, removed his tuxedo jacket, untucked his shirt, turned around and lifted it at the back. From where she stood, Mel could see the obvious curvature in Charles's back. His condition was severe and obvious to the naked eye when exposed, even though it hadn't been when covered by his clothing. She believed this part of the story, but something niggled at her about the discharge. Why take the man on in the first place? His story of that didn't make a lot of sense, given what she knew of the medical checks that soldiers endured. It was obvious he couldn't be a soldier in the normal usage of the term. What did Charles have to offer that they still thought him useful? She gave a subconscious shrug. What did it matter? The only thing that was worth exploring was the possibility that Charles had stolen the painting.

Mel ran through a mental scenario, seeing Charles reaching upwards for the Turner above the fireplace.

His back wouldn't allow him to stretch far, or even straighten enough to reach above the fireplace though he tried to do it. Charles looked around the room, then pulling up one of the chairs, climbed awkwardly up on to tapestry cushioning. His balance was precarious, but the thief was determined. He reached upwards, tugged at the frame, managing, despite his disability, to lift the painting off the picture hook. But, the frame was heavy. Charles struggled with it. The weight tumbled against him, knocking him off the chair, to land painfully on his back, while the frame crushed him down onto the expensive rug.

The noise of his fall brought both Mel and Derrin running into the room, catching Charles in the act of stealing the Turner.

Charles tucked his shirt back into his trousers and pulled his jacket on.

'I assume you have seen enough?' he said.

Derrin looked over at Mel, who gave him a quick nod.

* * *

Derrin returned alone after taking Charles back to the group. He sat down next to Mel at the window seat.

'What do you think?'

'He couldn't have lifted the frame, but that doesn't mean he wasn't capable of cutting the picture from it where it was. Though it would have been difficult and possibly painful to bend his body, while standing on a chair, to do that. Even so…'

'Maybe he had an accomplice. *Eleanor?*' Derrin suggested.

'I haven't ruled it out. I can *see* the situation. Eleanor could have helped him for certain. She's fit enough but I just don't get the motive at this point to justify her doing it. Her family is wealthy. Charles is wealthy. As she said, they don't *need* anything. So, why steal? Plus, with Charles' obvious claustrophobia, would he risk gaol time? I somehow doubt it.'

Derrin agreed. 'It does seem very unlikely to me. What do you know about Clara's family?'

'It wasn't something we talked about back in the day,' Mel said. 'But I knew she was from a very well-placed family. Though, not the wealthiest. We could talk to her. Rule her out?'

Mel's instinct told her that Clara was the least likely suspect, but you could never tell. Either way she would need to be interviewed.

'Okay. Let's go and get her in here,' Derrin said.

'I'll go,' Mel said.

Mel left the room and walked down the hallway to the study. Mr Williams was waiting at the door with Charles.

'You're still out here?' Mel asked.

'Need not to be locked in again. Could do with a brandy though to be honest,' he said. 'It's been a very trying few hours.'

Mel experienced a moment of empathy for Charles, even though she didn't like him much, which in and of itself was an odd sensation. He had trauma from a very serious war-related incident and she, perhaps more than most, could understand the debilitation of those times when past experiences weakened you. She fought with her own every day. None of that empathy however could change this slight unease she had when she looked at Charles. He gave the impression of being mild natured, but she felt there was something lurking beneath it. A sense that he wasn't all he appeared to be. And wasn't as nice as he seemed either. Those bursts of anger and frustration could be explained away by his trauma, but no, it didn't completely sit with Mel.

'Come back in the study. I poured some brandy earlier but never drank it. You're welcome to it,' Mel said trying to convey some sympathy. 'And just between us, we won't lock the door. Mr Williams is here to monitor if anyone tries to leave.'

She opened the door and Charles followed her inside.

The first person she saw was Michael, who didn't appear to have moved since Mel was last in the room. Now though, opposite him, and sitting beside the fire, was Eleanor.

Mel picked up the brandy glass which was on the small table between Michael and Eleanor along with Derrin's untouched drink. She passed it to Charles.

'Feel free,' she said and then she turned to Clara who was sitting on one of the sofas with her maid next to her. The girl looked even more uncomfortable than when she was standing earlier by the window.

'Clara?' she said.

'Me?' Clara said.

'Come with me please,' Mel said.

Clara got up from the sofa and she cast a quick glance in her maid's direction. The girl, however, was not looking at her, her eyes were focused elsewhere in the room. Mel turned to see who or what she was looking at.

At that minute, Charles Harris dropped the half-drunk glass of brandy to the floor. He took a step towards Mel, his hand pointing in her direction, as a burst of white foam filled his mouth. Charles crumpled to the floor as a seizure took his body.

'Charles!' screamed Eleanor jumping up from her seat by the fire and falling to her knees beside his spasming body.

Clara knelt beside Charles.

'We need a doctor!' she said. 'It's some kind of seizure!'

As Clara turned the man into the recovery position with great expertise, Mel bent down to take a look. A waft of almonds reached her nostrils, and Mel knew right away it was too late. Nothing she or anyone else could do would help. Charles had been poisoned and it was obvious to her it was a large dose of arsenic.

'Williams?' Mel yelled. 'Get the inspector. Now!'

She glanced at the other untouched glass on the table near the fire and the dropped and spilt tumbler that lay on its side, the glass miraculously unbroken. Her eyes scanned the room, taking in the shocked expressions around her. Seconds later, Derrin hurried in, pushing his way through the people now gathering around Charles, Eleanor and Mel.

'Step back,' said Derrin.

Clara stood up and moved back and away, merging with the other spectators.

Mel gave an imperceptible shake of her head and she and Derrin exchanged a look.

'Oh my god! He's dead!' cried Clara's maid, the first to realise what had happened.

Derrin kneeled by the body and checked Charles's pulse. Then he stood.

'Sit down. All of you,' he said. His voice was harsher than Mel had ever heard it. He looked over to Williams who was hovering by the door.

'Get Toby,' Derrin said. 'We'll move the body into another room.'

'Body?' cried Eleanor, throwing herself across Charles's prone corpse. 'Charles! Charles!'

Eleanor sobbed until Mel and Derrin pulled her away. The girl didn't resist too hard, but turned in Mel's arms and cried on her shoulder. Mel held her, not fully comfortable, but unable to push her former friend away. After a few moments, Mel led her back to the chair by the fire, placing her exactly where she had been when Mel had entered. Eleanor turned and gazed into the dying embers of the fire. It wasn't cold but her body trembled and shook and she wrapped her arms around herself as though she were inside a freezing cavern.

Mel's eyes swept the room, her perfect memory taking in the anomalies. But she said nothing for the time being and waited while a half-dressed Toby arrived and he and Mr Williams picked up Charles's body and took it from the room.

'How did you know to turn him into the recovery position?' Mel asked Clara.

'I did my part during the war,' Clara answered.

8

'WHAT IS YOUR NAME?' MEL SAID LOOKING at Charles's chauffeur. 'Frank Carter,' he answered.

'Carter, go and stand where you were when I came in.'

'But, I don't remember where I was when you arrived, Miss,' Carter said.

Mel placed her hand on his shoulder.

'Take two steps left, and one backward,' she said.

Carter looked around confused.

'Do as she says, Carter,' said Derrin. He had moved back towards the door which he had closed after Williams and Toby had left with Charles's corpse.

Carter moved into position. Mel stepped back and looked at him again, a far-away expression in her eyes.

'What's your name?' she said turning to Clara's maid.

'Mabel Bailey,' Clara chipped in.

'Let her speak for herself please,' Mel said. 'Mabel. Move right on that sofa. You were huddled up to the armrest when I came in. Do that again.'

Mabel reacted slowly, looking to Clara as though needing permission. Clara nodded at the girl and she slid back into place on the sofa.

Without being asked, Clara sank down on the sofa next to Mabel and took up the exact position she was in when Mel had come in.

Eleanor, still in shock, didn't move — Mel ignored the fact she wasn't where she had been when she had entered the room. Michael was and so, satisfied, she turned her attention elsewhere.

Once she had them all back where they had been standing or sitting, Mel stepped back to the door and, standing next to Derrin, observed them all. She committed their positions to memory again for future analysis. Though the reason she had for doing this was not too clear even to her, Mel had wanted to reconnect with the subtle conversations or connections that had been happening when she had entered the study.

Mel's gaze fell on the tumbler which was still on the floor and for that reason affecting her concentration as it was out of place.

'Can I have your handkerchief?' she asked Derrin.

He gave it to her and she picked up the glass, sniffed it and placed it down on the table between Eleanor and Michael. Then she picked up the untouched tumbler, sniffing the contents. She placed the tumbler down in its former place and glanced over to the decanter in the corner.

Derrin went over to the decanter. Using the sleeve of his jacket, he took out the stopper and, bending at the waist, sniffed the contents. Then he returned to his place by Mel's side at the door.

Mel took one more look around the room. In her mind, she moved Eleanor back into position, super-imposing her across the devastated figure that now slumped in the armchair. Then satisfied, she and Derrin picked up the tumblers and the decanter and took them out of the room.

'I'd advise you not to drink anything from any of the other decanters,' Derrin said to the group, before Mel closed and locked the door, leaving them all trapped inside.

There was a general roar of sound coming from within the room as the implication of poisoning hit home to them all. Mel and Derrin placed the glasses and tumblers on the sideboard in the hallway.

'Arsenic,' Derrin confirmed.

'I thought so,' Mel nodded. 'What about the decanter?'

'There's a trace of the odour, but not as strong as in the glasses,' Derrin said.

'So, the glasses and decanter were probably poisoned after we poured them?'

'I think so, but since neither of us drank from them before we noticed the missing painting, then I can't be sure,' Derrin said.

'I am sort of glad for the stolen painting, just in case, though the odour was that strong, I like to think one of us would have smelt it first.'

She sniffed the decanter and the glasses again.

A shadowy pawn moved with stealth around the room, as Mel, a silent watcher, saw each of the occupants taking up their starting positions. The glasses were spiked first, one then the other, as someone leaned over them making an innocent move into a deadly one.

Mel came back into the present. She couldn't see the poisoner moving to the decanter right then, but she left the idea churning in the back of her mind.

Drawn by some strange urge to revisit times long since past, Mel fell back in her memories. The detail was as clear to her that day as it had been back then.

* * *

London, 1943

As the police arrived, the speakeasy doors exploded and the occupants ran, pushing and shoving each other out onto the streets and scattering in every direction. But the police weren't interested in the illegal booze, or the revellers who were out after curfew, they were responding to the gun fire, and had been positioned in earshot as backup to Derrin's operation. Derrin showed his credentials to confirm who he was, while Mel slunk away with her colleagues as pre-arranged, as though she hadn't been involved at all.

As the female RASC privates ran through the streets, Mel noted that Georgie wasn't with them. Thinking the woman had slipped away through a back door of the club, she stored what she had observed for another time. She and Derrin would no doubt talk about what had gone down in their debrief.

Back at the base, she pretended to go to bed, but snuck out of her room as soon as the other women went to sleep. By then, Georgie hadn't returned. Mel was worried for her. Anything could happen on the London back streets during those times. Mel wouldn't be out there alone by choice, and not unarmed, and she was now very well equipped at looking after herself.

Mel suspected they had taken Eric Stafford back to the base and he'd received medical attention there, and not in a regular hospital. He had been lucky, or maybe just practised enough to react when he saw Mel squeeze the trigger, and had ducked his head as the bullet flew towards him, receiving a blow that took a huge chunk of his right ear, and had cut a deep graze across his temple. The shot had caused enough damage to render the man unconscious, but not anything life threatening. Mel was glad she hadn't killed him, though she had intended to at the time, but his survival might mean information for Derrin on other traitors.

Mel went to the warehouse at the back of the base. It appeared so innocuous, a possible storage space, but was in fact a clandestine operations unit. She had a pass that allowed her full access and so she was let in by the night sergeant on duty. Anyone who worked in this part of the base was bound by the Official Secrets Act and Mel knew that what happened here had to remain undisclosed indefinitely. The only person she would ever be able to discuss it with would be Derrin or someone else in the same circles.

Once inside and past the checkpoint, Mel headed to the interview rooms. She checked the roster and saw that Derrin had a 'female suspect' in room three scheduled for interview. She went to the observation room attached to it and went inside. Through the two-way mirror she saw Georgie and knew that Derrin had taken the opportunity to detain her for questioning. She was somewhat relieved that Georgie was in safe hands, but Mel was also concerned for her. What would it mean if she was found to be a traitor? At that point, Mel had never been involved with the capture of a female collaborator. It felt different, even though it shouldn't have: a traitor was a traitor no matter what their gender.

'I was just having fun,' Georgie said.

Derrin leaned across the table and sniffed.

'Not a drop passed your lips tonight,' he pointed out. 'You see, I'd be able to smell cheap booze on you if it had.'

'Well, I don't need to drink to enjoy meself,' Georgie said.

'How do you know Eric Stafford?' Derrin said.

'Who?'

'Don't play dumb with me, Georgie, we know you have history. Stafford is a traitor; do you want to join him on the gibbet or in a firing squad?'

Georgie gasped, her composure slipping.

'I didn't do nuffin',' she said. 'I just know 'im from before I enlisted.'

'How do you know him?' Derrin asked.

Georgie sighed. She put her arms on the desk and dropped her head down onto them. Mel could tell she was defeated.

'He loaned me some money, when my old man was killed,' she said. 'But… I couldn't make his interest rates. I enlisted to… get free of 'im.'

Georgie's words, unlike her defeated posture, didn't ring true to Mel. She leaned closer to the glass, watching every tell-tale sign that Georgie made.

Derrin sat back in his chair. He looked benign and Mel had seen him do this with previous suspects. He didn't believe her either.

'Look, I'd like to help you, Georgie, but you have to give me more than a cock and bull story like that. You see I know you weren't married and you never had a husband that was killed in the war. In fact, you were one of Stafford's doxies? Weren't you?'

Georgie's expression changed from frightened widow to hard-faced criminal in a split second and then dropped completely to that of a woman trapped by circumstances. Mel knew she was all these things, probably coerced into prostitution by Stafford in the first place.

'I wanted a better life,' said Georgie now. 'I signed up to get away from 'im. That's the truth. Then he saw me tonight and threatened to kill me if I didn't 'elp him get that soldier.'

'What did he want the private for?' Derrin asked.

'I dunno. Didn't ask. But I knew if I didn't do what he said, he would do for me,' Georgie continued.

'But you're in the army, Georgie. You'd be protected. So don't give us that scared, weak woman baloney. All you had to do was report him to your Sergeant and we'd be able to arrest him.'

'You don't know Stafford. 'E 'as ways of getting to people. 'Ow do I know the sarge in't in 'is pocket?'

Derrin came into the observation room after he finished talking to Georgie, who couldn't give him much more information on the night's incident other than her part in it. She stuck to her story, no matter how much Derrin asked her the same things in various ways.

'She's telling the truth,' Mel said when he came in. 'I saw she was worried tonight. There was genuine fear whenever she looked at Stafford. Georgie is smart or she wouldn't be in the RASC, but she was too exhausted to have been able to sustain that level of consistency to her story. She wasn't trying to fox you once you exposed her earlier lies.'

'I agree,' said Derrin. 'Even though she couldn't tell us much about Stafford's dealings, she has confirmed that Stafford gave her the drug to stick in the private's drink. So, she can be used as a witness, albeit it a potentially hostile one.'

'You really think she will be hostile?' Mel said.

'She's scared. But it all depends on who she is most afraid of. Men like Stafford can be very persuasive. While she worked for him, she would have been terrified to put a foot wrong because of potential repercussions. She would have seen what he was capable of, experienced violence at his hands. It's how pimps work.'

'But she's been free of him all this time, it doesn't make sense that she'd still be scared,' Mel said.

'I've seen this sort of thing before. This is common in victims. It's brainwashing. She had been so conditioned in the past that just seeing him again put her right back in his control. All he had to do was tell her he could get to her anywhere… even here. Which he did, and she believed it.'

'Good grief,' Mel said.

But Derrin's words made complete sense to her. It was something she would watch out for in the future.

'How is the private?' Mel asked.

'He's recovering. She gave him chloral hydrate. Knocked him clean out. A typical Mickey Finn as you rightly observed. Good job you saw it happen or things might be different for him right now.'

'But who is he?' Mel asked. 'Why did they want him?'

'An ordinary soldier by all accounts, home on leave from the front. When Stafford is able to be interviewed, I'll get it out of him what it was all about. Maybe the kid owed him money. It seems to be the only thing Stafford cares about.'

The observation room telephone rang and Derrin picked it up.

'Yes General?' he said. Then he listened for a short time before hanging up. 'Our young private is more interesting than we thought.'

'Why?' Mel asked.

Derrin hesitated, as though he wasn't sure if she should be in the loop of what he now knew. He thought for a moment and then decided.

'He's been in on tactical planning for a big push into Germany,' Derrin said.

'Stafford wanted *information*, not money?' Mel said.

'It might well be that the intel was to sell. In which case we finally have Stafford for treason,' Derrin said. 'He's going to wish he hadn't been so quick to move when you fired at him.'

Mel nodded.

'While we are on that subject, good reaction. I'm always impressed by how fearless you are in the face of adversity.'

'Thank you,' said Mel taking the compliment even though she knew she hadn't been fearless, only practical: allowing Stafford's men to take her just hadn't been an option and the thought of it had terrified Mel far more than the consequences, or guilt, of shooting someone.

A few days later, Stafford, now recovering from the bullet wound, was brought in for interrogation. By then the other girls in the barracks had noticed that Georgie was missing. Despite asking, no one would give them information as to where she was. Mel knew that Georgie was being detained indefinitely. Most likely she would be held and kept safe until after any trial to condemn Stafford. After that, she had no idea what the army would do with her, but she liked to believe she would be freed, and relocated to avoid anyone who might be working with Stafford from finding her.

Many other decisions had been made regarding Georgie. Although Derrin didn't think it likely Stafford had any reach inside the barracks or in the service, they couldn't be certain. Georgie was, therefore, being held under a completely anonymous name as a precaution because they had agreed that keeping her invisible was the best way to ensure her safety. That and a strict thoroughly vetted guard detail that was on rota, watching the woman twenty-four hours a day.

Stafford hadn't been allowed any visitors, and was also not listed anywhere as being on the base or in military custody. His gang may therefore think he was dead. In many ways, the secret service wanted to keep it that way. Therefore, all paperwork relating to Stafford was marked Top Secret, and was full of redactions, protecting the names of Derrin and Mel, should there be a mole inside.

'Stafford's gang will be in chaos for a while,' Derrin told Mel. 'There will be a period of re-organisation among them.'

All of which gave Derrin and his team the opportunity to work on Stafford, and learn what he knew and especially who he worked for.

But, despite Derrin's belief there was no one inside helping Stafford, it had occurred to Mel in the days after his arrest that someone had to have been feeding him information. Otherwise, how would they know the young private would have key information that could be sold to the enemy? She hoped that if this was the case, Derrin's precautions of hiding Stafford, also nameless in the system, would mean that this insider wouldn't know he was there and might, as Derrin hoped, think he was dead.

'I've taken the precaution of listing a John Doe in the mortuary, with injuries consistent with direct gunshot wounds to the face,' Derrin confirmed, when Mel expressed her concerns.

After that they believed that they had done everything they could to hide his presence at the unit from any interested party that might be an infiltrator.

Before Stafford's interview, Mel had gone into the observation room so that she could study his responses and give her opinions on his lies and truths. She saw two soldiers bring Stafford into the room. They handcuffed him to the table which was rivetted down into the floor, taking no chances that Stafford would be a threat to the interviewers. Opposite Stafford, on the other side of the table, were two empty seats.

The door opened and Derrin came into the room with a soldier who stood by the door. Derrin sat down. He was wearing his first lieutenant's uniform and Stafford weighed him up, a small smirk tweaking the left side of his lips. The smile – if it could be called that – did not reach his eyes and Mel knew murder in a gaze when she saw it. Stafford was dangerous: he had no morals, no guilt and no inhibitions.

Derrin took one of the chairs opposite, his face blank and indifferent, and Mel could tell by his relaxed posture that he wasn't intimidated at all by Stafford.

'Army officer,' Stafford said. 'Knew there was sumfing off with yer.'

'I'm not here to talk about me, Mr Stafford,' said Derrin. 'What did you want with the private?'

'I didn't want nuffink. I was 'elpin' yer,' Stafford smirked. 'And no one'll say otherwise.'

'That's not true. We have a witness. A person you coerced into giving the soldier knock out drops.'

Stafford's smirk had remained on his face. 'Just sum whore init, mate? 'Er word against mine. She prob drugged 'im to rob 'im.'

'In order to say what the person does, or once did, for a living, you'd have to know who we were talking about as a witness,' Derrin said.

Stafford's mouth drew into a line. 'Well, I was suspicious when you and that little tart took him outside, so stands to reason you meant Georgie. She was known in the area… before she joined the forces.'

'Known? As in you forced her into prostitution?'

'I don't force no one to do nuffink they don't wanna do. Not me business what someone chooses to do with their own bodies. Women like her… well you can't stop 'em. Making money is just the excuse.'

Derrin stood and went out of the door, leaving Stafford to stew a little, but the thug looked as though he thought he'd won this round with Derrin. Mel knew that Derrin was only just getting started with him.

'I want you to come in with me and help with the interview,' Derrin said.

'Me? I'm not an interrogator,' Mel had said.

'No, but you're a woman and he'll hate it. His sort always do.'

'Okay,' Mel said.

'One other thing, I'm going to refer to you as Major Greenway.'

Mel nodded. The powerplay was just beginning and Stafford wouldn't know what had hit him.

9

South Yorkshire, October, 1946

'IT'S CRUCIAL THAT WE GET THE ELECTRICITY working again,' Derrin said. 'I could drive to the station and get help, but someone in that room is very dangerous and I don't want to see Avonby exposed by leaving here,' Derrin said.

'I could drive to the station for help,' Mel suggested.

Derrin looked towards the front door. It was now almost three in the morning and dark out.

'No. I don't want you to do that alone. Plus, I need you here. The more we wear this lot down, the more likely we are to discover who the killer and thief is.'

'Or who *they* are? There could be more than one,' Mel pointed out.

'Indeed, and we know how dangerous a trapped rat can be: a pack even more feral. So let's be on our guard,' Derrin said.

'I have an idea,' Mel said. 'When it gets lighter we can send Toby on my motorbike to the police station but in the meantime, while the suspects are all locked up, I would like to check the electricity wiring on the outside of the house. It could have been cut, and might give us a clue if there is an accomplice.'

'I'll come with you,' Derrin said.

Leaving a very tired Mr Williams by the study door, Mel and Derrin went outside of the house, locking the front door behind them. Since Mel now had the only keys, no one could get in or out of the building without her.

Mel led Derrin straight to the power cables that were fed around and into the house from the pylon in the next field, which in turn linked to other pylons leading across the country to the power station. Now Mel studied the grey painted cables that went into the house, looking for signs of any tampering.

'It all looks fine, which suggests this is a power station issue and not deliberate sabotage,' Mel said. 'So, the lights may just come back on at any point. Then we can call the station and get backup here. Although…'

'What is it?' Derrin said.

'If we can solve this mystery first, and get the painting back, I won't have to involve Lord Jonathan.'

'You don't think he'd react well?' Derrin asked.

'He'll be heartbroken. Every evening, he sits and looks at that painting when he's home. He loves it. And, he might not be too happy that I let my old friends visit with this result.'

'Then we had better get it back for him,' said Derrin. 'Mel… About us.'

Mel gave a tight smile. 'We'll have time for conversation, when we solve this problem.'

'Okay. But I'm not avoiding the discussion. So, you know.'

'I know. I want that talk too. Something else always seems to come first though, doesn't it?'

Mel unlocked the front door and they went back into the house. They found Mr Williams sound asleep in his chair.

'I hate to wake him,' Mel whispered. 'What did he and Toby do with the body?'

'Cloakroom,' Derrin said. 'How about some more interviews in the meantime? Clara?'

'I think we'll jump to her maid, Mabel, next,' Mel said.

'Why?'

'A hunch.'

* * *

Mel experienced a pang of guilt when she saw her former friends Eleanor and Clara on the sofa in the study. Eleanor had cried herself to sleep and now lay, huddled in the foetal position, with her head in Clara's lap. Clara had been dozing against the arm of the sofa. Around the room, all the occupants had changed places again and they found Mabel sitting in a corner on her own, away from the rest of the group. The girl was sitting on the floor, legs pulled up to her chin and her arms wrapped around her knees as though she was sleeping. But for some reason Mel didn't think she was asleep.

Mabel's segregation jarred with Mel, and she wondered what it meant in the dynamic of the assembly. Was Mabel on her own by choice, or did she feel ostracised?

Mel's gaze skirted slowly over everyone in the room and came to rest on the chauffeur who sat by the window and was more alert than anyone else in the room. She glanced at Derrin to see if he had noticed. An old expression niggled at her mind, something about how you didn't need to watch a crook, as he (or she) would always be watching you.

She turned her attention back to Mabel, realising that this was the time to take the girl away from the room and talk to her privately.

'We'd like to speak to you next,' Mel said.

Mabel looked spaced out, as though she really had been asleep when they came in, or had taken some draught to send her off. Now she looked up at Mel, bleary eyed, but terrified.

'You'll be okay,' Mel said.

'She can't tell you anything,' Clara said. 'She was with me upstairs when your wretched painting disappeared.'

Mel pulled Mabel to her feet. The girl was tiny boned and overly thin, as well as small in height. Mel wondered how old she was as she appeared childlike in frame and behaviour. Surely she was no more than eighteen? Mabel looked over to her mistress, Clara, a terrified expression on her face.

'Just tell the truth,' Clara said. 'You've nothing to worry about.'

The girl left the room with Mel and Derrin without a word, and followed them down the hallway to the drawing room.

Mel had noticed that the other occupants in the study were subdued. Exhaustion was a factor, something that she and Derrin were used to working through. But Charles's death must have been a blow. Especially given the implication that a poisoner was among them. Even so, Mel tried not to have too much empathy: one or more of them was responsible for what had happened to Charles and for the theft of the painting, and she was determined to find out who before the night was over.

'Sit down,' Mel said to Mabel, indicating the chair by the window as they entered the drawing room.

Mabel glanced out of the window and then took the seat. She turned her face up to Mel and Derrin as they loomed above her. Her eyes were round and a frown furrowed her brow.

'Right Mabel, we are going to ask you some questions,' Derrin said. 'Firstly, how long have you worked for Miss Taylor-Smith?'

'Only a few months, Sir,' Mabel said.

'How old are you?' asked Mel.

'I'm just turned twenty-two, Miss… I mean Your Ladyship,'

'Miss will do,' Mel said. 'Where did you work before you went into Clara's employ?'

'I worked for a friend of Miss Clara's: Miss Susan. Miss Clara offered me a job, so I left to work for her,' Mabel explained.

The girl's hands were shaking and she wrapped them into the folds of her skirt to hide the fact that she was terrified.

'Do you mean Susan Erskine?' Mel asked now.

'Yes, Miss,' Mabel said.

'You worked for Miss Erskine for how long?' Derrin asked.

'A couple of years. She was looking for a personal maid. My ma worked for her ma… I mean Mrs Erskine… in the kitchen. I was between jobs. The lady I worked for had left the city to avoid the bombings, so I was out on a limb, so to speak.'

'It is very unusual to leave one service for another. Why did you leave Miss Susan's? Was there a problem?' Mel asked. 'Did she fire you?'

'Oh no, Miss!' Mabel said but her eyes darted around the room as though she was looking for an escape route.

'You do know you can get into a great deal of trouble if you lie to a police officer, don't you?' said Derrin, picking up on the girl's terror.

'I haven't done nuffink,' said Mabel almost in tears. 'Honest, Sir. I just didn't like Miss Susan much. She was mean sometimes. Slapped me across the face for dropping her hairbrush. Pinching me, just because she liked to. She made me so nervous all the time that I'd do all the wrong things because of it. In the end, Miss Clara said to come work for her. She was always so kind to me, so I knew fings'd better there.'

'All right,' said Mel noticing the girl's tremors worsening. 'You're not in any trouble. For now. We just need to know more. About Miss Clara. And Miss Eleanor. And also Miss Susan since she has a bearing on your current employment.'

Mabel looked up at Mel with round wet eyes.

'But what would I know about anyone, Miss?'

'Come now,' Mel said. 'I know for a fact that personal maids know everything about their mistresses. I don't believe you will be any different. Not unless you're a complete idiot and I don't think you're stupid at all Mabel. So, tell me about Miss Eleanor and Mr Charles. What do you know about their relationship?'

'Oh, Mr Charles is very strong *willed*.'

'In what way?' asked Derrin, not correcting her 'is' to 'was'.

'Well, I guess he's used to getting all his own way and Miss Eleanor is such a sweet, kind person, she don't like to upset 'im.'

'What happens if Mr Charles is upset?' Mel asked.

'He gets a little… angry,' Mabel said. 'Like tonight.'

'Did anyone else find Charles's anger upsetting?' Derrin asked.

Mabel looked down at the floor, she appeared to be thinking and Mel wondered if the girl was replaying the events in the study, just as she did herself.

'No one was happy about it,' she said at last. 'When he was going on like that, Miss Clara pulled me into the seat next to her. She was looking at him as Miss Eleanor tried to calm him down, but she had this worried look on her face and I don't like to see Miss Clara upset. She don't deserve it.'

'Charles was upset about being locked up, wasn't he?' Derrin said.

'No. It were somefink else,' Mabel said.

'Do you know what?' Mel asked.

Mabel looked away, 'No. But I think Miss Clara did.'

* * *

'What have you done to Mabel?' Clara said. 'She was in a terrible state by the time she was returned to the study.'

'Please sit, Miss Taylor-Smith,' Derrin said. 'I can assure you; your maid was unharmed.'

'She's a sensitive soul,' Clara said. 'I don't like to see her so distressed. I mean, she was shaking from head to foot and bright red in the face. You must have done something.'

'No,' said Mel. 'We merely asked her some questions.'

'What about?' Clara said.

'You,' Derrin said.

'She's a nervous sort,' said Clara. 'And very loyal to me.'

'She told us she previously worked for Susan Erskine. I was surprised that Susan could afford a personal maid,' Mel said. 'How was that possible?'

'Oh, Sue came into some money. Some distant relative left her a bundle.'

'When did that happen?' Mel asked.

'During the war. Probably about six months after you enlisted. There was a house associated with the inheritance and so she moved out of her mother's home and took up residence in her own. Quite an impressive place to be honest. After that, she seemed to be the only person thriving during those awful times.'

'Who was the relative?' asked Derrin. 'What was the association and why leave Susan the money and not her mother?'

'Well, I believe he was on her father's side. But you know Sue,' she said looking at Mel. 'Always so secretive.'

'You poached Mabel from her. That can't have gone down well. Susan definitely wouldn't like that,' Mel said.

'She should have treated the girl better,' Clara said raising her chin and her eyes gleamed with an anger that Mel had never seen before.

'How did she treat her?' Derrin asked.

10

Six months earlier

'Hurry up, you lazy little slut,' said Susan. 'I'm already late and it's down to your clumsy fingers. Can't you ever do my hair right the first time?'

'I'm sorry Miss Susan. I'm doing me best,' Mabel said, her hands trembling as she pressed pins into the most perfect coiffure she had ever done for her employer.

'Ouch! You stuck that in me!' Susan turned and slapped Mabel hard across the face.

In tears, Mabel rushed from the room. As she ran down the stairs she met Clara who was on her way up to find Susan and see what was taking so long.

'Whatever's going on here?' Clara asked.

'Oh, Miss,' said Mabel, tears streaming freely down her face, highlighting the burgeoning and swollen cheek that Clara could see would soon develop into a ripe bruise.

'Did Susan do this?' she asked.

Mabel cried harder, 'I try my best. She just don't like me, Miss.'

Clara went upstairs and seeing the delightful styling of Susan's hair realised that her friend just didn't deserve the young maid.

'Oh that stupid girl!' Susan said. 'She's made me late again. I shan't be long; I just need to get my throw.'

'Did you just slap that poor girl?' Clara asked.

A cruel smirk and a little snigger confirmed that Susan really didn't have any compassion or regret for the impact her actions had on Mabel.

'She's so pathetic,' she said. 'I just can't help myself. If she wasn't actually good at what she does, she would have been gone long ago.'

Clara had been shocked to see this mean streak in her friend. But then she recalled how Susan had been at school and how she was always targeting the weaker girls among them with the odd demeaning comment, always said in such a way to imply she meant well, when it was really the opposite. Clara herself had been on the receiving end of such barbs, and sometimes they had stung. She had, like so many others, always excused Susan though. She was, after all, the poorest among them and had to fight for her place there. Even though Clara, Eleanor and Mel had never treated her like she was a poor relation.

Looking back, Clara had found herself wondering why she was friends with Susan at all. Perhaps they had given her so much leeway because she had less than them? She wasn't really their sort after all, even with the sudden upsurge of wealth. But Clara had been in a habit of remaining friends with Susan, especially with Mel's absence and Eleanor taken up with Charles most of the time. There were so few friends to be found in their circle during wartime. Clara realised then how often Sue used her new status to put her down too. The war had been harder on Clara's family than it had been on Susan, who had continued to thrive during those awful years, especially because of her mysterious inheritance. Now that they were all getting back to some normality and Clara's family fortunes were stabilised again, Susan had taken to being nicer. As though she was useful again.

Why didn't I see this earlier? Clara had thought.

Susan pulled on the throw.

'Well? Are you going to gawk at me all day or are we going to the theatre?' she said.

Clara found herself babbling an apology. A habit, she realised, she had developed in the last few years around Susan. She didn't like herself for it, and thought less of Susan because of her horrible attitude.

Later at the theatre, it was as though someone had thrown a

light switch on, which was illuminating her relationship with Susan for the first time. That night, Clara woke up to her bad behaviour, making her feel differently about her supposed friend. She saw the way Susan operated, and realised that she was being used for her contacts and social status. But this was nothing new, she always had been. Clara's family were old money, and the truth was, Susan did not have such a pedigree, nor did anyone really know where this sudden prosperity had come from, her capital that was like a bottomless pit, or the proverbial money tree, based on the frequency by which her once middle-class school friend bought clothing. She was even wearing French designs that she had shipped over that had been made by Christian Dior and buying expensive and rare Coco Chanel perfume. Rare because the woman had been suspected of being a Nazi collaborator and was somewhat out of favour in Europe. Until then, Clara hadn't questioned it much, nor asked too many questions about the money, because to do so was vulgar and frowned on.

'Where is it you say this deceased relative lived?' Clara asked Susan at the interval.

'What?' she said. Susan's eyes had narrowed and her back stiffened as Clara questioned her.

'The one who left you the money?'

'Isn't that Lord Mountbatten?' Susan said. 'I thought he was in India. Do introduce me Clara.'

Clara had found herself swept along on the tail of Susan's need for important associations. She had not been able to resist making the introduction, but she was very aware that Susan had, once more, dodged the question of where her money came from.

* * *

South Yorkshire, October, 1946

'You never got to ask her again?' Mel said.

'She always changed the subject. Once even implied that my interest was vulgar and intrusive. Sue has a way of turning things back on me and always makes me feel bad because of it. But I saw her get meaner to Mabel and I didn't like it. Eventually, I asked the girl to come and work for me. I didn't really need her, but I just felt this urge to rescue her. I don't know why, but I've never liked bullies. And Mabel is talented.'

'What impact did that have on your relationship with Susan?' Derrin said.

'She was a little put out, but she covered it by saying she pitied me the trouble the girl would cause. And I almost think she meant it too. It shows you how two completely different personalities just don't work together. Mabel is a sweet, dear creature, and I haven't regretted it. And Susan got another maid almost immediately and I have never seen her acting in the way she did towards Mabel with the new girl. It was odd and I did find it jarring,' Clara said. 'But what does all this have to do with now? And your painting? You can't think that dear girl is involved somehow? I swear she's never done anything to disappoint me, and I've always found her to be unfailingly honest.'

'I'm not able to say why your relationships are relevant yet. Just know that I don't ask questions without good reason,' Derrin said. 'I do want to know more about your friendship with Miss Parkinson and what you know of her fiancé Mr Harris.'

'*Know*? Well, they met at a party from all accounts. I'll be honest I hadn't seen too much of Eleanor for a few years. She had distanced herself, and she and Sue didn't get along once Sue became a little… well… over-the-top. The truth is, she only reached out to me again just before Sue told me about Mel's family. I think she was having the wedding jitters and needed an old friend to lean on. When we reconnected, it was a relief to have someone else other than Susan at that point because I wasn't feeling as friendly or as close to her as I had been.'

'How did Susan know about me? I haven't exactly been sharing it around or been in touch with anyone until you and Eleanor reached out,' Mel asked.

'I don't know. But she always does get in on any gossip. And it was implied that it had come to her through a source close to you.

She claimed to be friends with so many people I just took it on face value.'

'So. *You* wrote to me? Did Susan suggest that?' Mel asked.

'Mmm. I can't quite remember how it came about. But she may have made some comment about how nice it would be to contact you. Then I met up with Eleanor for lunch. She seemed happy and I'll admit, I was a little jealous of her and Charles. I haven't had too much luck myself in the love department. But still, I shared with her that I wanted to visit you and suggested she might come with me. She was a little circumspect at first. Then, when I had heard back and you invited me over, she confirmed she wanted to come as well. I thought this would be a great opportunity to rebuild our friendships. Truthfully, I was looking to ditch Susan at the earliest opportunity. I know that's an awful admission, but she never really was our *sort*, was she? So, I made the arrangements as you know. At the last minute, Eleanor said Charles *had* to come as well. I was a little disappointed, as I just wanted it to be about our old friendships and thought Charles might get bored.'

'She told us she had to encourage him and he hadn't been keen, but thought it would do him good,' Mel said.

'Oh!' said Clara. 'Maybe I misunderstood...'

'Perhaps you ought to tell us what she said, from your perspective?' Derrin said.

'She told me... Look I really don't want to shed any suspicion,' Clara said.

'It's important you tell us the truth,' Derrin said. 'It may prove her innocence...'

'She said he wouldn't let her come *without* him. That's why I sent you the letter asking if there was room. I had noticed that Charles could be a little *possessive* at times. I was worried about it to be honest. I could almost see some of those tendencies in Charles that Susan had. A bit of an edge all the time. Something bubbling under the surface as though he would explode at any moment. And we saw some of that too this evening, didn't we? All that shouting. It scared poor Mabel half to death.'

'Yes. She mentioned how uneasy he made her feel. What did Charles say or do in there, that might have got such a reaction?' Derrin asked.

'He didn't like being locked in. Eleanor told me while he was being interviewed by you that it was a phobia. Something to do with his service in the war. I tried to be sympathetic but… well his behaviour didn't ring true.'

'What do you mean?' Mel asked.

'He kept looking around, trying to make sure everyone was paying attention to him. Like it was some kind of… performance,' Clara said. 'I don't… didn't… know him very well of course. It could have been completely genuine. But I found it odd.'

***

Mel returned after escorting Clara back to the study.

'What do you make of all that?' Derrin asked.

'I think Clara is onto something with Charles's behaviour. I wonder if anyone else observed him "looking around" and what their take on it was? I wasn't sure about his potential CSR or Shell Shock. We all know that such moments of anxiety aren't as easily calmed.'

'Yes. I did notice that once we brought him out of the study, Charles was still. It wasn't even an effort,' Derrin said. 'You know first-hand that isn't how it goes.'

Mel's cheeks flushed slightly with the mention of her own weakness.

On instinct, Derrin pulled Mel into his arms and held her. At the mention of her CSR, she had been made aware of her own fragility and was fighting off the tremors. Derrin's warm embrace helped her regain her composure, gave her strength and somehow revitalised her energy. She sank into him, enjoying being held. It was a moment of tenderness that they rarely shared and she was reluctant to pull away, hoping it would last for longer.

When they drew apart, Mel noticed that Derrin was energised too and she realised that his impulsive hug was as much for him as it was for her. They looked into each other's eyes for a time, as though unable to quite let go, until a slight awkwardness came between them.

She gave Derrin a smile, which he returned, the light and warmth reaching his eyes reflecting in the continual glow from the candlelight. They shared mutual understanding which Mel believed spoke more than any words they could exchange. Derrin gave her a soft kiss on her mouth as though he was sealing some silent pact. Then he stepped back, and released her hands.

Mel turned her mind back to their situation. It had been a long night and much had happened, but they had barely scratched the surface of this mystery. She had so many concerns that they wouldn't solve the case before the morning when they would have to involve the police regardless. Something she didn't relish because at such a time she and Derrin would lose control, and possibly access to the suspects, which might mean the painting would never be found. The thought of this happening sent real terror running through Mel's veins but it spurred her on, making her more determined to solve the crime and find the thief and killer before she had to surrender everything to another party.

'Next up?' she asked.

'The chauffeur, Frank, I guess.' Derrin said.

'I'll fetch him,' Mel said.

'No. I will.'

'You think he'll be hostile?' Mel asked.

'We don't know him, so I'm being cautious.'

11

MEL AND DERRIN RETURNED TO THE INTERVIEW room together to continue the interrogation of Eric Stafford. As Mel came in, and took a seat opposite, Stafford's eyes narrowed and the viciousness returned to his expression. Mel kept her own expression blank, and slightly bored, as though Stafford's fate was sealed regardless of what he told them.

'Major Greenway will be asking the questions now,' said Derrin, standing beside her.

'Major? Don't make me laugh!' Stafford said, his arrogance and disrespect evident.

'Marm?' said Derrin.

Mel nodded.

Derrin walked around the table and without warning backhanded Stafford across the face. If he hadn't been firmly attached to the rivetted table Stafford would have been thrown back in his chair. As it was, the chair tipped on its rear legs, and Stafford's arms were yanked at a painful angle, but then the chair bounced back, crashing down on all four legs into its original position.

A deep cut appeared on Stafford's cheek as it blossomed red and began to bruise.

'You'll show respect to the Major, you scum,' said Derrin.

Mel caught the eye of the soldier standing by the door. He was only young, a new recruit, who had just reached the subscription age, and he too was looking at Mel with a modicum of fear and respect. Especially as she hadn't reacted with any shock at the violence dished out to the prisoner. There was something so concerning about a woman who didn't show her emotions and the soldier now looked at her as if she were Lady Macbeth threatening to dash the brains out of her newborn babe.

Stafford's arrogant demeanour slipped for a second.

'I remember you,' Stafford sneered. 'Little bitch who shot me in the face.'

Mel smiled now, she lost the bored expression as she leaned back in her chair.

'How is the ear, Mr Stafford? You won't be such a pretty boy from now on will you?'

Mel's words hit home as Stafford had always been vain about his looks and Mel's bullet had left his ear deformed beyond repair. He would spend the rest of his life wearing hats that covered it up.

Stafford's fury burst out and he began to yank hard at the handcuffs and table.

Mel remained calm as she watched the man struggle against the chains, even though she knew if he managed to free himself he would lunge at her.

'Sit still, or Lieutenant Bradley will hit you again,' she said, her voice cold.

'I'll fucking kill you both,' Stafford said. 'My men…'

'Your men think you're dead, Stafford,' Derrin said. 'No one is getting you out of here anytime soon.'

'The only thing that can save you now, is answering our questions,' Mel said. 'Tell us what we want to know and I'll get leniency for you. No gibbet or firing squad, just a quiet cell until the war's over. Then, who knows, you might be released to go about your business?'

'You haven't got the authority for that,' Stafford said, but Mel could hear the doubt in his voice.

'The Major has the ear of the prime minister,' Derrin said.

At the mention of Winston Churchill, Stafford looked up. He studied Mel for a long moment before saying, 'I bet she does.'

Stafford's smirking expression was even more grotesque because of the blood that now dripped from his busted lip.

Mel had never met a viler person, and she had, over the last few years, come across many forms of lowlife. But Stafford was irredeemable, and even if she had the authority to save his life to trade for information, she doubted it was worth it. Even so, if it made him talk, she would pretend she did have the power.

'You aren't helping yourself, Mr Stafford,' Mel said. 'Any moment now, the lieutenant will be getting out some tools that will encourage your cooperation, and I'll just stand by and watch. You see, I may be female, but I have a very strong stomach, and I have seen some work done inside these walls. At no point will I intervene on your behalf, or have any sympathy for you. Some of us just aren't made that way.'

A flicker of doubt crossed Stafford's features. He was a tough guy, but money was his main motivation, and he was beginning to wonder whether his life was worth what he knew. He could tell that Mel meant what she said, just by her cold and detached tone, which showed no empathy at all for the proceedings. Even so, he wasn't ready to give in and so it took Derrin a few more well-aimed punches before the man's resolve weakened further.

'What do you want?' he asked eventually.

Mel and Derrin kept their expressions blank. This was not yet a victory, only the information, should it prove to be true, would give them the win they were looking for. And there was always the risk that a man like Stafford would lie to string them along to save himself.

'Why were you trying to take the private?' Mel asked.

'He owed me money.'

'Wrong answer,' said Derrin and he hit Stafford again.

The blow fell right on the cheekbone and Mel heard the painful punch echo through the man's face as the cheekbone crunched. Stafford's eye began to swell shut. The handsome features were a long way from what they had once been already, any more hits and his face might be permanently scarred.

'I'll ask again,' said Mel. 'What did you want with the private?'

Derrin had suggested to Mel that Stafford's tough-guy image was only relevant when he was dishing out pain. Receiving it was always the moment of truth on real bravery or strength, and the likes of Stafford hadn't been trained to take torture. That was a very different specialism.

Blood-filled spittle dripped down onto the table in front of Stafford. Mel ignored it.

'Who were you working for?' Mel asked.

Stafford looked scared then, as though giving out such information would mean his death warrant.

'I dunno.'

Derrin moved in to dish out another blow and Stafford hung his head. He couldn't take any more already or maybe he really did value his looks.

'Wait,' he said. 'This fellow. 'E comes into the speakeasies. Offered a bounty if we could deliver the private to 'im. I dunno what he wanted.'

'You're going to tell us everything about this man,' Mel said.

'He'll kill me if 'e finds out,' Stafford said.

'That's a big *if* Mr Stafford,' Mel said. 'If you don't tell us, we *will* kill you, and it won't be an easy passing.'

By morning they had a name for Stafford's contact and details of exactly what he had wanted to learn. It was as they suspected: Stafford's contact was searching for details of the Allied forces' plan to end the war. What they needed next was to capture the spy and find out how he'd known about these plans in the first place. After all, any leak meant there might be a mole.

But before either of them could rest, Derrin's team set off to arrest the conspirator and bring him to the base, to face the same kind of justice he would have delivered to a very innocent young private.

* * *

South Yorkshire, October, 1946

While she waited for Derrin's return, Mel reflected on those times past. What a crucial find Stafford had been. Many arrests followed, and it was at that point that she and Derrin had ended all land-based treachery that might well have meant a different outcome to the war. The inside traitor was found too and executed for treason.

The Allied forces had invaded Germany the following year, bringing down the Third Reich. Hitler, hidden in the Führerbunker in Berlin, had taken his own life rather than be captured and tried for his crimes.

Stafford, like many other traitors, was tried and shot, an execution that neither Mel nor Derrin had any motivation to witness. Nor any guilt about. Though Mel remembered the outburst of anger and desperation when Stafford learned he'd been duped. It had been a very ugly scene, though she hadn't witnessed it first hand, and had just heard how the man was dragged in front of the firing squad, screaming with impotent rage and crying like a baby as he had begged for his life.

'Ironic,' Derrin had said. 'As he hadn't given anyone else he'd dealt with the slightest mercy and was responsible for the deaths of more than a dozen street girls.'

Now, Mel didn't know why she was bringing up these memories, except that the man had been misogynistic, abusive and a thoroughly unpleasant character. All traits that she had heard about tonight at different levels. Some even attributed to her former friend Susan, and Eleanor's dead fiancé, Charles. But what did it all mean? A thief, after all, wasn't as bad as a traitor, but a thief who was also capable of murder and attempted murder, that was a different thing all together.

It made Mel twitchy in a way that usually led to some inner revelations. She was starting to believe there was a link somewhere, she just had to find it. Like all games of strategy, life was full of red herrings and misinformation. It had deceptions, and deflections.

In the back of her mind, Mel saw the people held in the study, their starting positions moved as soon as Charles was wiped from the board. But who had taken him down? Was it a knight, a pawn or the queen herself? The picture wasn't clear yet. Neither was the role of each of the players on that board. Mel, however, was working on the stratagem anyway. She would, despite the perpetrators' efforts to thwart her, get to the end of the game. She knew it, not with arrogance, but with some inner instinct and surety. The killer and thief would slip up. They had to, because there was no way out of Avonby until the answer was found, and Mel and Derrin were both determined to solve this riddle in as short a time as possible.

Mel sighed.

There was something else going on here that hadn't revealed itself. She had a nagging sensation in the back of her head. A biting pressure, almost, that wouldn't let up. But the headache wasn't pain, more a swirling of unanswered questions that wouldn't leave her because they hadn't yet formed. Solving a mystery was, after all, nine-tenths of asking the right questions and one-tenth of getting the answers. But for now, those questions weren't obvious. All they could do was keep probing until they presented themselves. And some of that would come from the next move the killer/thief made.

They will have to make that soon, Mel thought as she glanced towards the window and saw the morning approaching. If the thief didn't escape custody shortly, then the daylight limited their chances of getting away scot-free. They were as much slaves to the passing of time as Mel and Derrin were, perhaps more so.

She glanced at the carriage clock that stood on the drawing-room mantelpiece. It was 3.43 a.m. Derrin was taking a while getting Frank, it should have taken mere seconds. Something must be wrong!

Alarm bells went off in Mel's head. She rushed to the drawing-room door just in time to see Derrin and Mr Williams struggling to open it. The occupants inside had decided to band together. They were trying to stop Derrin from entering the study.

She reached into her pocket, then realised she didn't have her pistol, it was safely stored in her locked chest upstairs in her bedroom. Mel rushed forward and pushed her entire weight against the door. With momentum and her added weight, the door gave, and the people behind it who were trying to hold them off fell back, some falling to the floor because they were weakened by fatigue in the first place.

Derrin withdrew a pistol from a hidden holster.

Old habits die hard, Mel thought, regretting she didn't have the foresight to bring hers down.

As Derrin held the suspects at gun point, all of them froze.

Mel's eyes went from one suspect's face to another's. She saw wide eyes and fear on the ladies and fury in Frank's. *Interesting.*

'Who was the instigator of this rebellion?' Mel asked staring them all down.

The group didn't move.

'We want out!' said Eleanor at last. 'There's a murderer in here.'

'Yes there is,' said Derrin. 'And you could be that person, Miss Parkinson.'

'Me? Kill Charles?' Eleanor said. Then she burst into another bout of tears.

Clara went to her. 'How much longer must this go on?' she said.

'There is a process and we must work through it. Eleanor, stop crying, your tears are wasted on us,' said Mel.

Eleanor gasped in her last tear and stared at Mel with an expression akin to fear.

'Who *are* you?' she asked.

Mel stood her ground.

'Carter. You're next,' Derrin said. 'And any more shenanigans from you lot and we'll be forced to tie you up.'

A collective gasp echoed through the room. Mel noticed then that Michael was still sitting in the chair by the fire. He wasn't moving and it was obvious he hadn't been involved in the attempted coup.

'Michael?' Mel said. She moved to him, put her hand on his shoulder and shook him gently.

Michael didn't wake. Instead, he slumped forward and that was when Mel saw the wound in his shoulder and the blood that had been seeping into the tapestry of the armchair.

'He's been stabbed,' Mel said.

Mabel let out a suppressed sob of terror.

'Is he… *dead*?' asked Clara.

Mel put two fingers to his neck and checked his pulse. It was there but faint.

'Unconscious,' Mel said. 'Mr Williams. Rouse the household. Get Daisy to bring bandages and hot water. We'll need plenty of towels. He isn't too injured, fortunately the knife missed a main artery, but the shock and blood loss are probably why he's out cold. Derrin, keep that gun trained on this lot. Shoot anyone that moves.'

'You can't mean that, Mel?' said Eleanor. 'We're your friends.'

'You've said that so many times tonight,' Mel said. 'But friends don't steal, and poison, and stab people for no reason. I want to know what is going on, and if I have to torture you all to find out, I will.'

'She means it,' said Mabel.

As Mel turned her eyes onto each of them individually, everyone in the room cowered except for Mabel and Clara whose similar expressions suggested they were in awe of her.

*　*　*

Mr Williams returned with Toby and Daisy and the provisions that Mel had asked for.

'Daisy, lay out some of those towels on this sofa to catch any blood. Good. Now, let's move him over there.'

Toby and Williams lifted Michael's body. His head lolled and Mel caught it so that he wouldn't injure his neck. They placed him on his side on the sofa so that Mel had access to the wounded shoulder.

'Give me those scissors,' she said to Daisy.

They managed to peel away Michael's dinner jacket but Mel had to cut away his shirt as it was clinging to his skin with the drying blood. As they pulled it away from the wound, more blood seeped out and Mel was forced to fold a bulk of towel against the cut as a compress. Once the remains of his shirt were removed, she began to clean the wound.

'Definitely a knife wound,' she said. 'Williams and Toby, can you search the room for the weapon? The inspector will cover you.'

The wound wasn't as deep or as severe as it could have been and Mel saw that Michael was in no real danger other than if infection set in. She sent Daisy to bring her some cooking whisky from the kitchen and when the girl returned, she poured a little over the injury to disinfect it. Then Mel pressed wadded dressing onto the wound and with Daisy's help, wove a bandage over and around the area, wrapping the gauze over his shoulder and around his torso to keep it secure. They placed another towel under his shoulders as extra security and lay him back down on the sofa.

Mel checked his pulse again and nodded to herself.

Only then did Mel turn her attention back to the group. No one had moved because Derrin was keeping them covered, pistol in hand.

'Eleanor,' Mel said, 'pull that chair from the fireplace and place it in the corner over near the window.'

'Why?' Eleanor said.

'Because you're going to sit there and not move from it.'

Eleanor looked over at Derrin then began to slide the heavy chair over to the corner that Mel had indicated.

'Mabel, go in that corner,' Mel said, indicating an opposite point in the room. 'Clara, sit on the footrest over near the fire. That way you'll be farther apart.'

Both women moved and went to where Mel directed without a word.

'Frank, sit behind the writing desk. I want to see your hands on top of the ink blotter at all times,' Derrin said.

Frank went over to the desk and sat down, back to the wall and facing into the room.

'Now what?' said Frank as he placed his hands on the desk.

'We're going to conduct the interviews in here,' Mel said. 'Daisy you can leave. Get some smelling salts and bring them in here. We'll use them to rouse Mr Chase soon. Toby, you're going to take my motorbike and go to the police station. We want as many officers as they can spare out here as soon as possible.'

'Are you sure?' Derrin said looking at her sharply.

'We've no choice. One of these people murdered Charles and they've now wounded Michael, possibly another murder attempt. We need help if we're going to discover the truth.'

Derrin nodded and Toby went to the door.

'Wait. Daisy? Before you get the smelling salts, take the door key, let Toby out, lock the door again, and then I want you to stay there to let the police officers in when they arrive.'

'Yes, Lady Melinda,' said Daisy. She took the set of house keys with a great deal of reverence and, wide eyed, went out of the study with Toby, closing the door behind her.

The key snicked in the lock and then there was silence for a moment.

'Frank Carter,' Derrin said. 'You're next and if I feel any guile coming from you, you'll feel the back of my hand.'

Derrin handed his gun to Mel.

Clara, Eleanor, Mabel and Frank all watched with amazement as Mel took and held the gun with obvious expertise and no nerves at all. Then Derrin walked across the room, sat down opposite Frank, and started firing questions at him.

12

ᴅᴇʀʀɪɴ ʜᴀᴅ ɴᴏ sᴏᴏɴᴇʀ sᴛᴀʀᴛᴇᴅ ᴛᴏ ɪɴᴛᴇʀʀᴏɢᴀᴛᴇ Frank than the key clicked in the door once more.

The door opened to reveal Toby and Daisy.

'Lady Mel,' Toby said.

Mel backed up, never taking her eyes off the room.

'Why are you still here?' she asked in hushed tones.

'Your motorbike. It's broken…' Toby said.

'What do you mean, *broken*? I only used it this morning,' she cast Toby a glance to fully take in what he was saying.

'Sabotaged,' Toby said.

Mel's focus returned to the remaining people in the room. 'None of them have moved from here,' she said. 'Not since we discovered the painting missing.'

'They musta done it before then,' Toby said.

'What about the inspector's car?' Mel asked.

'Tyres slashed,' Toby said.

Mel's eyes went to the window of the study. Was there someone else out there?

'Is the front door locked?'

'Yes,' said Daisy. 'Did it just as you said. Then Toby came back and I let him in and locked it again.'

'Good. Give me back the keys. Then gather everyone in the house together. I want all the house staff back in here,' Mel said. 'Get those smelling salts too, while you're at it.'

'I thought we were ruled out,' said Toby.

'It's for your own safety. If everyone is here, I can keep an eye on you,' Mel explained. 'Derrin? Can I speak to you please?'

Derrin took his attention away from Frank and, seeing the serious expression on her face, came to her immediately.

'Mr Williams. Please watch this lot. Anyone moves, call me,' Derrin said.

Williams stood up. He took a hefty poker from by the fireplace and held it firmly.

'I've got this Inspector,' Williams said.

The occupants of the room knew he would execute his orders to the letter, and possibly do some damage to anyone who tried anything in the meantime.

Mel gave Williams a nod, 'Yes you have.'

Outside, Toby explained what he had seen to Derrin, describing in detail the smashed engine of Mel's motorbike and the roughly slashed tyres on Derrin's car. When he finished his story, Mel sent him and Daisy to fetch everyone else.

'I don't know how any of them could have vandalised my bike or your car at any point during the evening. They were in our company the whole time,' Mel said.

'Agreed,' said Derrin. 'Unless they did it just as they arrived, there has to be an accomplice.'

'I'm now thinking it is probable that the electricity *was* cut off, perhaps not outside the house but via its source – maybe it was disconnected from the closest pylon. Which would mean that the collaborator understands how to handle electricity. Or they bought someone's help who worked for the electricity board. Either way, a great deal of thought and planning has gone into this heist. It wasn't just a mere opportunist burglary and subsequent violence.'

'No. They came prepared. Arsenic and a knife inside, a potential accomplice outside. It all makes sense. I think a full body search may be in order. Someone in there still has a knife, and may have evidence of the poison on them. Let's get back in there, I have some very hard questions to ask,' Derrin said.

'Okay. But before we do, I think you should keep hold of this,' Mel said handing back the pistol.

Derrin studied her for a second, his expression unreadable, and Mel didn't know if he understood why she had given him the gun back.

Recalling Stafford had reminded Mel that she once responded to anxiety in a very direct manner. Although those days had passed, she still didn't trust herself or her judgement in certain situations. She was more likely to react than think, especially if she felt under threat. Derrin took the gun back without question and stowed it away so that it was once again invisible and somewhere holstered in his clothing. Then they returned to the study.

As she opened the door, Mel noted that everyone had remained in their places with Williams watching their every move.

Mel checked on Michael and found he was still unconscious.

'Why do we have to stay apart like this?' Eleanor asked.

'Because someone in here poisoned Charles and stabbed Michael,' Derrin said. 'It'll be harder for that person to do any other damage if you can see them coming. This is for your own safety.'

'*Goodness*!' said Clara her hand flying to her throat in a flutter of uncontrolled panic.

'We know there is another person involved,' Mel said. 'You could come clean now and end this charade. We know there's an accomplice outside.'

Eleanor looked around before saying, 'I doubt anyone will speak out. Not when they can be accused of murder.'

'A fact that makes them all the more dangerous,' Derrin pointed out.

Eleanor shrunk into her seat, her arms wrapped around herself.

A knock on the study door signified the return of Daisy, Ruby, Toby and Mrs Weston. Mel ushered them inside.

'Good. Everyone is here so we can continue to keep you all safe,' said Mel.

Daisy handed over the smelling salts, and Mel put them in her pocket for later use.

The Avonby staff took up seats away from the suspects but were on full alert after being filled in by Daisy about the sabotage and the murder. Mel was sorry for Ruby who appeared to be tenser than the rest, which was no surprise after what she had been through previously. It was not an ideal situation and Mel found herself wishing that she hadn't invited her former friends over. Then this would never have happened.

Derrin turned his attention back to Frank. He ordered him to stand up.

'Hands on the wall above your head, feet apart,' he said. Then he frisked him, searching pockets, patting down his legs and arms, looking for any obvious storage or holsters for a hidden knife or pistol. He found nothing. When he finished searching Frank he made the man sit again.

'You said you had worked for Charles Harris for some time?'

'About seven months,' Frank said.

Mel watched Eleanor as Frank spoke. She didn't at any point contradict him, or interject. She would know the answers to these questions as Charles's fiancée and so Mel assumed that Frank must be telling the truth or she would have spoken up. Eleanor showed very little emotional response to his replies and had, by outward appearance, cried herself out for the time being. What Mel saw was a woman who was numb and subdued, who didn't even have the energy to deal with her own shock and grief. Even so, Mel was aware that this could all be an act. After all, Eleanor's comment about 'being accused of murder' could well have been a warning for anyone who might speak up if they were involved somehow and she could be implicated.

'And your role in the army?' Derrin asked Frank.

'Sergeant,' said Frank. 'I was on the western front if you must know.'

All eyes turned to Frank at that point. Knowing he had been on the ground on VE Day gave them a new respect for the man. But Mel and Derrin only took his words at face value: people lied about their part in the war all the time, exaggerating their bravery and physical prowess. They would only know more once they could check out Frank Carter's credentials through official channels, and that would be a long way off. Plus, the fact that Frank was a soldier and had seen action would likely make him more capable of murder in Mel's book. Although she hadn't seen combat in that sense, she knew she was able to act if the circumstances were right after what she had experienced. What situation might make a man like Frank resort to murder and theft? Mel reasoned it wouldn't take much if he felt the act warranted, and silencing a witness might be a good enough reason for murder too.

Derrin questioned Frank further as Mel tried to concentrate on the man's answers, but she was distracted when Michael moved, waking with a pain-filled groan.

'Michael?' Mel said, rushing towards him. 'How are you feeling?'

'What… Hap…?' Michael said.

'You were stabbed in the shoulder,' Mel said.

As Michael came round, he went from confused to shocked and then tried to sit up, which only resulted in causing him more pain and the knife wound to weep through the bandage.

Mel pressed another towel into his shoulder to catch the seeping blood and she and Daisy wrapped more bandages around it, securing the towel in place to prevent further blood loss.

'Keep still, you've reopened the wound,' Mel said to Michael. 'Did you see who did this to you?'

Michael shook his head. 'I remember feeling tired and nodding off by the fire. Nothing else. Not even…' He glanced at his shoulder. 'I didn't *feel* it?'

Mel's mind went to the last time she had noticed Michael moving and it was before Charles had been poisoned. He'd been leaning forward talking to Eleanor at that point.

'What were you saying to Eleanor just before I came back with Charles and he drank the poisoned brandy?' Mel asked.

'Charles was *poisoned*?'

Mel could tell Michael's surprise at Charles's death was genuine. Now that she thought of it, Mel recalled that Michael hadn't moved when Charles had begun to seize. Maybe it was at that moment that the killer struck him too, while everyone else was distracted?

'We weren't talking. I had just leaned forward as I noticed he was sleeping,' Eleanor said. 'Then Mel took the glass and… *Oh God…*'

'It's okay,' said Clara who stood to go to her friend as tears came down her face again.

'No!' said Mel. 'Please stay where you are.'

Clara sank back onto the footstool. 'She's upset,' she pointed out. 'I wanted to comfort her. Can't you see that having to answer all these questions just keeps bringing the whole horrible thing back to her?'

'That can't be helped,' Mel said. 'Until we find the killer.'

'The moment of truth now,' Derrin said. 'Who of you, other than Michael, wasn't paying attention to Charles's seizure?' Derrin's look went from one to the other of them. 'Well?'

'One of you must have seen something,' Mel said. 'Just think. It probably wasn't much at the time.'

Heads shook in subconscious denial. Mel noted that Mabel's head didn't move. The girl was looking down at the ground, hands squeezing together in a scared wringing motion. She was visibly distressed.

'Mabel?' Mel asked. 'If you saw something it might be important. Just tell me. Anything at all.'

'Nuffink,' said Mabel. 'I saw nuffink.'

For the first time, Mel didn't believe the girl at all but she decided to leave it and pick a better time to question her when others weren't so focused on their conversation. She was acutely aware that Mabel had good reason to be scared: the killer was in this room and it could be anyone.

'Stay calm please and just relax. That goes for everyone else,' Mel said.

Derrin finished his questioning of Frank but at the end of it, neither he nor Mel felt they had got anything much out of him. Even when pressed Frank claimed to know nothing and had only just heard he was driving to Avonby with Charles and Eleanor a few days earlier.

'Now what?' asked Clara. 'You've spoken to all of us and we can't tell you anything.'

'Can't, or won't?' Derrin said. 'I don't believe for one minute that you're all telling the truth.'

He didn't voice what he was really thinking, which was that they would wait this out until the culprit cracked or until they could safely send for some reinforcements.

'In the morning, you will all be taken into the station and this house will be thoroughly searched again,' he continued.

'Searched? For what?' asked Eleanor.

'The painting. Or had you forgotten where this all started?' Mel said.

The room fell silent, and then Mel noticed that Clara was fidgeting far more than she had been earlier.

'Clara?' she asked.

'I need to… powder my nose,' Clara said.

'Ah,' Mel said. 'Stand up.'

Mel approached Clara and began to pat her down.

'What are you doing?' Clara said.

'Looking for weapons. There is still a knife around here somewhere.'

'A *knife*?' gasped Clara.

'The one used on Michael,' Derrin said.

'She's clean,' said Mel. 'Come with me.'

'Go with them, Williams,' said Derrin.

Mel and Williams led Clara out of the room and down the hallway to the guest water closet near the front door.

'I'll be out here,' said Mel.

Clara pushed the door open and as she went inside Mel noticed a black smudge on the back of her dress.

As Clara tried to close the door she discovered that Mel's foot was in the way.

'No, we'll keep it ajar,' Mel said.

'But…'

Clara objected further but Mel wouldn't change her mind and so she gave in went inside, leaving Mel guarding the door.

The toilet flushed, and running water indicated that Clara was washing her hands. As she came out, Mel stopped her in the hallway.

'Mr Williams, bring that candle closer please,' Mel requested.

'What is it?' asked Clara.

'There's something on your dress,' Mel commented. 'Turn around.'

Williams shone the light over Clara's back and Mel studied the mark. She leaned closer, sniffing the stain, and then touched it very gently with the edge of her little finger.

'It's coal dust,' Mel said. 'Why would you have that on your dress?'

'I don't know,' said Clara.

'More light, Mr Williams,' Mel said.

Clara turned around, stopping Mel from examining the stain further.

'Oh well, it could be from anything,' Clara said.

'Who has been touching your dress?' Mel asked.

'No one. Don't be silly. I probably smudged it near the fireplace or something. In fact, I think I remember doing that when you demanded we all come downstairs.'

Mel turned Clara back around. 'It's a finger print.'

'How can it be? Surely I'd know if someone touched me. Especially with dirty hands,' Clara said.

'Why are you upset then?' Mel asked.

'I don't like to be tardy. I wish you hadn't mentioned it. All I want to do now is change my clothing. Can we go, please?'

Clara marched off, back towards the study, followed by Mr Williams.

Mel paused for a second, her mind exploring the possible scenarios for how Clara had a coal dust fingerprint on the back of her dress, and didn't follow them. She was as restless as everyone else. Nervous that they hadn't found out anything yet. The fingerprint on Clara's dress could be important. Mel was concerned that it might be evidence that could become contaminated. But short of marching Clara upstairs to change, she wasn't sure what she could do. She was in a quandary. She could force Clara to change, but where would that lead? What if the fingerprint meant nothing at all?

Every detail signifies a clue, she thought, making her mind up.

Going upstairs, Mel went to Clara's room. Inside she found another dress, discarded across the bottom of the bed. A simple blue day dress that she had probably arrived in. She picked it up and took it with her.

Downstairs, she returned to the study, calling Clara outside once more.

'What is it now?' Clara said, her patience frayed.

'Change into this please,' Mel said. 'I'll help you in the water closet, to make sure the mark isn't smudged.'

'Really!' Clara said and even though she was frustrated, she allowed Mel to lead her back to the bathroom.

After she had helped Clara remove the evening dress, Mel left her to put on the other one while she waited outside. In the interim, she studied the fingerprint, and then decided that the dress needed to be stored in a safe place for the police when they were eventually able to call them.

She opened the cloakroom door and looked inside the dark room. Light from the candles in the hallway spilt into the room and she saw Charles's sheet-covered body on the floor in the centre.

She experienced a moment of reverence: a feeling that the newly dead were not quite gone, and could see and hear. Mel respected life above all else and her experiences had taught her that murder always had consequences beyond the person who was killed. It also, more often than not, had motives. Those motives might lead to the answers she needed. If the original objective was to steal the painting, why had Charles been killed? Had he witnessed more than he had admitted to? Did he know who the thief was? Or was Charles's murder unrelated?

But no. Mel didn't think it was even related to the theft. The culprit had come prepared. This was no accident, or even opportunist killing. After all, it wasn't as though there were any chance arsenic vials around Avonby that could have been used to rid the thief of a witness on the spur of the moment. This thought confirmed to Mel that Charles's death had always been on the cards to the killer.

Perhaps the theft had given them the perfect opportunity. But who would want Charles dead, and why?

Mel looked long and hard at Charles's body as though it could give her the answers.

Stepping inside, she placed Clara's dress carefully over one of the empty coat hooks. Then, hearing Clara come out of the bathroom, she turned and left the room, pulling the door closed. Removing her house keys from her pocket, Mel locked the cloakroom for good measure. She didn't feel superstition, but was more concerned that evidence could be tampered with.

'Were you just in there, with the body?' Clara asked shuddering.

Lost in her own thoughts, Mel didn't respond as she escorted Clara back to the study. A thought was niggling again at the back of her head. Something she may have seen earlier, but couldn't bring to the surface of her tired thoughts. She was irritated and felt as though she was losing her edge. Her mind was too calmed by Avonby's beautiful landscape, her analytical brain made lazy from lack of use.

I should have cracked this by now! Mel thought and her frustration surged to the front of her emotions, a vague fury fuelling them. She wanted to go back into the room and slap the truth from those remaining as she knew that one of them had the answers. The question was, who?

One thing she was certain of though, Charles's death and the missing painting were not really related.

The coal dust!

'Clara!' she called now, running after her and Williams.

They had paused just by the study door to wait for her.

'Tell me the truth,' she said. 'Do you know where the painting is? Or why Charles was killed?'

'I don't *know* anything,' Clara said. 'I'd tell you if I did. I can't…'

Tears slipped down Clara's cheeks and her normal composure disappeared with the flood.

'What aren't you telling me then?' Mel asked. 'I know you're holding something back.'

'Please. Stop. Leave me alone. *I can't do this.* I want this all to end,' Clara said.

'Then talk to me! The sooner we solve this the safer everyone will be.'

'It's just… I didn't notice until your footman Toby knocked on my bedroom door. Mabel had just reached for the top button of my dress. As she went to open the door, I saw the dirt on her hands. After Toby told us we had to come down, I told Mabel to wash her hands.'

'Did you ask her why she had coal dust on her fingers?'

'No. I didn't know it was coal dust. She was just dirty. That's all I knew. But what does it matter?'

Mel didn't answer. She knew it was important somehow but couldn't explain why because she hadn't put all the pieces of her puzzle together yet. She likened it now to the parts of her motorbike engine: Mabel, Clara, Eleanor, Frank and even Charles were all components that would fit together in a certain way. But that pattern was, as yet, unclear.

But as Mel let Clara go back into the study her mind whirred and clicked, misfiring like the broken engine, which she could envisage spread out all over the shed. She knew every piece having taken the engine apart several times over the past years when it had gone wrong.

She saw the bike now, and juxtaposed Mabel's dirt-covered fingers. But the coal dust and engine oil were not a match and so she dismissed any connection with the sabotage. Besides, she couldn't see the young maid having any part in the destruction of her bike or the slashed tyres of Derrin's car. She just wasn't the type, and as far as she knew, hadn't been outside since she arrived.

Her eyes went to the front door. Mabel hadn't done it, but someone else had. That part of the puzzle was clear. Were they still out there, and if so, why hadn't they cut and run as soon as the theft was discovered and the house went into lock down? There were still too many questions and no significant answers for Mel to connect. The waters of this mystery were murkier than ever. For the first time in her life, she didn't see the moves and couldn't anticipate the game. It was like a black fog was over her head. All sounds, faces and especially motives were blurred beyond recognition.

13

WHEN MEL ENTERED THE STUDY SHE FOUND the other occupants, locked up now for several hours, were all in need of the bathroom. After Mel gave the women a pat down, she and Williams escorted them all one by one, returning them safely to the room after each comfort break.

Frank was the only person who didn't seem to need this break and therefore wasn't subjected to another frisk but since Derrin had searched him already it didn't seem important. He remained in the corner, his eyes wandering to the window at frequent intervals as though observing the subtle changes in the sky.

Once everyone was comfortable again, Mrs Weston and Ruby were sent for jugs of water and some glasses to drink from.

'No one but them will go anywhere near the jug or the glasses, and I advise you to not let your glass out of sight,' Derrin said.

'Why not just search us properly?' Eleanor said. 'Surely then the culprit will be obvious.'

Frank turned his head back to the room as she spoke.

'We all have rights, that's why,' he said. 'They can't do it. Chain of evidence.'

'What do you mean?' asked Clara.

'Well, one of them could plant somethin' on us,' Frank said. 'Who's to say she didn't steal her own painting?'

Frank tipped his head in Mel's direction.

'Why on earth would I do that Mr Carter?' Mel said.

'Insurance money. Jealousy of your cousin. How'd I know?' Frank said.

'Well, you seem to know plenty about Lady Melinda's life,' said Derrin.

'Heard how she shoulda inherited everythin' but her cousin had to have it all,' Frank said.

'Where would you hear something like that?' Derrin asked.

'It weren't just me. Heard her and Mr Charles talkin' about it,' he said looking at Eleanor.

'There were rumours, Mel. Nothing mean has been said, honestly,' Eleanor said. 'Charles investigated you when we heard Clara was in touch and he learnt what had happened. He said he sympathised. That this was a "stupid, archaic" inheritance rule. It honestly didn't seem fair to us.'

'What do you mean he investigated me?' Mel asked.

'Well, he asked someone to… Really it wasn't for any erroneous purpose, it was just a little natural curiosity. I'd been wondering what had become of you and he found out.'

'I think I'd be careful where you cast aspersions, Mr Carter,' Mel said returning her attention to Frank. 'Rumours and gossip usually never lead to positive things.'

'Indeed,' said Eleanor. 'What a vulgar thing to bring up.'

'No more vulgar than you and Mr Charles discussing it in the back of the car,' Frank said.

'Really!' Eleanor said. 'You're in Charles's employ! How can you be so disloyal?'

'In case you 'aven't noticed, Mr Charles dying means I'm out of a job.'

Eleanor fell quiet.

'You see I 'ave nothin' to gain today,' Frank said. 'And when the other coppers get here, I'll prove it.'

'If you can prove your innocence then, why not do it now?' Derrin asked.

'Oh no, what I 'ave to say is going to fall on many ears.'

'In that case you can remain quiet until then. I don't think any of us needs to hear any more from you for now,' Derrin said.

* * *

Derrin felt that Frank was twisting what he had heard to create dissent among the suspects and perhaps even throw suspicion Mel's way. Not that he or anyone else would listen. Derrin knew how hard Mel worked on the estate, and that she had a good relationship with Lord Jonathan, if not Lady Laura. No, Derrin was not suspicious of Mel. She was the one person he would always trust. Hadn't she saved his life more times than he had saved hers in the past?

Derrin knew Carter's sort though. He wasn't unlike many criminals they had dealt with in the past. He claimed now that killing his boss was detrimental to his own livelihood, but stealing an expensive painting could bring him in thousands of pounds that would mean the man might never have to work again.

Like Mel, Derrin had been watching and observing the silent interactions between the suspects. Mabel was the only person who never looked up, or at any one of them. Derrin wasn't sure whether this was good or not. What it meant in the scheme of things could be explained away so simply given the woman's apparent nervousness. She was terrified, he was certain. But was that because she had seen something? That was what he most wanted to know, but how to draw the answers from the girl was the question…

Leaning against the study door, Derrin's eyes fell on the small woman. She was sitting quietly, happier to be on her own at the side of the room. Maybe she did feel safer that way. He wasn't sure. But she'd stopped fidgeting now, and was more at ease. As the clock on the mantel struck five, Derrin observed a glimmer of sun coming up. It was later now in the morning as the summer had waned into autumn. It would probably not come up fully for another two hours, but already the need for the candles was lessening, and the grounds outside were becoming visible. That was when Derrin thought he saw someone running across the lawn…

He stood upright, moving away from the door he had been leaning against and hurried towards the window to get a better look. But, by the time he reached it, the lawn was empty.

Mel came to his side.

'What is it?' she asked in low tones.

'I thought I saw someone, outside,' he said.

It was still too dark outside to make out more than the outline of the bushes beyond the expansive lawn, but Mel squinted, looking hard for any sign of movement. She said nothing during her silent study of the gardens, but Derrin suspected she was wholly invested in his observation that someone was out there.

'Is it worth separating Frank from the others?' Derrin whispered.

'You think he'll tell us what he knows if we do?'

'Possibly,' Derrin said, glancing around the room.

In the far corner, Mrs Weston, Toby, Daisy and Ruby sat huddled together and were nodding off. Mr Williams remained by the door, poker still in hand, lest anyone should try to run. Mabel hadn't moved from her earlier position; Eleanor appeared to be dozing in the chair by the window; Clara was slumped on the footrest, looking decidedly uncomfortable; Michael was asleep again on the sofa, and Frank, the biggest anomaly of them all, was watching Derrin and Mel: alert and ready as though expecting an affray at any moment.

He reminded Mel so much of others of his ilk. Men she had met in the army; men who had been avoiding service, and some soldiers, afterwards, who told stories of the awful scenes they had seen. Stories, Mel understood, that felt fantastic and untrue to anyone who hadn't been there. Perhaps it was the human condition to disbelieve any horrible events you hadn't witnessed first-hand. Mel didn't know, but she had been inclined to believe those who spoke out about the horrors. Especially on the Western Front, where there had been the most losses, and the greatest acts of heroism. Mel glanced at Frank again. Was he a hero, or a fantasist? She didn't know, but the nagging doubts inside her wouldn't go away. Partly because Frank implied he knew more than he was saying, and partly because she just didn't like him and was suspicious, Mel tried to envisage him on her chessboard, forcing her lagging mind to work hard for a few moments. What piece was Frank? A pawn in someone else's game? Or a knight trying to protect the queen?

Who is the queen? Mel thought toying with the idea of Frank being the knight.

Casting her gaze over the room, in much the same way that Derrin had done, her eyes fell on Eleanor. She and Frank didn't seem to like each other much but was that genuine, or were they pretending? They were closely connected to Charles Harris and either of them might have a reason to want to kill him.

A shudder ran down Mel's spine as though a premonition was lurking somewhere out of reach. A moment of clarity that her weary brain just couldn't get. Then she realised that Clara was watching her again. This time with an inscrutable expression. She could see the tiredness around the woman's eyes though and experienced a pang of guilt. All they wanted to do was go to bed, but that was impossible as Mel daren't let anyone out of her sight – not until the painting was found and the murderer revealed. For she would never forgive herself if anyone else died.

Mel remembered, then, the weird spot of coal dust on Clara's dress. How did Mabel get that on her fingers? Daisy had filled the coal buckets for all the rooms and there were tongs to pick up the coal pieces. So, it wasn't likely she had just been reviving the fire as she surely would have used the tongs?

There was only one way to find out though. She turned her attention to the small figure across the room, huddled in a corner.

'Mabel?' Mel said. 'Come outside in the hallway with me.'

Mabel jumped to attention, and realising her attempt to be invisible wasn't working, changed her demeanour completely. She lost all sign of being pathetic and weak, as she climbed to her feet and headed towards the door with Mel in tow.

The study door closed and Mel found herself face to face with a very different Mabel as they stood in the hallway. The girl was no longer twitchy and afraid; she now appeared resigned.

'What can I do for you Lady Melinda?' Mabel asked. Her voice was still low, but the nerves had gone. It was like someone had flicked a switch, removing all the young woman's fear in one move.

'I need you to tell me your movements this evening.'

Mabel nodded. 'I 'ad 'oped I wouldn't need to.'

Mel examined this sudden change in attitude. Was it a defence mechanism, or was the real Mabel coming out at last?

'You know something Mabel. There's a murderer among us. So, if you've seen anything, now is the time to tell me.'

Mabel sighed. 'I've been thinking through what I seen earlier. At first, I didn't fink it was anythin', but then, well… I'm now wondering.'

They sat down on the chaise in the hallway.

'What did you see?' asked Mel.

'Mr Charles wasn't as nice as what he appeared,' Mabel said. 'I saw it. That mean streak, just like Miss Susan has.'

14

5:45 p.m., the night before

MABEL WAS WALKING AWAY FROM MISS CLARA'S room when she heard raised voices.

Miss Clara was dressed, and her hair was coiffed, Mabel didn't need to do anything more for the night and so she was heading back slowly to the servants' quarters, where she was grudgingly sharing a room with the scullery maid, Daisy.

She hadn't been too pleased about that, as Miss Clara had promised she would have her own room in a fancy place like this. Daisy was nice enough as it turned out, and Mabel had no choice but to share, so she had settled her carpet bag containing her meagre overnight needs in Daisy's room and then she had headed off to help Miss Clara get ready for the evening.

She had been dallying as she left her employer's room, looking at the lovely paintings and admiring the beautiful wood panelling on the walls of the landing. Avonby was such a magnificent building and Mabel, a fan of beautiful structures, couldn't help but appreciate the details.

When she heard the quarrel taking place, she loitered for a different reason other than the attractive décor in the manor house: she wanted to hear the fallout from the other guests. And Mabel, like most personal maids, loved to collect gossip.

The argument was coming from a room close to the servants' staircase, and Mabel recognised the voice of Miss Eleanor.

She slid up to the room, discovering the door slightly ajar. She peered inside, seeing Charles and Eleanor, and Eleanor was wearing a floaty peach dress with short sleeves. Charles's cheeks were ruddy with anger, and then she saw him grab Eleanor's arm and twist the skin viciously.

'Ouch!' Eleanor had said. 'You absolute beast!'

Eleanor pulled her arm from his grasp but the red mark was obviously going to bruise. She backed away from Charles and Mabel had seen the ugly expression on his face. He had enjoyed hurting his fiancée and she knew it. Mabel's hands flew to her mouth but not in time to stifle her shocked gasp.

'Who's there?' Eleanor said, becoming aware that they were being observed.

Mabel hurried away, scooting down the servants' staircase quickly to avoid being seen.

Down in the kitchen she came face to face with Daisy.

'Oh there you are! We're going to eat after the guests have been served, so go and wait in the kitchen. They'll be some nice leftovers too, if we're lucky,' Daisy said.

Mabel was shaken by what she had witnessed. Mr Charles was usually nice around her, and she had seen a bit of him lately as he and Eleanor had visited Clara on numerous occasions. She hadn't suspected he was that 'sort' of man – a bully – and she had thought Miss Eleanor was happy. But Mabel knew now she couldn't be: she was anything but content if Charles was hurting her like that.

'What's up with you?' Daisy asked, being too familiar considering she and Mabel had only just met.

'Nothing. I erm…'

'Go sit down at the table. I expect you're hungry and thirsty now,' Daisy said, her voice kind.

Mabel had nodded and did as Daisy suggested. She was soon served some hot vegetable soup and the gorgeous fresh vegetables were nicer than anything Mabel had eaten in London. She was beginning to like the countryside. But regardless of that she remained distracted, and couldn't stop thinking about Miss Eleanor.

***

Mel hid her surprise. This was not what she expected Mabel to tell her. She had been expecting some story about the coal dust. But she sat back on the chaise and listened to Mabel's retelling of the previous evening's events without saying a word to interrupt until she had finished. The story was a little meandering, and splattered with Mabel's comments about the beauty of Avonby, her disappointment in having to share with Daisy, along with what she had observed between Charles and Eleanor in his room.

'So you're saying Charles grabbed and pinched her and it was deliberately malicious?'

'Yes Miss, and that's why she musta changed her dress too. She wasn't wearing that black one earlier with the long sleeves, she was wearing this floaty peach dress, all taffeta and pretty it was.'

'But short sleeved?' Mel said.

'Yes Miss. She couldn't hide the bruising in that dress. I'm sure that's why she changed. Though, I obviously didn't see her leave Mr Charles's room.'

Mel absorbed this new information. If Eleanor had changed, she must have done it straight after the incident because she and Charles had come downstairs on time. It also meant she was used to Charles's outbursts and had come prepared. It upset Mel to think that Eleanor was suffering abuse by her fiancé but it also changed the dynamic of their relationship. Maybe she wasn't so upset about his death after all?

Earlier, when Charles was having his main meltdown, Eleanor had been behaving like the concerned and loving fiancée. Mel analysed Charles's behaviour from a different perspective, rerunning it in her mind, as was her habit, while shirking the awful tiredness that had been wearing her concentration for the last few hours. In those few moments of analysis, she was alert again. Focused. Her faculties returned full fold. *At last!* The relief that she could think again was enormous. Now she remembered Charles yelling, his eyes casting around as though he had been looking for the attention he was receiving. She remembered also the tentative touch of Eleanor's hand on his arm as she tried to calm him. Replaying the scene now, Mel turned her focus to Eleanor instead of Charles. Yes the woman had been jittery, and clearly frightened by Charles's public outburst. She had taken an involuntary step backwards, knocking the table by the fireplace, glancing over her shoulder at the two glasses that were there.

There was something else too… Something that had been near the glasses, an envelope opener. A long thin blade. What was that doing on the table just then? Was that Jonathan's? Mel couldn't recall seeing it before. But yes, her photographic memory saw it as clearly as if she were stood once more in that room, at that time.

As Mel came back to the present she found Mabel watching her.

'You weren't here then, were you Lady Melinda?'

Mel didn't explain her process to Mabel as she didn't know how to. She merely went into herself and explored her memory in minute detail. It was a skill that few people had.

But she was annoyed with herself for her lapse earlier. What was wrong with her? Her brain just hadn't been working and she didn't know why. She should have noticed the knife at the time! She should have remembered seeing it after they discovered Michael's injury. But she just hadn't. Her mind was so murky.

She stood up, the envelope knife she had seen could have been used on Michael, it was sharp enough – but why had Michael felt nothing when the culprit stabbed him?

Mel remembered that even with the ruckus of Charles's shouting, Michael hadn't seemed to move. It was almost as though he had been drugged and couldn't wake.

Mel herself had been suffering with a pressure behind her eyes, compounded by the continued tiredness, which seemed to have lifted after leaving the study.

There was still more she wanted to ask Mabel, but a niggling in the back of her mind made her want to return to the room now and take a serious look around the chair Michael had been sitting in. A chair that Mel had been about to take prior to discovering the painting was missing. And that reminded her, the envelope knife hadn't been on that table then either. So someone had put it there afterwards.

'Come with me,' Mel said.

Mabel stood up she was looking oddly revived too, as though the air were somehow cleaner out in the hallway and they had both woken up from a fugue that was suppressing their natural exuberance.

Mel opened the door now and what greeted her inside the study made her realise that something was very wrong indeed.

She saw Frank collapsed over Jonathan's desk, Clara waning, her head down on the table by the fire, Derrin was slumped by the door with Williams who appeared to have nodded off, the poker slipping from his fingers. Michael was deep asleep on the sofa. Eleanor was unconscious in the chair beside the fire and the staff of Avonby, furthest from the fireplace and at the back of the room, all looked drowsy.

'Derrin,' Mel said shaking him now.

Derrin groaned but didn't come round.

'Mabel! Get me that jug of water off the table,' Mel said.

Mabel reached for the jug and Mel dipped her fingers in flicking water over Derrin's face. He roused, pulling himself up off the floor the moment he realised he was no longer standing.

'We need to get everyone out of this room,' Mel said. 'There's something poisoning the air.'

Derrin woke Williams, and with the rest of Avonby's staff – the most alert and least exposed – they managed to wrangle all the occupants of the room out into the hallway.

Michael was the last to be lifted outside and placed on the chaise that Mabel and Mel had recently occupied. He too began to come round, though a bowl had to be brought urgently for both he and Eleanor who were not only displaying signs of tiredness but were also dizzy and nauseous.

Frank, left on the floor for lack of seating to put him on, was slow to come round. Williams, Toby, Mrs Weston, Ruby and Daisy were all quick to rally.

'What happened?' asked Clara as she held her head, a fierce headache making itself known.

'We've been exposed to something. I suspect it is a present left by our culprit,' Mel said.

She glanced at the open study door. They would let the room air a while before they could investigate.

'Let's get you all into the drawing room,' Derrin suggested.

Mel nodded her agreement. They had to contain everyone either way, but they couldn't go back into the study until they discovered the source of the contamination.

Once everyone was suitably awake and able to walk they were moved from the hallway and down to the drawing room.

With the wind taken out of the suspects' sails, Mel and Derrin left Toby and Williams to watch over them while they went back to search the study. Using the water in the water closet sink, Derrin wet two handkerchiefs and they each tied one over their mouth and nose before entering the room.

'There was no odour,' Mel commented. 'But I did detect something chemical when I returned. I'm glad now that I took Mabel outside, it was only then my head started to clear. Plus, I remembered seeing an envelope knife earlier. I'm cross with myself for not recalling it sooner.'

'Charles was distracting everyone and perhaps that was intentional. Smoke and mirrors are a magician's friend for a reason,' Derrin said.

'But where has the knife gone?' Mel said. 'We searched everyone.'

Now they pulled away the chairs and the table from near the fire and looked at the floor under all the furniture in the room. When they finished the search Derrin's eyes fell on the fireplace.

'What's that?'

They both moved closer, and seeing a partially burnt piece of cloth dangling from the grating Derrin bent down to examine it.

'This is our culprit,' he said. 'And I'll lay money on it being dowsed with chloroform.'

'Are the side effects of exposure drowsiness, dizziness and sickness?'

'Yes. I think someone put this over Michael's mouth and nose first, knocked him out before stabbing him through the chair.'

Mel shook her head. 'It doesn't make any sense. What's the motive?'
'At this point, I don't know.'

Mel looked around the room and then sank into herself again, her mind's eye adjusting to recall mode and the positions that she had placed everyone in just after Charles's murder. But this wasn't the placing she was most interested in – it was prior to that – before she took Charles away to question him. She flicked through her memory, bringing up the montage image she wanted. He – Charles – had been standing behind Michael as Michael had taken the seat near the fire. Michael had been tired even then, and had promptly closed his eyes. There was a flurry of movement as the Avonby staff were given the freedom to go to bed and Mel had turned away to deal with something. Ah yes, she had ordered cocoa for them all to make the stay slightly more comfortable.

When she had turned her attention back to the remaining occupants of the study, Eleanor had taken the seat opposite Michael, and Charles was by the window, hands in his pockets. He had been ruddy in the face even then. Mel had asked Eleanor to come with her as the first person they would interview, and when Charles had got upset, Michael, she was sure, hadn't moved or reacted. He remained, slumped, head tucked into the side of the chair. Charles had then been taken outside and left with Williams.

Mel saw it all again clearer than before now that her head was free of the fumes from the chloroform.

It was possible that Charles had been hiding something as they left the room. He had been overly pleased to be outside and Mel was sure that Williams didn't have his eyes on the man the whole time they were gone. Could he have concealed some evidence outside in the hallway?

Acting on this hunch, Mel went back outside and examined the chair that Charles had been sitting on as he waited for Eleanor's return. It didn't take long for her to discover a small vial stuffed down the side of the seat cushion. Taking the handkerchief from her face, she carefully picked up the vial and showed it to Derrin.

'Charles chloroformed Michael, then he threw the evidence of the deed into the fire. Then he made a fuss until we let him out and that gave him the opportunity to hide the vial out here, in anticipation that he might be searched,' Mel explained. 'I wonder if he knew the fumes would affect everyone else in the room, or whether that was a mere unexpected benefit?'

'Charles stabbed Michael, then?' Derrin said.

Mel looked back at the chair.

'No sign of the letter opener unfortunately,' Mel said.

'Could he have hidden it elsewhere? In the drawing room when we took him there for the interview?'

Mel shook her head, 'No. I didn't take my eyes off him the whole time he was in there, or until I brought him back and he drank the brandy.'

'Of course!' Derrin said. 'It must still be on his person! We need to search the body — because if it is there it proves our theory without doubt.'

The two of them hurried to the cloakroom and Mel unlocked the door. There was now no need for a candle as the dawn light was filtering through the window close to the room. Derrin went inside and searched Charles's body while Mel waited at the door. She wasn't squeamish but too many cooks could always spoil a broth and she knew she would just get in Derrin's way.

'Well?' asked Mel.

'Not here,' Derrin said.

'Pat down his legs,' Mel suggested but the search of the corpse failed to bring any more evidence up, which meant that their assumption of Charles knocking out Michael also couldn't be fully substantiated, even though they both believed it to be true.

After locking the cloakroom once more, Mel turned to Derrin. She was still replaying the scenarios in her head, and now she felt there was some real movement on the chessboard. Perhaps there were not one but two killers in the room, with motives that were, as yet, uncertain.

'I still think Charles stabbed Michael. Otherwise, why did he chloroform him to ensure he wasn't detected?' Mel said. 'What I don't understand is why attack Michael in the first place? They only met for the first time this evening.'

'We need to find the knife,' Derrin said. 'Its location might tell us something.'

'And speak to Eleanor again,' Mel said.

Derrin nodded. 'She may be able to give us some insight into Charles's access to chloroform, and why he would want to stab Michael. Oddly the injury isn't that bad, it doesn't seem as though it was aimed to kill.'

They decided to go and search the study once more now that everyone was in the other room. But before they did, they removed the decanter and glasses from the hallway and stowed them in the cloakroom with Charles's body, along with the chloroform vial, to ensure that all the evidence was being kept together and to avoid any chance of contamination.

They pulled out every chair and sofa in the study, searched under the desk and inside the drawers, but there was no sign of the knife that had injured Michael.

Finally, they tipped up the chair Michael had been sitting on when he was drugged and attacked. There, in the lining under the seat, they found the knife.

'This somewhat confirms our theory about Charles,' Derrin said.

Mel's mind went back to where Charles had been standing and she moved him across her metaphorical board, observing in her scenario that this was indeed very likely. She could even imagine the subtle stabbing and extraction of the knife through the back of the chair, then an elusive bend when he shoved the knife under the seat. She even imagined the twist of his waist to suit Charles's deformed spine.

'Eleanor must know something,' Mel said. 'Let's get her in here.'

15

ELEANOR WAS BROUGHT FROM THE DRAWING ROOM and now sat on the chaise while she and Derrin stood over her. She looked tired, but more awake than she had earlier before they discovered the chloroform exposure. Mel could sense something else in her former friend as she sat upright, almost glowering at them, in the way you might if you were being held against your will.

'I don't know why you need to talk to me again,' Eleanor said. 'I already told you what I know. Which isn't much by all accounts.'

'We do have a few more questions,' said Derrin ignoring Eleanor's tone which bordered on irritated and grumpy.

'Why did you change your dress this evening?' Mel asked.

'What do you mean? I came to dinner in this!' Eleanor said, pointing to the long black satin dress, which was now looking less elegant as it was wrinkled and dull.

'Before dinner you were wearing something else. A peach dress, I believe,' Mel said.

Eleanor fidgeted on the chaise; her hand went instinctively to her arm.

'I just changed my mind…'

'Eleanor, did Charles hurt you before dinner?' Derrin said, his voice soft and empathetic.

'No. Of course not!'

'Then what is wrong with your arm?' Derrin pressed.

'I bruised it. I can be very clumsy sometimes,' Eleanor said.

'May I see it?' Mel asked.

Though reluctant, Eleanor pushed up the sleeve of her dress. Mel and Derrin saw then a ripe bruise, consistent with the very hard squeeze of a man's fingers. They also noted several others that were faded enough to go unnoticed under casual scrutiny.

'How long has he been doing this?' Mel asked.

'Oh no. You don't understand…' Eleanor denied.

'A witness saw him hurt you last night,' Derrin said. 'He's dead now. You have nothing to fear and can tell us the truth.'

She crumpled in an instant, and all signs of her previous attempts at arrogance dissolved as tears began to roll down her cheeks.

'He's been beastly ever since the engagement party. I just didn't understand what was happening. All was lovely, and then as soon as the ring was on my finger it was like the devil had got into him. At first the bruises were "accidents" only last night I saw he actually… *delights*… in it.'

'Were you going to leave him?' Mel asked.

Eleanor nodded and shook her head as though she wasn't sure what she would have done. 'I needed this engagement, and the marriage. But things were getting worse and his behaviour, even in front of others… I was telling myself I couldn't go on like this. The wedding is in two weeks and what would he be like once that deed was done?'

Eleanor shed silent tears that appeared to be more like relief than sorrow to Mel. Mel had seen many cases of women falling foul of men who claimed to love them. Charles it seemed was the bully that Mabel claimed he was, a conclusion that even the young maid had come to after witnessing just one incident.

'I had thought this weekend might be good for us. But all I could think of all evening while I was pretending to enjoy myself was how I wanted to get as far away from Charles as I could,' Eleanor said, once she was able to speak again.

'Did you tell him that?' Mel asked.

'Oh no! He would have turned if I had. I was trying to make sure that everything went smoothly. That he would be calm and well mannered. He is very charming in company and it's when we are in social situations that I like being with him the most. But in that room, locked up, it turned that side of him back on, despite everyone being there to see it. He appeared to be worse than ever. I did my best to deflate his anger as you saw, but his behaviour horrified me.'

'Was his story of being buried alive true?' Derrin said.

'I believed it,' Eleanor said. 'I thought it was the cause of his… moments… that is, until last night.'

Derrin glanced at Mel and they had a silent exchange, following which, Mel took over the main questioning.

'Had Charles met Michael before?' she said.

'Oh no. Never. And I hadn't known he was coming until Clara told me.'

* * *

Two weeks earlier

'Oh, do sit down Charles,' Clara said. 'You're making me nervous with all this pacing.'

'I'm sorry,' Charles said.

He took a seat next to Eleanor as Clara poured tea into some petite china cups.

'Help yourself to the cucumber sandwiches,' Clara said.

'Not for me,' Eleanor said but Charles took a tea plate and helped himself to a generous portion of sandwiches, which he ate in silence.

He appeared to Eleanor to have too much energy: he was always on edge. She was wondering why that day he had insisted again on joining her for tea at Clara's. He did often go there with her though, and she was starting to have the suspicion that he didn't want her to be alone with anyone, in case she revealed how he was behaving in private. Even so, Clara was the only friend of hers whose company he enjoyed, and she had encouraged the friendship, hoping that after the wedding he wouldn't mind her seeing her friend too much because he did like her.

'I have some gossip,' Clara said. 'Michael Chase is back in England.'

'Michael? Really? After all this time…' Eleanor said.

'Who is Michael Chase?' asked Charles, showing interest in the conversation for the first time.

'An old friend,' Clara explained. 'Went off to India with his father years ago.'

'A friend of yours too?' Charles asked Eleanor.

'Yes. When we were children. I haven't heard a word about him since he moved away,' Eleanor said.

'Anyway,' Clara continued, 'he's coming to Avonby!'

'What? I thought this was a girls' trip,' Charles said, 'or I'd have never agreed to it.'

'Oh, don't be so archaic Charles,' Clara said. 'You're engaged to Eleanor. You don't *own* her!'

This comment hit home and Charles went silent, refusing the fruit cake that Clara offered. Eleanor sensed his change of mood, and began to feel tense. For fear of Clara noticing she made their excuses as soon as it was decent to leave after eating.

As they waited for Frank to pull up with the car, Charles was in a foul mood. It was as if leaving Clara's and there being no one around to moderate him gave him free rein to be difficult. He made it clear, in an angry outburst, how he felt about her meeting some 'other man' at Avonby.

'Oh, don't be absurd,' Eleanor said. 'Michael was this spotty, gawky boy. Never in a million years would I consider any form of relationship with him. To be honest he always had a thing for Mel and we all knew it.'

'But why did Clara have to invite him to the weekend with you all?' Charles seethed.

Eleanor tried to laugh off the situation.

'Darling, she's desperate for a boyfriend. She probably has him in her sights already.'

'Well, I'm positively put out now,' Charles said.

'You needn't be. I'm not interested in anyone but you. Why are you acting so jealous all of a sudden?'

Charles stiffened beside her and at that point Eleanor knew that the casual way she was speaking, which he took so easily from Clara, was a mistake coming from her. Charles didn't like to be called jealous or pulled up for any shortcomings, she had learnt that almost from the start of their relationship. She now regretted trying to smooth out his suspicion so directly when it had probably added fuel to the fire.

The black Rolls-Royce pulled up at the kerb and Frank got out to open the door for Eleanor and Charles. Eleanor slipped in first, but as she was sliding across the seat to the other side to allow Charles room to enter, he put his foot in and ground it over the top of hers.

Eleanor yelped and Frank quickly looked into the back of the car to see what was wrong. He saw Eleanor looking down at her foot, which was dirt covered. Her stocking was ripped and her shoe was badly damaged, not to mention the scratches on her skin from Charles's sole which bled and the large welt that would obviously leave an ugly bruise.

'It's nothing, Frank. Just an *accident*. I thought she had moved over quicker than she did. Sorry darling,' he said to Eleanor. Then he leaned over and kissed her head as if it would make everything better.

Eleanor bit her lip and fought the tears that had sprung to her eyes. She was unsure if indeed the accident was as Charles had said, it all happened so quickly.

'Can you take me home please?' she murmured. 'I need to change my shoes and stocking and wash the wound.'

'To Miss Eleanor's please Frank. Then you can take me to my club.'

Eleanor had remained silent all the way back, but as Frank pulled up in front of her house Charles turned to her and said, 'I'm coming with you to Avonby, and if you don't like it then you aren't going.'

'Yes Charles,' she said wishing that Clara hadn't mentioned Michael and that his anger would dissipate soon, for she felt it bubbling still. She climbed out of the car, sickened and afraid.

* * *

'Charles wasn't going to come to this weekend. I'd initially asked him, but he thought at that point it was just us girls having a small reunion. I had been glad he had said he wouldn't come. To be honest,

I wanted to speak to you and Clara alone. Get some advice, like in the old days,' Eleanor said as she finished her story of Charles's bad behaviour and Mel fought with herself over the sympathy she wanted to offer. She was torn between her dislike of Charles's conduct and the need to remain neutral until they discovered who had killed him. After all, his behaviour did give Eleanor the strongest motive.

'It's fair to say,' Derrin said, 'with this in mind, you do have reason for wanting to kill your fiancé.'

'You can't think I poisoned him? That's monstrous!' Eleanor said. 'He didn't deserve…'

'Yes. He *did*,' Mel murmured.

'And who else, but you, has reason to see Charles out of the picture?' Derrin pressed. 'By your own admission he was abusing you. You could *almost* be forgiven for ridding yourself of someone like that.'

'Oh no. I could never… all I had to do was leave him. And I was getting the strength to do it. You must understand, girls like me don't find men of Charles's standing that often. I thought I was lucky at first. Don't you think that if I wanted to kill him, I'd surely have waited until after we were married? Then, I'd have been set for life…'

Mel couldn't argue with Eleanor's reasoning as it did make more sense than killing him now. However, his death after the marriage was certain to rouse more suspicion. Plus, people didn't always act rationally when they perceived themselves to be under threat. Mel herself had reacted with instant violence in the past and she thought again of her shooting of the criminal, Eric Stafford, but she also recognised that a reactive murder in the heat of the moment was far different from a murder that had been planned. For a start, in law, one would be deemed self-defence, another first-degree murder.

'Eleanor, do you have in your possession any arsenic?' Mel asked.

'Good heavens, no!'

'Then you won't mind us examining your toiletries to make sure, will you?' Mel said.

Eleanor shook her head. 'I don't mind,' she said. 'I've nothing more to hide.'

Mel gave Eleanor a long look: this one thing she said didn't ring true at all.

* * *

When Mel reached Eleanor's room, she found the door slightly ajar. She went inside, and throwing the curtains wide to let in the burgeoning morning light, she turned to take in the room with her most critical eye.

Eleanor was not the tidiest person. The woman's toiletries were scattered all over the dressing table as though she had been in a hurry to use them. Or as if she had been searching for something in a panic. A small pot of concealer was left open and Mel saw then the remnants of a woman rushing to hide her bruises from a group of people whose opinion might matter to her. It was, after all, a degrading experience being beaten by the person who was supposed to love you.

The peach dress was thrown over the chair by the bed, and the disarray confirmed the observations of Clara's maid, Mabel. Eleanor had admitted switching her dress, but if she hadn't Mel would know it to be true by the state of the room.

Mel opened every jar and every bottle and sniffed the contents to make sure that none contained arsenic and she found no trace of almond among the products, and no surplus bottle with any mysterious or unidentifiable contents. She was, therefore, fully committed to the idea that Eleanor was innocent, until her eyes fell on a piece of paper that was lying crumpled by the bin under the dressing table.

Mel picked up the paper and discovered it was a note written on Avonby stationery.

Dear Elle,
I know what is going on and I'd like to help you.
He shouldn't be treating you like this.
Come and find me and we'll talk.

There was no signature or anything else to identify the sender and because the paper had been put into all rooms, on Mel's instruction, no immediate clue as to who had used it.

Mel sniffed the paper looking for traces of perfume or cologne and there was a vague smell of something that she tried to place but had to shelve for future consideration, knowing her subconscious would work on it until the answer came.

She folded the paper and put it in her pocket, then she finished her search of Eleanor's room and headed back downstairs.

* * *

When she returned, Derrin and Eleanor were still talking, but Mel suspected he hadn't gleaned any more information from her. They looked relaxed with each other; Eleanor's tears had long since dried up. Mel didn't know if Eleanor had ever loved Charles or whether the marriage would have been one of convenience for her, but what she was sure of now was that her former friend was relieved deep down to be free. She suspected that this emotion made her feel conflicted and guilty, as though she were somehow betraying Charles. In the end, Charles didn't deserve either her love or loyalty, and certainly not her grief, though it was obvious that Eleanor was experiencing all of this in a complex wave of emotion that overtook any comfort her newfound freedom might bring.

As she reached the bottom of the main staircase, Mel met Derrin's eyes.

'No arsenic,' she said. 'But I did find this.'

She handed Derrin the note and he read it quickly.

'Who was this from?' he asked.

'Oh, I'd forgotten about that!' Eleanor mumbled.

'Who gave it you?' Mel asked.

'That was placed under my door after dinner when the lights had gone off and we'd all retired. I didn't see it at first, as I was stumbling around the room, trying to find my nightdress by candlelight. Then there was a knock on my door, and I opened it to see Charles there. I was tired and I didn't really want to see more of him by then, but as he stood in the doorway, he saw the envelope and picked it up. He'd opened and read the note before I had a chance to.'

'What happened then?' asked Mel.

'He got angry. Started ranting that it was all Michael, and he'd known all along there was something "going on". I tried to placate him, but he wouldn't believe me.'

'But… why would he assume Michael had sent the note?' Derrin said.

'Well, after he… pinched me… we thought we heard someone outside his room. Charles rushed to the door and he saw Michael walking down the landing towards his room. We knew then, he must have heard our quarrel and perhaps he'd seen what Charles did as the door wasn't properly closed,' Eleanor said. 'That's your witness isn't it?'

Mel and Derrin didn't correct her assumption, even though they knew it was Mabel who had witnessed everything and not Michael. It wasn't too much of a stretch to imagine Michael might have heard the row too and perhaps he had sent the note.

Mel studied the handwriting recalling that she and Derrin hadn't talked to Michael at all yet, and therefore hadn't heard his take on what had happened and who might have drugged and stabbed him. She toyed with the idea of sharing that they knew Charles had done it, but thought better of it.

Is this the motive for Charles's behaviour, she wondered. *But why would he bring chloroform with him to a dinner party in the first place?*

Charles was already prepared to take some drastic action! It was the only answer.

'Do you know what chloroform is?' Mel asked now.

Eleanor shook her head.

'It is the drug that affected us all in the study,' Derrin explained. 'This substance can also be used to render someone unconscious. Someone used that on Michael last night, and then burnt the evidence in the fire. But despite knowing to use this chemical, they didn't seem to appreciate that burning the rag it was on would affect everyone in the room. At least, we don't think they did.'

'This substance…' Mel said, 'is administered by putting a cloth over someone's face and mouth, making them breathe it in. Did you, by any chance, see Charles do that to Michael?'

Eleanor's face paled.

Eleanor shook her head again but she was clearly frightened by the description of the drug. 'I didn't see him do it to Micheal… but I think… Charles has used it on me…'

* * *

After Mel had returned Eleanor to the drawing room, she went back to the hallway to talk privately with Derrin to digest and dissect the latest information.

Eleanor hadn't wanted to go into details about what Charles had done, except to say that she had 'fallen asleep' when visiting him at his parents' house once and when she came round the next morning she didn't feel well and was violently sick. The symptoms she had described to them sounded so like the ones caused by chloroform exposure that Mel and Derrin were left in no doubt that she had, for some awful reason, been drugged by Charles in the early days of their relationship.

'He must have used the entire vial to dope Michael,' Mel said. 'After all, it had to be a lot to affect the entire room.'

'Yes. And coupled with the fumes from the fire, in an enclosed space. These are all factors he may not have considered. But… what on earth was wrong with the man?' Derrin said, angry and disturbed by the revelations. 'If he wasn't dead already I'd be tempted to kill him myself.'

'It's despicable,' Mel said. 'Poor Eleanor.'

'Well, whoever poisoned him, I think he had it coming,' Derrin said. 'I know I'm not supposed to say that, when it is a cut and dried case of pre-planned murder. Malice aforethought. And no jury would let someone off for behaving like that but… the man deserved it.'

'He did. At this point, though, I'm sure Eleanor isn't the guilty party, but someone else seems to have done the job for her.'

'What about the note? Did you sense anything when you showed it to Eleanor again?' Derrin asked.

'She became very guarded as soon as she saw it. That in and of itself was suspicious. I'm not completely sure she doesn't know who the writer was.'

They talked about the note that Mel had found and concluded that it was possibly from Michael.

'It's obvious he saw Charles's behaviour,' Derrin said. 'We should talk to him.'

'He's much recovered now,' Mel said. 'I'll get him.'

'Yes. Let's speak to him now,' Derrin said.

'Before I go, I think the kitchen staff should go about their duties, and get us all some tea for a start. That will make us all perk up a bit too. And it doesn't seem as risky now that daylight is here.'

Derrin agreed and Mel went back to the drawing room and soon returned with Michael, Mrs Weston, Ruby, Toby and Daisy. The latter four went off to start their day-time duties, despite everyone being tired from the lack of sleep and the worry of the murderer among them. It was strange how they all picked up with the daylight streaming in through the windows, and Mel observed that they appeared less afraid now that it was no longer night time.

Everything always seems better in the morning, she thought.

The house was in chaos with the study turned upside down as it was. Broken glasses and empty wine bottles were still evident on the mantlepiece, but despite this, Mel decided there was little point in sorting it out, when the police would probably make more mess when they arrived. So, she left Derrin in the hallway and went to the drawing room once more to give the instructions and bring Michael out to learn what he knew.

After the Avonby staff went about their business, Michael took a seat on the chaise and Mel and Derrin pulled up a couple of chairs that they had taken from the study, placing them on an even level to the man, which showed that they were not treating him as a suspect, but rather a victim.

'How are you feeling?' Mel asked.

'My shoulder is sore,' he said. 'But you did a good job bandaging me Mel, so I'm not as bad as I was earlier.'

'Good,' said Mel. 'What can you tell us about the incident?'

'Well, when your painting went missing, I was tired and truly believed you would find it quickly, so I dozed in the chair. I was half asleep when I felt something cover my face. The next thing I remember was waking up on the sofa.'

'Do you have any idea who would do this to you?' Derrin asked.

Michael frowned and shook his head.

'We think we have the culprit,' Mel said. 'But we are still looking for motive. Can you tell me if you saw or heard anything unusual when you arrived yesterday?'

'Can you give me a clue what I should have seen?' Michael said.

'Don't play dumb. You saw Charles and Eleanor last night before dinner…' Derrin said.

'Okay. Yes. I heard them arguing and then I saw that little maid hanging outside the door, eavesdropping. When she ran away, I thought I'd let that bounder, Charles, see me. Thought it might curb his bad temper if he knew he was being watched.'

'So, you saw what he did?' Mel asked.

'Nope. But I heard Eleanor cry out, and I knew he'd hurt her somehow. By that point I hadn't even met him yet, but I already didn't like him.'

'Eleanor received a note last night, did you put it under her door?'

'No. What did it say?' Michael asked.

Mel drew it from her pocket and showed him.

'Not me, I'm afraid. Though I had planned to have a word. Really, what a lovely girl sees in a chap like that…' Michael said.

'We are all in agreement there,' said Derrin.

'The thing is,' Mel said, 'Charles drugged you and then, we think he stabbed you with an envelope knife that he had taken from Jonathan's desk in the study. Do you know any reason why he would do that?'

At that moment, Daisy turned up with a tray holding some tea cups and a plate of buttered toast. She placed it on the chaise beside

Michael as there wasn't a table nearby to put it on. She was followed by Ruby and Toby who were equally laden, and who took the rest of the drinks and food to the drawing room for the remaining suspects.

Once the serving staff had moved on, Mel and Derrin continued talking to Michael, who helped himself immediately to the tea and toast.

'I exchanged words with him,' he admitted. 'It was before you came to get us from our rooms. Before, I guess, your painting was stolen. He came banging on my door, threatening to "thump" me if I went near Eleanor again. He was talking about a note… that one, I suppose… and didn't believe that I hadn't sent it. A few minutes later, your butler found us and made us all come downstairs. After that, and with the painting missing, I didn't think much more about it.'

'Was Eleanor there at the time? Did she see you and Charles arguing?' Derrin asked.

'No. But obviously your… Mr Williams… saw us. If he hadn't come when he did I might well have landed one on Charles,' Michael explained. 'The man is a cad.'

'Was,' Derrin reminded him. 'So, I guess I need to ask, did you poison the brandy?' Derrin said.

'Might I point out that anyone could have drunk from that glass last night, so what makes you think Charles was the target in the first place?' Michael said.

'We know that could be true, and have discussed the possibility,' said Mel, 'but last night everyone saw how partial to the brandy Charles was. Eleanor and Clara had both cried off from drinking it, preferring wine. Myself and Derrin had abandoned the glasses earlier and I'm certain that if it had been in there when we poured, one of us would have smelt the tell-tale almond aroma. The other observation we noticed was, the decanter appears to have been spiked after the fact, as though to draw attention away from the glasses being the source of the poison. But there is barely any arsenic in the decanter. And plenty in the glasses. Someone knew that at some point Charles would take one of those glasses. Someone who might have been relaxing in a chair, pretending to sleep?'

'Oh really, old bean, you couldn't possibly think I did it. Haven't you just said that Charles drugged and stabbed me? I was out of it, almost from the moment I sat down in the chair.'

'That's true. But the key part of what you said was "almost". You had time, when you first went into the room to poison the glasses,' Derrin pointed out.

Michael shook his head furiously. 'I never would have put others at risk like that. Anyone else might have drunk it, yourself included. Besides, I'd never met the man before tonight, so why would I even have such a thing with me? Unless you think I'm just some insane poisoner who carries arsenic around and doesn't care?'

The ferocity of Michael's denial wasn't lost on Mel. She found it difficult to imagine him bringing arsenic with the specific motive of killing Charles. Even after seeing his bullish behaviour, there was no time to plan such an assault. She had to admit this part of the puzzle didn't add up at all. She saw now in her mind's eye, Charles moving around the room, owning every space, his arrogance seeping through every pore of his body. He had thought himself in charge of the whole scenario of the game he was playing, and Michael had got caught in the crossfire of his abuse of Eleanor. All this pointed again to Charles's own mental issues, which were compounded by jealousy and obsession.

'He could be lying,' Derrin said after Michael returned to the drawing room. 'He could have planned to stop anyone else but Charles from drinking the brandy. He was sitting right next to it.'

'I don't think so,' Mel said taking the wind from Derrin's sails as she explained her thoughts. 'Sadly, with Eleanor being the only other person sitting by those glasses, I'm swaying towards her as the culprit of the poisoning, after all. Despite what was said earlier.'

'But the same scenario stands that someone else might have drunk from the glass other than Charles. Michael might have,' Derrin pointed out.

Mel's mind swept back to those first few moments again in the study. Eleanor sat down opposite Michael while Charles remained standing – ready perhaps to take his revenge on a man he had only just met. Then Eleanor saw Charles use the chloroform on Michael. She could be excused for thinking Michael was out of the picture and safe from harm as he was unconscious not knowing of course that Charles was planning to stab him.

'We are at an impasse,' Derrin said, interrupting her thoughts.

He glanced towards the large oak front door and the small windows either side. The morning was fully awake, a fact that should have lifted their mood, but did the exact opposite as it made them both aware that time had all but run out.

'It's perhaps time to send Toby over to the farm to get a lift to the station,' Mel said.

'Yes. And it looks like we have failed by being distracted from finding the Turner, to solving a murder.'

'I wish we could find that at least before we have the police tramping all over the house.'

'Another search then, with daylight on our side?' Derrin said.

'Yes,' said Mel her mood improving with the suggestion. 'After that we are going to have to act, we can't keep everyone locked up for much longer.'

16

WITH MR WILLIAMS KEEPING AN EYE ON the suspects, now waiting, not so patiently, in the drawing room, Mel and Derrin decided to take another look at each of the guests' bedrooms. Mel was satisfied that Eleanor's room and belongings had been sufficiently searched, but they hadn't seen Michael's, Clara's or even Charles's possessions.

They started in Charles's room which was very tidy in stark contrast to Eleanor's room. Derrin went straight to the toiletry bag on the dresser and opened it to find another small bottle of chloroform wrapped in a muslin cloth.

'Same fabric that was burning in the fire?' Mel said.

'Yes, and this bottle is half empty. It confirms that original cloth was very well dowsed with half of this bottle and the full contents of the one we found empty. But when and how did he do it without being observed?' Derrin said.

They continued to search the room; Mel found a box with some female jewellery inside.

'Eleanor's?' Derrin wondered.

'I don't think so, it's not her taste which is quite modern,' Mel said.

'Then whose?' Derrin said.

Mel's mind was still on the chloroform. 'Derrin, I think Charles had been planning to use the chloroform on Eleanor again last night. It's possible he had the dowsed cloth in his jacket pocket as he went to her room, with the other bottle in his pocket in reserve. She said she wasn't in the mood for him, and he would have known that because of his earlier conduct. Maybe he even sensed she was about to break things off.'

Mel saw the scene in her mind, Charles turning up, the cloth in his hand, or pocket. Him finding the note, and then his anger switching towards Michael, whom he appeared to have some kind of irrational jealousy about.

She explained her suspicions to Derrin and looking back inside the toiletry bag, he agreed that her theory was not only possible, but likely.

'Charles didn't return to his own room, as he went to Michael's. He could have dowsed the cloth again in between Eleanor's room and Michael's, making sure it would work on Michael. After their argument, he didn't have time to return to his own room because Mr Williams brought them both downstairs,' Mel said. 'After that, there was no opportunity to go anywhere else because we locked him up.'

'I think your theory is reasonable. We may need to get Williams to confirm what he saw. He hasn't mentioned interrupting a quarrel, but then we haven't had any time alone with him since this whole thing started.'

'True. And Williams might at least back up Michael's alibi. For you see, if he and Charles were arguing, that would have been around the time we discovered the painting was missing. As I got Williams and Toby immediately and made them gather everyone else, I find it hard to imagine that Michael could have stolen and hidden the painting before he returned to his room. There wasn't time.'

'If we can rule out Michael at this point, it does narrow the field,' Derrin said.

'Let's finish the searches, then we'll go and speak to Mr Williams,' Mel said.

* * *

As Derrin didn't want to leave Clara and Eleanor alone with Michael and Frank in the drawing room, Toby was asked to take Mr Williams's place in there while Derrin and Mel spoke to him.

After the change around, Mr Williams came out into the hallway and reluctantly took a seat on the chaise.

He looked worn down by the night of mostly no rest and Mel felt very sorry for him, so she explained what they needed to know to save the butler's time and energy.

'Oh yes, I did come upon Mr Harris at Mr Chase's room last night,' Williams said.

'We don't want to put words in your mouth, so can you explain what you saw and heard in as much detail as possible?' Mel said.

* * *

Several hours earlier

Williams was all ready to retire when Lady Melinda rang the service bell from the study. He pulled on his uniform and hurried back upstairs only to receive the biggest shock of his life: Lord Jonathan's prized painting was missing!

'We need to rally everyone into the hallway,' Lady Mel had said, but at that time, he hadn't thought the Avonby staff were suspects too.

After Williams spoke to Mrs Weston, and fetched Toby, Daisy and Ruby, he headed upstairs on Lady Mel's instructions: orders that were backed up by Inspector Bradley. Toby had gone in search of the ladies with Daisy, and Williams came up the servants' stairs alone to find the two gentlemen.

As he reached Mr Harris's room, which was nearest the stairs, he discovered the door ajar and Mr Harris absent. Williams had felt immediately suspicious of Mr Harris, especially with the painting missing, and he wasn't sure what to do, continue the task of rallying everyone, or go downstairs to tell Lady Mel that Harris was missing.

Raised voices alerted him that a disagreement was taking place down the corridor. Williams hurried to see what was going on and found Mr Harris at Mr Chase's room. Both men were squaring off each other and it looked as though a serious altercation was about to take place.

'I know your game, Chase, and Eleanor is engaged to me. You

have no right to send her private notes. What happens between us is our business,' Charles was saying.

'A girl of her class deserves better than your sort…'

'And what is my sort exactly?' Charles asked.

'You're a brute, Harris and I intend to have a word with Eleanor in the morning about your uncouth behaviour,' Michael said.

Williams observed how controlled and polite Michael remained during this exchange and how irate Charles became. Mr Harris was, in Williams's opinion, not a gentleman. Even so, he knew he had to address him as such, and make sure that his own behaviour was beyond reproach.

'Excuse me gentleman,' Williams said, interrupting urgently when he thought that Charles might attack Michael. The man literally wiped his mouth and put his fists up, ready for a bare-knuckle boxing match.

'What is it?' Charles snapped.

'Lady Melinda requests you all come downstairs right away,' Williams explained.

'Why should we?' Charles said.

'It's very important,' Williams said. 'She'll explain when you go to her. And Inspector Bradley is also there.'

'Of course,' said Michael. 'I'll come right away.'

Michael was in his dressing gown, and so went to dress, putting on the tuxedo he had worn earlier while Williams waited for him with Charles. At this point, Charles's temper seemed to fade, but Williams was uncomfortable with him nonetheless. There was something bubbling under the surface, despite the outward appearance of him calming down. Charles Harris had a darkness inside him and Williams had met his sort before. It was an innate cruelty that seeped out, despite the man's attempts to hide it.

* * *

'So, Mr Chase was already dressed for bed?' Derrin asked.

'Yes, Inspector,' said Williams. 'It took him some time to get ready again.'

'And did Chase and Harris discuss anything more afterwards?' Derrin asked.

'No. They were silent, and as you know, I brought them downstairs.'

'Is there anything else you can tell us?' Mel asked.

'Not about that Milady, but… Mr Harris was very difficult when he arrived,' Williams said.

'What happened?'

'Well, I was watching for their arrival as you told me to, so I was on the ball when the doorbell rang and opened it immediately. Miss Eleanor was standing on the doorstep. She looked like she had been crying. Then Mr Harris was ordering Frank around. He was making him get the bags out of the car. I called for Toby, and we helped him bring them in of course. But there was so much complaining about everything. And well, Frank was certainly unhappy though he tried not to show it.'

'Did Frank say anything to you when he was in the kitchen later?' Mel asked.

Williams shook his head. 'No, Lady Melinda. He was very professional.'

'One other thing,' Mel said. 'What did you think about Frank and Charles's relationship?'

'Think?' Williams said.

'Did you get the impression Frank liked Charles?' Derrin said.

'No. I think Frank hated him, if I'm honest,' said Williams. 'Mr Harris was not a good employer.'

'If Frank didn't say anything to you, then what was it that gave you that impression?' Mel asked.

Williams was thoughtful. 'It was when Mr Harris grabbed Miss Eleanor's arm as he walked up the stairs to their rooms. I was following on, Frank was in front of me, and I saw his fingers tighten on the bag he was carrying. At first, I thought he'd almost lost his grip and then I realised he was tense. Upset even. And I think it was because of the way Mr Harris was behaving towards the lady. Frank definitely didn't like it. I also think he's very pleased he's dead.'

'Why do you say that?' Derrin asked.

'I caught his eye as Toby and I lifted the body to remove it from the study and well, there was this gleam in his eye and a tiny little smile. If he'd have spoken just then I'd have expected him to say "good riddance".'

'Thank you, Mr Williams,' Mel said.

'Will that be all, Your Ladyship?' Williams said.

Mel nodded. 'You've been very helpful. But as Toby is now in the drawing room, why don't you take a break and get something to eat and drink in the kitchen. After that, will you go to the farm and get them to call the police station if their phones are working? And if not, ask them to send someone to the station?'

'Yes indeed, I will,' said Williams and the relief that these awful few hours might be ending was evident on his face.

Mel watched him hurry away and then on the spur of the minute called after him. 'Mr Williams!'

'Your Ladyship?'

'Be careful when you go outside,' Mel said. 'Get straight to the farmhouse and don't stop for anyone unfamiliar.'

Williams nodded, then he turned and hurried down the servants' stairs to the kitchen.

'That was interesting,' Mel said. 'Williams all but pointed the finger at Frank for Charles's murder.'

'Do you think he was right?' Derrin asked.

'I'm still not seeing a clear picture on that score. He is man enough to be offended by Charles's behaviour towards Eleanor, but is he a poisoner? I mean, Frank is more the sort to take him outside and give him a leathering.'

'I would think so too, except for the fact that his job would be on the line. And there lies a motive for *not* killing him as Frank has already pointed out,' Derrin said.

Mel gave a deep sigh, 'Well, that's it. The decision has been made and this terrible business will soon be out of my hands.'

'We've done everything we can without reinforcements,' Derrin said. 'And there's no sign of the painting still.'

'I'm upset that we can't solve this,' Mel said. 'And Jonathan is going to be mortified about the painting.'

'When are they due to return?' Derrin asked.

'Monday or Tuesday, I'm not entirely certain as they've put it off a few times already.'

Mel fell quiet. Now Michael Chase's story was corroborated and even expanded on by Mr Williams, she knew that he wouldn't have had time to remove and hide the painting, then get back to his room, let alone change before Charles arrived at his door. With Mr Williams as a reliable witness, Mel had no doubt that he wasn't guilty of the theft. He had been a very unwitting target for Charles's jealousy and rage and nothing more. Which left them now with three plausible suspects: Clara, Eleanor and Frank. Eleanor and Frank had the greatest motive because as far Clara was concerned, Mel couldn't see any reason at all for her to be involved. The thought of her seeming innocence was a source of chagrin for Mel, as she couldn't place Clara anywhere in this story at all, except that it was she who pushed for the reunion, and pushed hard. Maybe that was something to explore more?

'One or more of them killed Charles and stole the Turner,' Derrin said as though reading her thoughts. 'But it does seem that Michael Chase is in the clear. I suppose I ought to let him out of that room.'

'Let's not for now,' Mel said, and then she fell quiet, deep in her thoughts.

At that moment the lights came back on in the house.

'Good lord!' Mel said. 'Maybe there wasn't any sabotage after all?'

'Indeed! I'll go and ring the station now, and can you tell Mr Williams there is no need for him to leave?'

Mel went off to the kitchen to take care of this task and she found Williams sitting at the table, finishing a much-needed cup of tea. When Mel explained that he didn't have to go out, Williams sank back into his chair and let his head droop into his hands. The man was exhausted but had been keeping going for her sake. She was relieved now that she didn't have to send him out alone, for the fear of an accomplice still lurking on Avonby grounds had been weighing on her even as she had given him the instruction to go.

Mrs Weston in the meantime had started a broth and Daisy had some bread dough resting ready to bake for lunch.

'I know we are all very tired,' Mel said. 'But let's try and go about our business until the police get here, and no one is to go outside or open any doors or windows until then. The painting is still missing, and we can't risk it getting away.'

'You think it's here somewhere then, Mel?' asked Mrs Weston.

'I do. But we just haven't discovered where our clever culprit has hidden it.'

'I hope you find it soon, Miss,' Daisy said.

Mel hoped so too, but she didn't say anything more. Instead, she left the kitchen and headed back upstairs to Derrin.

17

THERE HAD BEEN LITTLE CONVERSATION BETWEEN THE suspects as each of them were pulled out and interviewed over the last few hours. They were all exhausted, but as time dragged on, they became even more frustrated.

'Will they ever let us out of here?' Clara said now. 'I don't know about you lot but I've had it with that rotten painting and if I'd been the thief I should have turned it over by now, just to put an end to this torture.'

'Indeed,' said Michael, but he was aware that the thief might well say something like that to throw suspicion off themselves. 'The only thing any of us can be sure of is what we've been party to.'

'Is that a confession?' asked Eleanor.

Michael smirked. 'Elle, old girl, you surely know me much better than that.'

'But we don't though, do we?' Clara said. 'I mean, was it a coincidence that I bumped into you at the station?'

'What do you mean?' asked Eleanor.

'Well, I always go through Euston on a Wednesday. Anyone might know that, if they had done their research.'

'What are you accusing me of now?' Michael asked. 'I had just arrived from India. I wasn't even thinking about reconnecting with you, Eleanor or Mel.'

'So you said. But how do we know that?' Clara said.

She and Eleanor sidled up to each other then, closing ranks as that had always done when they were teenagers, Michael noticed.

'Not that I have to, but I'll tell you how I saw it,' Michael said.

'I'd like to hear that story too,' Frank said.

* * *

Returning to London was a bittersweet experience for Michael, having had no contact with his former school friends during his exile in India. Now, Michael was obliged to return, not only because Mountbatten was planning to give Indian territory back to the indigenous population of the country, but because his father's estate needed to be sorted out. As the only child of General Philip Chase and Lady Penelope Baring-Chase, Michael was the sole heir and beneficiary. He was struggling with the idea that everything was now his and, on top of losing his father, he had to deal with making a life for himself back in England. He knew so little of what remained in London, he wasn't sure what he was coming back to, or even how to start again. The prospect was daunting, but there was nothing left for him in India, and so he had little choice in the matter.

As all these thoughts and fears went through his mind, Michael was oblivious to the young woman who was staring at him as she waited for a taxi, right next to where the porter was standing with his trunk.

As he reached the porter, their eyes met and Michael felt a spark of something akin to recognition.

'M… Michael?' she said.

'Why yes,' he answered, and then it came to him. She hadn't changed that much after all; except she was no longer a girl but a woman. '*Clara?*'

Clara nodded. 'What on earth are you doing here?' she asked.

As Michael went into his explanation, Clara showed such warmth and understanding that he could see their friendship rekindling without much effort in the future. He was relieved at having seen her that day. It was an amazing coincidence. A pleasant homecoming that he hadn't expected at all.

'You must tell me all about India,' she was saying. 'Why don't we go for tea? I know a lovely shop near here.'

'I'd like that,' Michael said.

Paying the porter to store his possessions for a while, Michael agreed to join Clara for afternoon tea and, instead of getting taxis, they walked a few minutes from the station to a small tea room that had somehow managed to survive the war, and was now thriving in the middle of a row of newly restored buildings.

After taking a seat by the small window, Clara began to update Michael on all that had happened to his friends since he had left. The biggest revelation was Mel, of course.

'Oh, but you simply must come to Avonby. It will be a proper reunion with you there too, and we can reconfirm our friendship group,' Clara said. 'I know Mel will be thrilled and I'm sure Eleanor will be too. You are staying in London, now that you're back?'

'That's the plan,' Michael said.

Clara was beaming at him and he did notice that she was indeed far prettier than he remembered. His thoughts were focused on this amazing good fortune at meeting again. He had been in such a depression during the long journey, feeling isolated and adrift as the British shoreline drew closer, and the air damp and cold. England had seemed so alien to him, after the warm, slow pace of New Delhi. He knew the winters would be hard compared to the heat he was accustomed to and he said this to Clara.

'Yes. It can be cold, but that's what a cosy fireplace is for. You'll settled again, once you're among friends. And surely, it's cleaner here?'

Michael didn't correct her on this somewhat uninformed comment and assumption. He had found New Delhi to be clean and welcoming. He also didn't point out to her that London, with its smog and foul air, was far dirtier than the streets of India.

After tea, which was pleasant, but not quite as good as the familiar Assam leaves he drank in India, Michael excused himself with the promise to be in touch, though he had been reluctant to leave Clara's pleasant company.

He had returned to the station and after collecting his trunk headed back to his old home in Hammersmith via taxi.

On the journey, he observed London was different in some areas which were nowhere near rebuilt, and yet the city had somehow managed to retain its essence. He was pleased to see some spectacular buildings remaining and knew that normal life was resuming here, though things would never quite be the same as before the war. How could they be?

By the time he reached his former home, Michael had decided to keep his promise to Clara and was very drawn to the idea of visiting Mel at Avonby. He had always liked Mel. She had been different from the others, less shallow and totally gutsy.

The meeting was very fortuitous, he thought and his spirits were lifted.

He had approached London with a feeling of trepidation, and isolation, and now here he was, with the very real opportunity to reignite old relationships. It made him feel less alone and for the first time since his father had died, he had begun to see an optimistic side to moving back to England.

'Oh Master Michael!' said the housekeeper opening the door for him. 'We've been expecting you!'

Michael smiled at his former nanny, turned house-keeper and now old retainer, who had dutifully remained in the house throughout the war and all the time that his family had been absent. It was a warm welcome and sweet homecoming after all, and Michael had let her usher him inside, while the taxi driver and the footman wrangled his trunk inside and up the stairs to the master bedroom.

But before he settled, he penned a note to send to Clara, saying he would like to join them on their trip, and left it with Nanny to send to Clara's home for him.

* * *

'That's not exactly how I remember it,' Clara said.

'Bit rich, old bean. I probably wouldn't have had the nerve to talk to you if you hadn't spoken to me first. And you were very insistent on me coming to Avonby, right from the first conversation,' he said.

'Were you?' asked Eleanor.

'Well… I mentioned we were visiting and Michael jumped on it,' Clara said.

Michael gasped at the blatancy of the lie. Clara really was a piece of work after all, and the sweet open kindness she had shown him all along had now disappeared. That small attraction he had been cultivating for her now shrunk to a small glimmer, not quite crushed, but viewed through a different lens. He looked at her with open surprise, and then he closed down his expression, knowing that he was giving away too much of himself to someone he had effectively just started to know.

He was about to point out that Clara had written to him so quickly after they parted that his own note hadn't left the hallway before hers arrived. But being a gentleman, he decided not to embarrass her further and with the rapid chatter that Eleanor and Clara were involved in, he couldn't have got a word in anyway.

'Can you lot shut it,' Frank said. 'And the sooner one of you owns up and turns that painting in, the quicker we'll be out of here.'

'Rude,' Clara said. 'You shouldn't even be held in the same room as us.'

'Neither should your maid in that case,' Frank said. 'But you ain't planning to throw her out are you?'

The mention of Mabel brought her once again to the attention of the suspects. She was sitting in the chair in the corner, gazing out of the window, and had been forgotten about until Frank mentioned her.

'She's hardly causing any problem,' Clara said. 'Unlike you with your insolent comments. I doubt Charles would have put up with any of this, if he were here.'

Frank glowered at her, silenced by the arrogance of her tone and the knowledge that he was not in the same class and never would be.

* * *

Toby was paying careful attention to the conversation, planning to recount it all to Lady Melinda, whom he knew would be able to make something important of it. Toby loved watching Lady Mel in action when she had a problem to solve. Sometimes she would go quiet, and Toby would hold his breath as she seemed to sink inside herself. When she came back from this quiet, thoughtful place, she would have solutions. It was like she could see things that other people couldn't. It was kind of spooky when you didn't understand it, but Toby admired her, and wanted to be as knowledgeable and observant as she was.

'You!' Clara said. 'Fetch Mel here, right now. I want out of this room. Now it is daytime, and the lights are back on, I expect her to get the proper authorities in to sort this all out.'

Toby sat back in his chair and folded his arms, showing a stubborn refusal to move. He ignored Clara even as she began to rant about how rude he was.

The drawing-room door opened and Derrin and Mel came inside and Toby realised they had been outside the door listening to the entire exchange.

'I *have* rung the station now, but it will be an hour or two before the day shift clocks in and will be sent over to Avonby,' Derrin said.

'This is your last chance.' Mel said. 'I've decided, if the painting is returned immediately, that I won't take the theft any further with the police. Though the death of Charles is another issue and something that neither the inspector nor I can help you with.'

'That's a good offer,' Eleanor said. 'Anyone wish to own up and at least put that to bed? I'll be happy if you find that dratted thing now.'

Mel and Derrin looked around the room and waited for a response, but none was forthcoming.

'Okay then,' said Derrin. 'Then the private interviews will begin again.'

There was a collective sigh as the suspects all glared at each other, hoping that the culprit would own up and they would at least be off the hook for theft.

18

'FRANK,' SAID DERRIN. 'YOU'RE UP NEXT.'

There was a kind of relief when Frank stood up to go with Derrin and Mel, as though he was so bored that even being questioned was a massive relief. He followed them now without a quibble and they all went out into the hallway.

'Sit on the chaise Frank,' Mel said. 'Something has been bothering me. When I went outside to check the electrical cables after the power cut. I noticed that Charles's car wasn't at the front of the house, unlike the Inspector's car. Visitors usually remain at the front, and I'm sure that Mr Williams would have told you that.'

Frank shrugged. 'Mr Charles insisted that I clean the car, so your footman, Toby told me I could take it to the garage around the back as everything I'd need was in there to get the job done.'

'You cleaned the car before supper?' Derrin asked.

'Yeah. Then I went into the kitchen via the back door,' Frank said.

'Well, let's confirm that shall we?'

Mel rang the bell that was near the front door. Mr Williams appeared and she asked if he could confirm Frank's story.

'I wasn't in the kitchen at that time, Lady Mel, but Mrs Weston and possibly one of the girls was,' Williams said.

'Ask Mrs Weston to come up please,' Derrin said.

As Williams left, Mel noticed that Frank appeared to be a little twitchy as though he feared his story wouldn't be corroborated.

'What's worrying you?' Mel asked.

'I don't fink I saw anyone in the kitchen when I came in,' Frank said.

'So, you're saying that no one saw you coming in from the back?'

'Yeah,' Frank said. 'I came in. 'Ung me coat up. Then I went to the room Toby had said I could sleep in. I had a lie down, because I was tired: it was a long drive from London to here, and we'd left before dawn.'

Mrs Weston appeared and was, as Frank said, unable to confirm seeing him.

'He did come from the servants' quarters corridor later for supper after Toby fetched him,' she said. 'But I had me back to the boot room door as I was basting the chicken around then.'

'Thank you, Mrs Weston, that will be all,' Mel said. 'But can you ask the others if any of them saw Mr Carter before dinner and if they can pinpoint his whereabouts?'

'I will ask,' said Mrs Weston and she went back downstairs.

'Well then, you can see I was telling the troof about being in me room,' Frank said.

'Not necessarily,' Mel said. 'You could have sneaked in another way. The house wasn't locked down at that point.'

'I have no answer to that,' Frank said.

'Let's talk about Charles,' Derrin said. 'You said earlier that you've worked for him for several months. What sort of man was he?'

Frank fidgeted again. 'He weren't a nice one, if that's what you mean. He were 'urting Miss Eleanor all the time. I saw it. So did his father. And I fink 'is mother knew it too.'

'What makes you say that?' Mel asked, her curiosity about Charles's parents piqued.

'They were trying to keep their eye on fings.'

* * *

Two weeks earlier

'To my parents' house Frank,' Charles said as he climbed into the back of the car.

Frank had picked him up outside the gentleman's club after collecting Miss Eleanor first from the bridal shop.

Frank noticed that Miss Eleanor was very subdued that day and he couldn't help wondering if she was having serious second thoughts. He couldn't blame her if she was, after witnessing, by then, several 'accidents' that usually resulted in Eleanor being physically injured.

'How was lunch?' Eleanor asked, her voice soft as though she were attempting to avoid confrontation and keep the afternoon light.

Charles was seething with anger and looked as though any moment he was about to explode.

'I'll tell you about lunch,' he said. 'I met someone who told me some very interesting things.'

'Oh?' said Eleanor. 'That's nice.'

'*Nice*? Yes. Nice!' Charles said through gritted teeth.

Frank had glanced in the rearview mirror and saw the worried look on Eleanor's face. She knew she was in some kind of bother, but not what it was she was supposed to have done this time. It was clear that Charles was always on the lookout for ways to punish her. And it had all started around the time of their engagement party. Frank didn't understand what had happened between them, but something had, and since then, Mr Charles had been on the warpath.

'Should I take the scenic route?' Frank said, hoping to give Mr Charles time to cool off before seeing his parents.

'No. Go there directly.'

Eleanor was looking out of the window now, trying not to show she was scared. She had seen Charles in these rages, just as Frank had, and she had good cause to be concerned.

'Lovely day today,' she said trying to lighten the conversation even as her voice trembled, 'considering it's autumn.'

There was a nip in the air that showed the change of season, but the blueness of the sky could cheer up the soul.

If a person has a soul, Frank thought as he glanced once more at Mr Charles.

'Shut your stupid wittering,' Charles said. 'I'm in no mood for it.'

Eleanor shrank into the seat beside him as if she wanted to just disappear. Her cheeks bloomed red and tears started in her eyes.

Frank felt a stirring in his heart that he hadn't felt for years. Not since before the war, when he had hardened himself to the atrocities he had seen and endured. He pitied her. And up until that point he hadn't felt anything other than disgust for the pair of them. But he was seeing Charles more as each day passed for the utterly vile brute he was.

Eleanor, he noticed, was slowly losing her beauty and more frown lines were appearing on her brow than she had previously had. She was overly thin now. And he suspected she barely ate, plagued with worry about her forthcoming marriage as he was sure she was.

Frank was surprised by himself as he analysed this doomed relationship. Why did the woman put up with it, even for one minute? Why would anyone?

Frank was plummeted back into his own childhood years and the awful drunken tantrums of his father, which invariably ended up raining down on his defenceless mother.

It was horrible how his father treated her, like she was something to wipe his feet on and to wait on him, hand and foot, when he was home. Even though he deserved nothing at all. The man was barely a provider, and Frank had been finding work from the tender age of eleven, just to make sure he and his mother ate. He hid his earnings from his father, who would have taken and used his hard-earned cash to satisfy his awful need for gin, which seemed to Frank to be the heart of the problem.

Frank wondered if his parents had ever been happy. He couldn't remember it. When his father had died, falling dead drunk under an oncoming carriage, his mother had carried on like he had been the best father and husband in the world. Even at his funeral she seemed to have forgotten the black eyes, the fractured ribs and the days of profound starvation that he had inflicted on them. His wake was a celebration of the lie that was his father's life. He could never understand why she hadn't told the truth about him. Why carry on the lie, right up to her own passing? Was it some latent need to retain the dignity she never had?

That day in the car, as he saw the destruction that Eleanor's future surely held, all the fury of his younger years came flooding back. He wanted to thump Charles. He wanted to see him crushed under the wheel of a car. He hated him.

They reached Charles's family home and Eleanor perked up as though she knew she would be safe here for a while, for Charles would never show his mean streak in front of his parents. But that day was different and Charles was in a frightful mood, one that would never be satisfied until he had inflicted something on her.

Frank pulled the Rolls-Royce into the kerb and quickly got out, hoping to head off the inevitable pinch or stamping on the poor girl's foot again. He didn't want to see that again, as he wasn't sure what he might do to Mr Charles today if he did. Probably something he would regret or end up in gaol for.

Frank opened the back door and reached inside to help Eleanor out and that was when he saw the meanness in Charles's eyes. He quickly pulled Eleanor up and out, just as Charles's cane slapped down where the woman had been sat. A blow that might have given her serious injuries. Maybe even a breakage.

He pulled Miss Eleanor behind him then, and glared at Charles, daring him to attempt more. The fury was in his eyes, but Charles was not a brave man and Frank knew it. He could bully a woman, but he'd never take on another man. Charles backed down, but Frank suspected he had only postponed something that would be inevitable.

'Ah here you both are. How lovely. Come on inside,' said Charles's mother, appearing at the door in an uncharacteristic greeting.

She exchanged a look with Frank and then peered into the car at her son.

'Charles?' she said and Frank couldn't help wondering if this simple word held some kind of warning, for immediately Charles's demeanour changed, and he climbed from the car and held out his arm to Eleanor as though nothing had occurred.

Eleanor was stricken with fear, having seen that awful moment when the cane had hit the car seat and she knew he had meant business. Frank thought then that this might be a turning point for the woman.

'I'll follow you shortly,' she said. 'I just need my reticule.'

With Charles moving away, Eleanor reached back into the car and picked up her purse.

'You deserve better, Miss,' Frank said to her.

'Thank you, Frank,' Eleanor said.

Eleanor turned and walked into the house, but there was no enthusiasm in her step. Frank was left wishing he could have done more.

Men like him shouldn't exist, he thought.

But it was out of his hands, other than in the spur of the moment when he could head off some awful deed. He shook his head, feeling that dreadful hopelessness he'd experienced as a child, when his father had been in a rage. He was afraid now, like then, but not for himself, for Miss Eleanor. She wasn't a bad sort, he could see that, and she'd fallen for the wrong man, as some women did. All he could do was wait and watch and hope that the woman had the sense to call off the wedding and walk away.

Frank locked up the car and went around to the back of the house to the servants' quarters where he was given tea and cake while he waited for his employer. But while he was there, there was a commotion and one of the servant girls ran in requesting a bowl of cold water.

Mr Charles had knocked Miss Eleanor's arm while she was pouring the tea and she had burnt her hand. By the description given, Frank knew this *wasn't* an accident, but would be claimed to be one. He was disgusted, but mostly sad that he had failed to protect Miss Eleanor, just as he felt he had his mother all those years earlier.

Later, while he was warming the car up for Charles and Eleanor's return home, Charles's father came outside to see Frank.

'We must watch over Miss Eleanor, mustn't we, Frank? She does seem rather prone to accidents,' Mr Harris said. 'Myself and Mrs Harris are a little concerned.'

'And I intend to take care of 'er. We don't want any serious ones now, do we? Perhaps Mrs Charles needs a word too?' Frank said.

'I'll take care of that side,' Harris nodded. 'Let me know if you have any future concerns, will you?'

* * *

'I promised I would. And I have been sending little messages to Mr Harris senior, to let him know how it was going. As you know, it weren't going well,' Frank said.

When Frank finished, Mel and Derrin were silent.

Mel now saw Frank in the study, moving in to drop the arsenic in the brandy glass, knowing Charles well enough that he would drink from it eventually. She even saw Frank watching as Charles drugged and stabbed Michael, that utter meanness coming out in a vile and final stroke that probably tipped Frank over the edge.

'So you…' began Derrin, but Mel cut him off when she took his hand and squeezed his fingers gently.

'We don't need to know,' she said.

Derrin glanced at Mel, surprised by this turn of events. They both suspected that Frank had been Charles's poisoner, but they were left with a quandary: the man deserved it, but murder was murder.

'Did you see Charles chloroform Michael?' Mel asked just by way of confirming her suspicions.

Frank nodded. 'And when he took the knife from the top of the writing desk earlier. I was watching, as I fought it was for Miss Eleanor, and was gonna step in. I swear he wouldn't have bin 'appy until he proper maimed her.'

'Why didn't you speak up earlier? You could have saved Michael being injured,' Mel said.

'I didn't see him use the knife to be troofull,' Frank said. 'Just the cloth over his face and I saw him chuck it in the fire. He was getting rid of evidence and I knew that. But I wanted to see why he'd done it to Mr Chase. I didn't fink they knew each other.'

Mel saw all of this in her mind's eye and realised that the pieces of the puzzle were starting to shape up and the characters on the board were taking their roles. She saw Frank now as the knight, protecting a queen, and she couldn't in all honesty hold any of it against him. Especially given his childhood.

'I need to speak to the inspector,' Mel told Frank. 'Please take yourself back into the drawing room.'

'You're trusting me to go meself?' Frank said.

'Yes I am,' Mel answered.

Frank stood and walked down the hallway, going meekly into the drawing room. Once inside he closed the door.

Mel sank down into one of the chairs.

'You know he has to take his punishment for this,' Derrin said.

'*Does he*?' Mel asked.

'Mel. It was murder. And he planned it,' Derrin said.

Mel shook her head and although she could see it, she still struggled to believe that Frank had brought arsenic with the sole purpose of killing Charles.

'It's that part I'm having difficulty with,' Mel said. 'You see, I don't believe he planned this. If Frank killed Charles, it was because he was reacting. Something went in Frank's mind for a time. His poor childhood was the first trauma. He was a soldier and has just survived the brutality of the front line, and then he finds himself working for a bully like Charles. A bully who is terrorising his fiancée and Frank, with his history, couldn't bear to see it.'

Mel's hand was shaking. She felt her own traumas trying to surface. Derrin sat down on the chaise and reached for her. He rubbed her cold fingers between his warm hands and then he pulled her to him, holding her until the tremors stopped.

Mel felt a small wetness streak against her cheek, and Derrin dashed his hand across his face, removing all sign of his own grief as fast as it had appeared.

'We can't let our own issues cloud our judgement here,' he said. His mouth pressed against her ear, his voice low, and even the keenest eavesdropper wouldn't have been able to make out his words. 'But I do feel the same. The more we hear of Charles's behaviour, the more I can forgive his killer.'

Mel nuzzled into his neck and enjoyed the warmth of his skin pressed against hers and the moment of weakness passed as his embrace gave her strength. She came back to herself from that pit of darkness that sometimes surfaced and made her feel fragile. It was so hard to accept this feebleness when at all other times she was a lioness ready for battle. One day, someone would understand what had happened to them during the war and, Mel hoped, would support them to learn to deal with it and take away these awful symptoms for good. But while the world refused to belief that there were any serious cases of CSR, she didn't think that would happen. They were expected, as always, to have a stiff upper lip.

Mel pulled her mind away from the thoughts that caused her episodes and back to the problem at hand. The death of Charles had overshadowed the loss of the Turner and it was time to up that search again. There were still so many unanswered questions and so much that they had to learn before they could resolve the crimes that had occurred.

'There's many missing pieces of this puzzle,' Mel said pulling the focus back onto the crime. 'The biggest for me is why was Charles so angry with Eleanor? She said all was great until just before their engagement, then he changed.'

'Let's talk to her again,' Derrin said. 'And this time we must be brutally honest about what we know of their relationship.'

Calmer, they drew apart. But Mel was reluctant to let go of the moment. A surge of passion came over her as she looked at Derrin, and she leaned in again. They kissed as though they were sealing the deal for a later encounter. She couldn't help recognising how conflict always brought out this urge to draw closer to him, and how that closeness frequently turned sexual, as though this connection they had could consume them and assuage the pain they were both feeling. Derrin's touch always made her feel better, and inside, she suspected it was the same for him too. Now she wondered how they had managed to keep apart so much. And were those moments of irritation and anger between them part of this desire to be individual, strong and independent, for fear of growing reliant on one another? Mel didn't know for sure, as she was better at analysing other people's emotions than her own. As for Derrin, what went on in his mind was for the most part unknown. A thought that was difficult for her to come to terms with, especially when they shared an almost telepathic connection when it came to solving mysteries.

Derrin stood up and pulled Mel to her feet, and she sensed the same reluctance to move apart that she felt. She became once more aware of her surroundings and glanced around the hallway as though she expected Mr Williams or Toby to be lurking. But no one was there, and their moment of intimacy remained unseen, a fact that Mel was grateful for, because she still didn't know what the future held for her and Derrin, and gossip amongst the servants was something to be avoided at all costs until she knew where she stood.

'Time to speak to Eleanor again, I think,' said Derrin again. He didn't release her hand and Mel understood that he was making sure she was stable and able to carry on as well.

She nodded and pulled back to show she was ready, but letting go and no longer having his touch was a wrench. Mel forced her mind away from her desire for Derrin, there would be time alone again soon, she knew they would need that, and her thoughts focused once more on the Turner. She had to get the painting back, and find out who had taken it and why they had done it in the first place, because somehow the theft felt personal.

19

ELEANOR WAS SITTING QUIETLY BY THE WINDOW when Mel and Derrin opened the drawing-room door. She didn't turn her head to look at them, but merely stood up, as though she knew the time had come to tell them her truth. She walked towards them, head down, hands clasped in front of her.

'Can I get you some water before we start?' Mel said as Eleanor took the chaise, which was now becoming the 'hot seat' for the interviews.

'That would be nice,' Eleanor said.

Before coming for her, Mel had sent for a jug of water and some glasses and Mr Williams and Toby had placed the tray on a small table they had brought out into the hallway from the study. Now she poured a glass and handed it to Eleanor.

The air was clean in the study, but since Mel and Derrin had experienced greater success interviewing in the hallway, they had opted to remain there. It was more open and felt less oppressive, and perhaps psychologically made the suspects feel less defensive. Although Mel also suspected that it might just be because they were all fatigued and couldn't resist any more.

As Eleanor drank the water, Mel glanced at the grandfather clock. Time was ticking onwards and it was approaching nine in the morning. She expected a contingent of police officers to arrive at any time, though Derrin had said he told them 'not to rush'. Even so, she supposed that they would be there by ten at the latest and then she would no longer be involved as the police took over the investigation. It was likely that Derrin would be relieved at that point too, and neither of them would have any further control over what happened. Derrin for his part might be seen to have a conflict of interest having been at the dinner party and because of his friendship with Mel. With this is mind, there was a greater sense of urgency to solve the crime and get back the painting, leaving the murder problem to the police thereafter. A prospect Mel looked forward to as she didn't really want to be the one to bring down Charles's killer because of her mixed feelings about him.

Eleanor finished the water and asked for more and when she had the second glass in her hand, Mel sat down opposite her and opened the conversation.

'When did Charles's attitude change towards you?' she asked.

'I told you already.'

'Did something happen to spark the change?' Derrin asked. 'And I'm not blaming you; I just want to see if we can pinpoint a catalyst.'

'What does it matter?' Eleanor said. 'He's dead and it's all irrelevant.'

'No, it isn't irrelevant,' Mel said. 'Something happened. And you need to tell us what it was. In the end, it might help you come to terms with it too. And that could aid you to move on from what's happened here.'

Eleanor's shoulders drooped for a second and then she forced herself to sit upright and Mel and Derrin could see the quiet resolve and strength that the woman had found deep inside herself.

Mel steeled herself: she knew the story that was coming would be unpleasant and hoped that Eleanor could sustain her determination and energy throughout the account.

'We went to a pub…' Eleanor began. 'The night before our engagement party.'

* * *

London, August, 1946

Eleanor was excited about the engagement party, which had been organised last minute for friends and family. They hadn't been planning one initially, and the wedding was already booked for the end of November, but Clara and a few other friends insisted it should be celebrated beforehand.

'And he can afford it, Elle, so why not?' Clara had said.

Eleanor had arranged it all with Charles's approval and money, and they had decided to go for a quiet dinner the evening before, just the two of them, to talk through the final arrangements.

Charles had been driving that night, after giving Frank the evening off, and he had picked her up from her apartment. He was smiling and happy and Eleanor thought they couldn't be any more in love if they tried. It was all perfect. She hadn't, at that point, seen anything in Charles that would suggest otherwise.

It was a warm evening, even though the summer was almost over in terms of the calendar, and Eleanor was wearing a new calf-length dress of dark blue silk, with a fox-fur stole around her shoulders. Charles remarked that Hollywood would come calling if a producer saw her looking like that. She took the compliment, feeling pretty, and had laughed with him at the absurdity of such an idea.

'We are so early for the restaurant booking, let's pop into that pub and get a drink. It's a lovely evening, still warm, and I would love to show my fiancée off,' said Charles.

'But we don't know anyone from around here,' Eleanor had said looking around at the somewhat dubious area.

'Then it will be even more fun,' Charles said.

He had pulled the car over by the entrance, and being a gentleman, opened the door for her to get out of the car. Then, taking her arm, led her inside.

The pub smelled of spilt beer and cigarettes. Eleanor's nose crinkled, but she said nothing as he settled her at a table with a drink; even so she did think it was a very strange place to bring her. She had never been in such a place before, and hadn't ever wanted to, but being with Charles she was sure she was safe and if her future husband liked to be spontaneous like this, then she didn't really mind.

It soon became clear that Charles had stopped at the place for some other reason. He did know someone there and he went off for a moment to do 'business' with them.

Eleanor felt exposed being in a common pub, and left alone, and she sipped her drink whilst trying not to draw attention to herself while he was gone.

When Charles came back, he kept rubbing his nose. As he approached Eleanor saw him stuffing a vial of something into his jacket pocket. He came and sat down at the table, picking up the half glass of beer he had left for himself and he took a big swig.

Eleanor noted immediately that he was acting oddly, he appeared to be hyperactive and was talking faster than usual. She also saw how dilated his pupils were. None of this change in behaviour was attractive or appealing and she was hugely uncomfortable around him for the first time since they met.

'Are you all right?' she asked eventually.

'I'm fine. How about you?' he said. 'Was the drink nice? I'll get you another one.'

Eleanor tried to object but Charles was out of his seat and heading to the bar, returning shortly with another gin and tonic which he placed in front of her and encouraged her to drink.

'I can't possibly drink more on an empty stomach, darling,' she said. 'What time was the dinner reservation?'

Charles ignored her comments. 'I like this place, always full of sociable sorts. They just got a jukebox last week. I'll put some music on and we can have a little jig. I know you enjoy that.'

'Oh no! That's not my thing at all,' Eleanor said. 'You are funny. Now stop joking around and let's leave. I'm hungry.'

Charles left his seat again and this time he went to the jukebox and began to feed coins into the machine and soon a variety of different tunes played through it. Eleanor was confused by his conduct which was so out of character that she really didn't know what to do. Any thought of dinner was now gone as she nursed the second drink.

Charles became the life and soul of the party, buying drinks for total strangers, as Eleanor looked on appalled by this sudden change of behaviour. As the evening drew on, the group drifted away and Eleanor began to feel even more concerned. He had begun to drink heavily and she knew he wouldn't be fit to drive the car.

She began to look for a way out of the situation. Perhaps she could hide his car keys and persuade him to leave and get a taxi. She was sure he would be embarrassed the next day. Her mind made all kinds of excuses for him. Was he drunk before they arrived at the pub? Was it because of his issues following the war? She had become aware of these problems almost as soon as they became involved. Charles, had in fact, opened up to her about it, wanting to have no secrets between them.

'Charles. Do you think we ought to leave?' Eleanor said approaching him at the bar.

That was the first time she saw the awful irritation on Charles's face and felt the brunt of his appalling attitude when she questioned him.

'Stop being a wet blanket,' he said. 'Look, I have something in here that will make you enjoy yourself more.'

It was then that he pulled out the small vial, and Eleanor saw it contained a white powder.

'Come on.' Charles took her hand and pulled her into the ladies' washroom. Blocking the door, her poured a line of the stuff onto the sink. 'You snort it like this.'

Then Eleanor saw him breathing in the substance through a rolled-up pound note.

'What is that?' she asked.

'Try it,' Charles said.

'No. I don't want to. It's making you behave… peculiarly,' she pointed out.

Eleanor went to the bathroom door and as she reached for the handle, Charles grabbed her from behind and placed a handkerchief over her nose and mouth. She struggled against him, feeling suffocated and scared, until the awful compound began to work and she slipped away into thankful oblivion.

***

A few hours later, Eleanor woke up. She was on the floor of the washroom, her clothing was in disarray, her underwear had been removed and she found it crumpled on the floor beside her. Her stockings were ripped and laddered and she felt desperately ashamed. Charles was nowhere to be seen and so she staggered to her feet, only to feel nauseated. She hurried to the toilet and threw up until her stomach hurt.

Afterwards, when the sickness subsided, Eleanor walked to the sink to wash her face. She looked at her image in the mirror and saw the haggard visage of someone who had been drugged and then molested. But who had done it? All she could remember was Charles's outlandish behaviour, trying to coerce her into taking something, and then blackness.

Her mind began to put the pieces together. Charles had put something over her face. He'd almost smothered her. What had he done, and why?

The bathroom door opened. Eleanor saw Charles standing in the door frame. She could hear the jukebox playing the song he had favoured the night before. *Surrender* sung by Perry Como.

'What… happened?' Eleanor asked now.

'You lied to me,' Charles said. His face was black with rage.

'What did you do to me?' Eleanor asked.

'You were holding on so much for the wedding night, teasing me. A man gets impatient,' he said. 'I thought I'd loosen you up and make it all official.'

'What? You mean you… brought me here… for *this*?'

'I know the owner. He left us alone while he locked up,' Charles said.

Sickness roiled in Eleanor's stomach and she ran back to the toilet, throwing up bile while her empty stomach retched again and again.

'Oh my God. You… I can't believe you *did* this… What is *wrong* with you?'

Charles then fell into a torrent of excuses. It was the cocaine he had inhaled, it had taken away his inhibitions. The alcohol on an empty stomach. She almost bought into the excuse until…

'You know I've wanted you. But you said we had to wait. Then I find out someone else has been there before…'

'*What*? You've forced yourself on me. You're disgusting,' she said.

'Who was he?'

'I'm not having this conversation with you. Take me home. Now!' Eleanor said.

Charles left the bathroom and Eleanor washed her face once more. As she came out, he held out the fox-fur stole and she put it around her shivering shoulders.

The jukebox was still playing the same song. A ballad she had once liked, she now found frightening.

'It seemed apt. I was trying to be romantic,' Charles said nodding to the wurlitzer. 'Come on, old girl, it'll all be all right. I forgive you lying to me and you need to forget this happened.'

'Take me home,' she said again. 'I don't feel well.'

'Ah. You'll sleep that off and then we'll have the party tonight as you wanted. I know you like the finer things Eleanor and I can still give them you. All you have to do is forget what happened here.'

'I don't know right now how I feel about our future together,' Eleanor said.

'Don't be rash. No one will want you. Not if you turn out to be pregnant,' Charles pointed out. 'Besides, you know I love you, don't you?'

Horrified, Eleanor said nothing as she followed him to the front door. Something behind her drew her attention and Eleanor stopped and grabbed Charles's arm.

'What was that?' she said.

'Nothing.'

'I heard moaning,' Eleanor said.

The groan grew louder. Eleanor looked over towards the brass-covered bar. She couldn't see anything but she knew someone was behind it, injured.

'What have you done?' she murmured, overwhelmed by fear of him for the first time.

Charles grabbed her arm, and pressed his mean face against hers. 'Behave yourself Eleanor or you might find yourself in her condition. Now come on and get in the car.'

Charles pulled her out of the front door of the pub, slamming it shut behind him, then he pushed her into the passenger seat of the Rolls, climbed into the driver's seat and started the engine.

As Charles pulled the car away, Eleanor took in her surroundings. The roads were empty and it was still not fully dawn; she was working out how long she had been unconscious and what Charles had done to her during that time. She felt tainted and afraid. Through the corner of her eye, she saw him now, vaguely smiling, and she couldn't work out whether this was the after effects of the substance he had taken or whether it was because he was completely insane and she hadn't realised it.

'I hope you're going to put on some nice underwear for me tonight,' he said. 'No need to be coy any more.'

Eleanor put her hand to her mouth and fought back another wave of sickness. Just a few hours ago she had been in love with Charles. The thought of him coming near her again revolted her now. He was a repulsive villain and no number of excuses were going to explain away his terrible deeds. He had taken from her a moment that should have been full of tenderness and joy, and turned it into an awful violation of her trust.

Eleanor knew that she couldn't marry him now no matter what, but how could she extricate herself, and what if, like he said, she was expecting? How could her family take that shame? Her mother would die of it!

It was an awful situation and one she had to disentangle herself from when she was sure it hadn't happened. But until then, she might have to play along, because she was afraid of Charles: she knew what he was capable of. There were still so many questions about the last few hours. What had he done to the person behind the bar? What had happened while she was unconscious? She couldn't remember it, but it was obvious.

Charles dropped Eleanor home and she sneaked into the quiet house before her parents saw the state she was in. In the bathroom she washed herself clean and then, wrapped up in her nightdress and robe, curled up in her own bed and sobbed herself to sleep.

* * *

Eleanor slept the day through, only stirring when her mother, Cynthia Parkinson, woke her at five in the evening.

'You and Charles were out late last night! Come on you need to get up and get ready for your party. Being "fashionably late" doesn't apply at your own engagement, you need to be there to greet everyone,' Cynthia said.

Eleanor sat up, rubbed her eyes and roused herself as her mother left the room. After sleeping the drug off, she felt physically better and was starting to justify Charles's actions to herself and, not wanting to upset her mother, she got up and dressed.

Later, with a smiling and normal-looking Charles by her side, Eleanor paraded her expensive engagement ring, all the time trying to shake off her disgust as they did the rounds and talked to everyone who had come.

'You okay?' asked Clara, taking her aside halfway through the night.

'Yes, why wouldn't I be?' Eleanor said and she forced a smile on her face that didn't quite reach her eyes.

She saw Clara's frown.

'I'm just a little tired. It's all a little too much,' she said, making, what she hoped would be a plausible excuse.

'Okay. You just don't seem yourself,' Clara said. 'Are you sure there's nothing wrong? You don't have to go ahead with this you know. If you have doubts.'

'All is well. Stop fussing, you're worse than my mother,' Eleanor said.

The party went well, was a success as far as these things go, and she and Charles looked like the ideal couple. He was so respectful and loving to her that by the end of the night, Eleanor had almost convinced herself it was a one-off and horrible incident that would never be repeated. She would of course, ban him from attending such disreputable places as that seedy pub ever again.

'You've done well tonight,' Charles said as the evening ended. 'But you have a lot of making up to do. Your lies have caught up with you. Who was he?'

'It doesn't matter,' Eleanor told him. 'It was years ago.'

'It matters to me,' Charles said.

She didn't enjoy the reminder and wished he would just leave this alone, and she then might be able to put the awful thing he'd done to her behind them too.

She told him this and Charles just laughed. Then he pinched her hard on the top of her arm.

This was just the beginning of his hateful attitude, Eleanor knew, because he couldn't forgive what he saw as a terrible slight, and Charles, instead of calling off the engagement, had decided to make her pay for it by marrying her to prolong her torture. It was an awful prospect that had sent her spiralling into a state of denial and panic, which invaded her mind at various times.

She had lost weight, barely eating because she was full of anxiety.

The strange thing was, no one commented on the change in her personality and she had come to realise that this was because they all thought it to be pre-wedding nerves. Even her mother made excuses for her small irritable outbursts and the lack of appetite, but never bothered to question Eleanor on it. She began to feel that only she could see what Charles was, and questioned her negative thoughts about him all the time. Even when his wearing comments were taking their toll on her and Eleanor was beginning to believe that she was worthless and faithless and stupid because he told her she was all the time when no one was in earshot.

The weeks wore on, and more and more things occurred afterwards, but she managed to avoid being with him still, in the biblical sense, and so Charles's frustration had grown. Accusations abounded, and no matter how she had reassured him, he wouldn't believe her.

The only relief happened when, just last week, her monthly time came, and she knew she could be free of Charles. She made sure to keep him at arm's length, and had continued to ever since.

* * *

When Eleanor finished her story both Derrin and Mel remained quiet while she gathered herself. Eleanor was in tears again and the extent of her abuse at the man's hands had stretched further than they had at first suspected.

'It was my fault, of course,' Eleanor said now much to Mel's amazement. 'I had held out on him, but you see, I'd fallen for someone before the war. We'd had a fling for a while, and then he threw me over for another girl. I was barely sixteen at the time. I had tried to forget what had happened and had almost convinced myself. I had felt so used you see. He broke my heart, and I didn't want to be in that position again. So, I made Charles wait, even though he'd already asked me to marry him. You see, it really *was* my fault.'

'Let's be clear. Charles's abuse of you was *not* your fault in any way,' Derrin said. 'He was a sickening individual. He raped you and has been hurting you ever since. He deserved to be punished for it.'

'I could have reported it, couldn't I? And we wouldn't be here now. He'd possibly be in prison, wouldn't he? At the very least I could have disentangled myself. I just couldn't. Not until I was sure that I wasn't expecting.'

Derrin and Mel both knew the justice system and the possibility of Charles getting away scot-free was very probable. The law would have seen it that they were involved, engaged and almost married. All Charles had to do was say it was consensual, because of their promise to marry, and a claim of rape was unlikely to stand up at all. After all, the law said a man could do what he wanted with his wife – he owned her. A law that, Mel knew, was wrong and should be changed, but they weren't there yet. Even so, Mel didn't point this out to Eleanor. It was a conversation for perhaps another day when this business was resolved, and if Eleanor needed further reassurance that she wasn't responsible.

'I'm so sorry this has happened to you,' Derrin said again showing a lot of empathy. 'And I do understand how difficult it is to free one's self from a bad situation. But Charles was wrong. His actions intolerable. No man should treat a woman in that way. I know it is hard to accept, but you weren't to blame for any of it.'

As he talked, Mel saw that Derrin's values totally aligned with hers.

'I know you're tired and I'm sorry to ask more, but do you know who was behind the bar and what Charles had done to them?' Mel asked.

Eleanor looked down to the floor.

'A few days after the engagement party, my father was reading his morning paper and I saw the murder on the front page.'

'Murder?' Derrin said.

Eleanor nodded. 'I picked up the paper once my father discarded it.'

'Who was it?' asked Mel.

'A charwoman called Joan Carter. I remember her name because I have thought about her every day since then. She was stabbed. The papers said the bar was broken into. Robbed. But Charles had the key and let us out. He'd also said the owner knew we were there. I suspected that Charles was responsible. Though I couldn't be certain, as I didn't see him do anything.'

'Thank you for telling me this. I will investigate it and see that some justice is done for Joan Carter or at least get some answers for her family,' Derrin said.

'Can I go back now?' Eleanor said, her voice shaky.

'One other thing. Did Charles steal the painting?' Derrin said.

'I don't think so. I don't believe he ever had an opportunity.'

Mel saw the tired circles around her former friend's eyes. The woman was broken and she was sure she had told them everything they needed to know for now. Not that any of it helped at all with the loss of the painting. But it did give a haunting motive for Charles's death.

'Do you believe her?' Derrin asked when Eleanor was back in the drawing room.

'About the rape? Definitely.'

'What about the painting?'

'Probably, based on the reports of Charles's movements after everyone retired. I think it is unlikely to have been him,' Mel said.

But something was irritating the back of her mind.

'I can't help thinking, what if she's lying about being there when Charles came to her room? Did she perhaps return to her room to find him there with the note? Perhaps she had stolen the painting and hidden it somewhere when the alarm was raised?' Derrin said voicing the question that was privately rolling around in Mel's thoughts.

Mel replayed this as a scenario in her mind.

She saw Eleanor standing on one of the chairs by the fireplace, a utility knife in hand.

Eleanor reached out and cut the painting from the frame, then rolled it up, sticking the canvas into the neckline of her dress.

As she saw this possibility, Mel considered also that Eleanor could be using Charles's behaviour and subsequent death as a distraction tactic, which would mean she was far more devious than she had taken her for.

'It's plausible. Charles would know if Eleanor had been missing from her room and could have pointed the finger at her. Perhaps he had even threatened it for fear that she was about to leave him. Which would make it essential for her to rid herself of him once and for all,' Mel said. 'There's still the question of motive for the theft though. I don't think Eleanor needs the money.'

'True. And Frank has all but admitted to killing Charles… Though there's still the question of where the arsenic came from,' Derrin said after she explained her thought process. 'We know that whoever killed Charles, it was unlikely to be on the spur of the moment. Is it possible that Eleanor and Frank are in this together? Maybe he did it for her, hoping it would look like natural causes, a seizure. He wouldn't have known about your experience during the war or that you and I might understand poisons such as arsenic.'

'True. But we haven't found any poison in either of their possessions,' Mel said.

'But Charles did have substances. What if he had arsenic too, and our killer took it and used it on him instead?' Derrin said.

'If he did, who was he planning to use it on?' Mel said.

'That is of course the big question,' Derrin said. 'If it was Eleanor he was planning to poison, then there might be a case for self-defence.'

'There is also the death of poor Joan Carter. Eleanor knew about it. Charles might well have feared her speaking out if she called off the engagement. I can't help feeling for poor Joan, who was just in the wrong place at the wrong time.'

'Definitely. And who covered the murder up for Charles?' Derrin said. 'It's something to look at, when we sort out this sorry mess. We can at least get some justice there.'

At that moment the phone rang in the hallway interrupting their thoughts.

'That'll be the station,' said Derrin.

20

As Derrin answered the call, Mel was left in a quandary. Although Derrin's suggestion might be plausible, she couldn't imagine Charles having arsenic in his possession without knowing or recognising the pungent odour when he picked up the brandy glass and drank from it. And, if he had been the person to bring the poison in, who was it originally intended for? Was it possible he did plan to silence Eleanor?

It felt as though she were surrounded by toxic secrets that when revealed, brought up more questions than answers.

Try as she might, Mel still couldn't see the full shape of this game, and she was sure it was because a key piece of the puzzle was still missing. Or maybe several pieces. Crucially the thief had yet to be caught, and the painting was still AWOL. Mel couldn't imagine where it was likely to be, except that she was certain it was somewhere in the house still. She might have to retrace the steps of every one of the suspects in detail. And there were still interviews to do to bring out any final bits of information on that score.

Mel glanced over at Derrin, still engrossed in the call from the York constabulary, as he recounted, probably for a superior, what had occurred so far. She noticed that he didn't mention who they suspected may have killed Charles. The jury was still out on that score for Mel. Somehow she hadn't quite been convinced that it was Frank, which was why she had prevented him from coming clean and taking the blame. He might have claimed responsibility to cover for the real killer, especially if he thought it was Eleanor. As she and

Derrin had discussed, it was likely to be some form of honourable need to protect her. It spoke volumes about the man that he was ready to take the responsibility, and possible death sentence, for his deceased employer's fiancée. Mel determined that she had to find out why before the day was out and she could at last get some sleep.

While Derrin was busy Mel made her way down to the drawing room and opened the door.

'Toby, why don't you take a short break until the inspector has done giving his report. I'll stay here for the time being,' she said.

'You sure, Lady Mel?' Toby said.

'Yes. Get a drink, food, whatever you need. It's not going to be long before the police take over from us,' she said.

Toby left the room and Mel took his seat by the door.

The occupants had watched and listened to the exchange and they studied Mel now with expressions that were mostly curious. The only exception was Clara who sat quietly studying her finger nails as if she were sitting in a waiting room and nothing untoward had happened at all.

Mel examined Clara's demeanour, recalling the incidental meeting she'd had with Michael, and that she had been the instigator of this reunion. Instead of a need to reconnect, was Clara's motive something entirely different?

As though feeling she was being watched, Clara looked up and Mel was struck by the unguarded loathing of her expression.

She kept her own gaze steady as she stared back, her face blank and unreadable, in the way she had learnt during the war. Inside she had many questions, and the first of which came to her lips.

'Where did your profound abhorrence of me come from?' she asked.

Caught as she was with her guard down, Clara did the only thing she could do: she came clean.

'I've always despised you. Your family had so many doors open for them at the sheer mention of the Greenway peerage. Even you, Mel, with barely two pennies to rub together, your father living off that meagre allowance granted by the estate, and then scrabbling for some crummy job in the home office when it dried up. The Greenway "get out of jail card" was played again. Your name had it all!'

'You're a Taylor-Smith with all the privileges that your family had. I don't believe you were jealous of what my parents *didn't* have. It's something else. And I want to know what it was,' Mel said.

Clara glared at her and the look contained such open hatred that Mel almost recoiled. Why had she never noticed Clara's loathing before?

'You had everything: looks, charm, intelligence. Utter outlandish bravery that no one ever condemned you for. You're not in the same mould as the rest of us. In fact, you're so different you shouldn't have been welcomed into the fold. But of course, you're a Greenway and so there was no question of turning you away. I'm not the only one that hated you. We all did. Except maybe Michael who was utterly besotted and would have run into a fire for you. Although maybe that's changed now, after all you've put us through these last few hours. What do you say, Michael? Still like Mel as much as you once did?'

'I think you'd better stop now, old bean,' Michael warned, a deep frown furrowing his brow.

'If that's the case then why are you here? Why visit Avonby, Clara?' Mel said, because she wasn't afraid to get the answers now that the torrent was pouring like an unstoppable waterfall from Clara's mouth.

'I wanted to see you finally brought low. Living like a servant in your own family estate. I wanted to see if you were hurting because of it. I know Lady Laura, did you know that? She hates you too, Mel and she sees you as the sponging leech your father was, draining the estate of funds that should be used elsewhere.'

'Steady on old girl!' Michael interrupted. 'That's just not right. The truth is Mel should be the rightful keeper of Avonby!'

'Yes,' said Clara. 'And I bet she hates that she isn't. I bet she despises Jonathan and Laura more than I detest her.'

Mel considered denying everything that Clara claimed but understood there was little point. Once such a thing was said out loud, it could never be erased from the minds of those who heard it.

But she didn't have to speak as Michael spoke up for her once more.

'Of course, all of what you say is utterly awful, Clara. Mel is no scrounger. This is her home and she has every right to be here. And while you claim to know the heart of Lady Laura, I happen to have had recent contact with Lord Jonathan and he couldn't sing Mel's praises enough. He openly admitted that Avonby is thriving due to her innovations. I honestly don't know how you can have the nerve to come here and say otherwise.'

Clara gave a cold grin. 'Let's talk about Lord Jonathan shall we?'

'*No*,' said Eleanor. 'Please don't Clara.'

'You don't get it, do you? Elle has even more reason to hate the Greenways,' Clara continued. She was enjoying her hateful rant now and didn't care who suffered for her revelations.

'Stop it!' Eleanor said. 'I'm warning you, Clara.'

'Are you? When I was there for you, even as you cried yourself to sleep after what Jonathan Greenway did?' Clara said.

As soon as the words were out of Clara's mouth Mel knew that Jonathan was Eleanor's first love, the man who had broken her heart. The man who had taken advantage of her when she was barely sixteen, and then thrown her over. She wondered now why Eleanor had never shared this secret.

A lot of past events now made sense to Mel. They had been friends so long by then, and she remembered that summer when Elle had gone away with her family to Europe, and when she had returned she had seemed more sophisticated than the rest of them. She had remained quite absent in their lives for a while after that. Clara had voiced a suspicion that there was a suitor, but Eleanor hadn't revealed who or even admitted it at the time. Now Mel was putting two and two together and she knew why she hadn't told them; it was Jonathan Greenway and Clara had been told the truth when the affair ended, but it had been kept from Mel all this time.

This revelation now shed a different light on the whole visit of Eleanor and Clara, and by default Michael, Mabel and Frank. Had Clara come just to gloat, or had she stolen the painting to cause trouble for Mel?

'Oh Clara! What have you done?' Eleanor said. 'None of this has any bearing on Mel, and certainly not my previous relationships, no matter who that is with.'

'You must hate him, surely?' Clara said. 'He threw you over for Laura and now look at all she has. All this should have been yours.'

'Well, it isn't,' said Eleanor. 'And it was never supposed to be Jonathan's either. He was just an ordinary man when we met, even though he was a Greenway.'

'I'm sorry. And I'll always support you, but you must have wanted to pay him back,' Clara said.

'Of course not!' Eleanor said. 'That's ridiculous. It was years ago and I'm over it.'

'That's enough Clara,' Michael said again. 'You shouldn't cast aspersions, when you seem to have the most disrespect for the family. You're just hurling this on Eleanor to avoid suspicion yourself.'

'I have an alibi for when that painting went missing,' Clara said. 'Mabel will vouch for me.'

'Mabel?' Mel said, looking at the maid who until then had appeared to be in her own little world.

'Oh yes. I was with Miss Clara,' she said. 'She sent for me as soon as she was going to bed.'

'Do you remember the time?' Mel asked.

'Of course, it was just after midnight,' Mabel said. 'The big clock in the hallway had chimed twelve. Then the lights went out. I was waiting up for her and was in the kitchen, even though she told me not to bother as she suspected it would be a late night with everyone catching up.'

Mel was glad when Toby reappeared to take over from her. She was completely shaken by Clara's revelations. She didn't want to believe that all her friends had despised her and she had been blissfully unaware of it.

'Don't take it on, old bean,' said Michael as Mel opened the drawing-room door. 'It's just jealousy. You've always been something special.'

'He's still besotted! What is it you have, Mel? Is it some kind of animal magnetism that some poor fools can't see through?' Clara sneered.

'That's enough!' said Derrin appearing at the door. 'Miss Taylor-Smith, sit down and be quiet. I could hear your ravings all down the hallway.'

Clara was about to retort, when Mabel came and took her arm. 'Leave it now, Miss,' she said.

Mel felt the awful tremors threatening to consume her as she followed Derrin outside. She was strong, but the appalling hatred that Clara had poured on her had left her feeling shocked and upset. How could someone who purported to be a friend behave like that? It was so completely reprehensible. Despite the knowledge that Clara had shown herself up, it didn't take away the feeling of embarrassment Mel experienced from the whole explosion. She was ashamed and guilty for being a Greenway, and that made no sense whatsoever, as she couldn't change or help who she was. To learn that Clara had been hiding this hostility towards her and her family for all these years had sent her imagination into overdrive and Mel was examining every interaction they had ever had to see how and where she had missed the signs.

'I'm off my game,' she said to Derrin. 'I did not see that coming.'

'It's a known fact that socialites are the best liars in the world,' Derrin said. 'They learn to hide their true selves from a young age. Did you know that through history there have been many aristocrats that have been very successful spies? Just negotiating society, they learnt to mask so well, they discovered a real talent for it.'

'I obviously wasn't as good at spotting it when I was younger,' Mel said.

She tried to shirk the feeling of foolishness, as well as a genuine grief, after learning her friendship with Clara had never been real or reciprocated. She had been thoroughly blindsided and found herself questioning all the friends she had ever had, and this strange antagonism towards her family name. Did Eleanor and Michael feel the same? Did so many other people she knew?

'What's happening with the reinforcements?' she asked, turning her mind to the problem at hand as she tried to steady her emotions and head off the stress-related reaction that her body was still having.

'Are you okay?' Derrin said.

Mel weighed up his question. She had felt like she was being surrounded, attacked from all sides, yet it was only Clara who made these claims. She took this thought forward, pulling herself together.

The change that came over her physical appearance wasn't lost on Derrin. He admired how Mel stood tall, back straight as she refused to be dragged down into the mire that Clara had tried to create. He knew she was robust, but also what a fierce blow Clara's words would have been. The betrayal of someone you thought was a friend could make anyone feel awful, but Mel had been through so much worse that some spite-filled words, although initially shocking, were soon washing away from her as she brought her sharp mind back to what was important. He didn't know if later she would unpick the vitriol and let it in, but he hoped she wouldn't.

'You can't make an omelette without breaking a few eggs,' he said now.

'You think she didn't mean what she said?'

'No, I think she did mean it. But she wouldn't have cracked like that and let it out if she wasn't rattled,' Derrin said.

'Hmm. I think you're right, which might mean we are closer to solving this case than we thought. But back to the police situation… Why aren't they here yet?'

'There has been an incident in Northallerton and I'm sure you heard about the "Glasshouse Riots" there earlier this year?'

'Military prisoners rioting over food rations?' Mel said. 'Yes. I heard about it. Awful business.'

'There was an attempted resurgence and all forces were called to the scene earlier this morning. It is on a need-to-know basis and the incident will never reach the ears of the press, or the public.'

'You shouldn't be telling me then, I assume?'

'No. But you're still under the Official Secrets Act and I don't expect you to share this anyway. But it does mean that my superior is leaving this problem in our hands for the time being.'

Mel was torn between disappointment and relief. On the one hand the extra time would give her and Derrin the opportunity to solve the case before the reinforcements arrived, but on the other, she had been ready to hand over the responsibility, especially after Clara's outburst.

'What now?' she asked.

'We bring out Mabel and see how much she sticks to the story of being with Clara immediately after the lights went out.'

'Right. But wait a second on that. Let's go downstairs into the kitchen,' Mel said.

'Why?'

'It's a hunch. You'll see when we get there,' Mel said.

21

As Derrin escorted Mabel back out to the hallway, Mel was waiting for the young maid by the chaise.

'We'd like to talk some more about the alibi you just gave Miss Taylor-Smith,' said Derrin.

'Right you are, Inspector,' said Mabel.

'Can you tell us in detail what you were doing before the lights went out?' Mel asked.

'I was in the kitchen, Lady Mel. I was waiting up for Miss Clara, like I said,' Mabel said.

'Did anyone see you there?' Derrin asked.

'Well, I did see Mr Williams, as he was waiting too,' Mabel said.

Mel noted the shift in Mabel's expression as she said this.

'What time was that?' she asked.

'I don't know, Miss, I wasn't looking at the clock. Mr Williams was walking around locking up for the night, I think. He musta seen me as I was sitting by the table. Mrs Weston had given me some hot milk before she retired.'

Mel nodded. 'That was kind of her. And you still had that milk?'

'Yes,' Mabel said. 'Look I don't know I can be much help.'

'Please indulge us, Mabel,' said Derrin.

'Yes, Inspector.'

'So, what happened then just before the lights went out?' Mel asked.

'Well, I heard the clock chime, and I fought, "that's late". Then the lights went off,' Mabel said.

'What did you do then?' Derrin asked.

'I found a candle, lit it, and went to Miss Clara's room,' Mabel said.

'You didn't see anyone else at that point?' Mel asked.

Mabel shook her head.

'Anything else, Miss?' Mabel asked.

Derrin went to ask a further question but Mel cut him off.

'That will be all for now,' Mel said, exchanging a look with Derrin which he appeared to understand.

* * *

Derrin returned Mabel to the drawing room, and came back with a still-hostile Clara. They had pre-agreed that he would interview her and that Mel would only observe and take note of the details and make comparisons with Mabel's story.

'Clara, I'd like to do a walk-through of your movements last night. Do you remember what time the lights went out last night?' Derrin said.

'No,' Clara said.

'Could it have been midnight?' Derrin asked.

'Oh. I don't know. Mabel said it was. Something about the clock chiming. But I didn't hear it or don't remember either way.'

Derrin asked her how long she waited for Mabel to appear at her room, once she arrived there.

'I think it was soon afterwards like she told you. I got in the room and removed all my jewellery. Then I was struggling to reach the buttons on the back of my dress so I rang the bell for help, and she turned up. I guessed that one of your servants told her I had rung and needed help.'

'That's when you saw her hands were dirty,' Mel interjected.

Clara became immediately hostile. 'I already told you that.'

Now she's let it out, she can't hide her contempt for me, Mel thought. *Interesting.*

'Did you ask her why her hands were covered in coal dust?' Derrin asked.

'No. She'd obviously stacked a fire without using the tongs. She's not the brightest girl sometimes.'

'I would like you to cast your mind back again,' Derrin said. 'Try and work out how long it might have been before Mabel arrived at your room after you.'

'I told you I don't know.'

'A guess?'

Clara sighed. 'Maybe fifteen or twenty minutes. I'm sure it was no longer than that,' Clara said.

'Can you describe how you saw the coal dust on Mabel's hands?'

Clara thought. 'Mabel knocked on the door. I let her in. I only had the one candle lit so it wasn't very bright in the room. I said I needed help with the dress. She went to unfasten me and she yelped. I obviously turned around to see what was wrong. Saw her dirty fingers and told her to wash them. That's it. I don't know why this is a constant fascination and I really don't wish to go over it again! So, if that is all Inspector…?'

'It isn't,' said Derrin. 'I am very likely to question you again very soon.'

Derrin led Clara back to the study this time.

'Why am I being brought in here?' she asked.

'I don't want you talking to Mabel again until I cross examine her.'

'This is ridiculous!' Clara said. 'That girl isn't involved; she wouldn't hurt a fly.'

'Then she has nothing to hide,' Derrin said closing the door on her and leaving her inside Jonathan's study.

'I don't suppose she'll enjoy being in there alone,' Mel said. 'But you did the right thing. Though if they are both lying then they clearly haven't got their story straight or didn't have the opportunity without being observed by the others.'

'My thoughts too,' said Derrin. 'Let's get Mabel again.'

<h1 style="text-align:center">22</h1>

'I DUNNO HOW THE COAL DUST GOT on me hands,' Mabel said when asked. 'I was downstairs. Heard the clock chime, and then I went to Miss Clara's room as I knew she'd need help.'

Mel visualised the girl's movements.

Mabel crept up the servants' stairs as the clock chimed. As she reached the top, the lights in the house went off, but Mabel was already in the dark and her eyes were adjusted by then. From her vantage point down the hallway, she could see Clara, Michael, Eleanor and Charles leaving the study, and Mel and Derrin, heading off towards the fuse box to see if they could fix it.

'And you maintain you were downstairs in the kitchen when the lights went off?' Derrin asked.

Mabel nodded.

'We know that's a lie Mabel,' Mel said.

'No! I ain't lying,' Mabel said.

'But you are. You see, you can't *hear* the grandfather clock from downstairs. The chime isn't loud enough. But you can hear it as you walk up the service stairs.'

Mabel gave a start and her cheeks flushed with guilt.

'So, what were you doing on the staircase at midnight?'

'Nuffink. I wasn't,' she denied.

'Mabel, this is very serious. If you own up now to stealing the painting and return it, I will not press charges,' said Mel. 'I'm being very fair under the circumstances.'

'I would if I could, but I didn't steal nuffink,' she said and then promptly burst into tears.

Mel sighed now, losing some of her patience. The tears of the women that night were now grating on her and she had lost all empathy for them. Time was passing and the painting was nowhere to be found. She was certain that Mabel, if not the culprit, knew who was and might be covering for them.

'You were on the stairs. You came to the top; the lights went out and then you saw us all leave the study. Didn't you?' Mel pressed.

Mabel wiped her eyes and nodded.

'After that you went in and you stole the painting, hiding it somewhere in the house when you realised we had returned and discovered the loss sooner than expected,' Derrin said. 'So where is it girl?'

'I was on the stairs,' she sobbed. 'But I didn't take anyfink.'

'What were you doing there?' Mel asked.

'I came to look at the main staircase. I didn't get to see it when we arrived, and I love looking at nice furnishings. And wood panelling. Dunno why but it makes me 'appy.'

'I don't believe you,' Derrin said. 'If that's so, why didn't you tell us earlier?'

'I didn't want Lady Mel to think I was snooping. And when the picture was gone, I didn't want anyone finking it were me.'

'Let's back track,' said Mel repeating what they had already agreed. 'When you came upstairs and the chimes finished, the lights went off?'

'Yes, that's right.'

'And, when we all went in our different directions, did you see anything else?'

Mabel stopped snivelling and began to think. 'It was dark but after you and the inspector went looking for the problem, someone came downstairs and went into the study. I was scared to move so I was standing by the umbrella and coat stand by the front door, hiding in the middle of thick coats that were hung there. Anyway, I heard sumfing that sounded like breaking glass. It gave me a bit of a start and I didn't want to be caught where I was, in case I got the blame for the damage. And I weren't wrong, not with one of them expensive wine glasses smashed as it were on the mantel…'

'What next?' Mel said, impatient with Mabel's meandering explanation.

'The person who dun it came out of the study,' Mabel said.

'Did you see who?' Derrin asked.

Mabel shook her head. 'No. It were too dark. But… I fought it was a woman.'

'How could you tell in the dark?' Mel asked.

'She came past and I smelt this waft of perfume.'

'Did you recognise the scent?' Mel asked.

'Yeah. It smelled just like the perfume Miss Susan gave to Miss Clara for her birthday a few months ago. It's Coco Chanel. Miss Susan gets it all the way from France and it's Miss Clara's favourite.'

'So, you thought it was Clara?' Mel asked.

'Oh, miss! She's been so good to me. I didn't want to dob her in. But you pushed me hard and I'm never going to forgive meself for betraying her like this. What'll happen to her?' snivelled Mabel. 'I'm sure she didn't do nuffink and it's all a misunderstanding.'

'If she turns over the painting, nothing. I'll forgive and forget, but if she doesn't then the police will take over when they arrive,' Mel said.

'Oh no, miss!' Mabel said.

'When you return to the drawing room, don't discuss anything with anyone in there,' Derrin warned her. 'For your own safety.'

His words gave Mabel a jolt and she nodded her agreement before returning to the drawing room with Mel.

* * *

'It seems very convenient that she has just thrown Clara to the wolves when the finger was pointing in her direction,' Derrin said.

'I know. I don't believe her,' Mel said. 'But I suppose we only have one option and that's to question Clara on what Mabel just told us.'

'Or we let her stew a while longer,' Derrin suggested.

'I'm open to that choice: I need to think,' said Mel. 'I wish I wasn't so close to this right now, as I appear to be unable to be objective.'

All Mel wanted to do was take a walk in the garden and ground herself for a time. She was dreading the forthcoming conversations she would have to have with Jonathan and Laura on their return, a situation that was adding pressure and making her blank out on what was really going on at Avonby. She chided herself, because the game should have revealed itself by now, and yet there were still too many things that didn't add up.

'Take a break,' Derrin said. 'We both need one. And the suspects aren't going anywhere for now.'

'What will you do while I'm gone?' Mel asked.

'Think. Perhaps go and speak to some of the servants again to gain some clarity on Mabel's movements,' Derrin said. 'Other than that I need to remain by the phone in case the yard rings.'

'Right. I would love to change, if you really don't mind?' Mel said.

'Take as long as you need.'

* * *

Mel went back to her room to freshen up. In the bathroom, she splashed water on her face and cleaned her teeth, all the time knowing that she was denying this privilege to the guests as they were held under guard downstairs.

Taking the opportunity to change from her evening dress, she pulled on a pair of slacks and a blouse. The comfort of the change, as well as the quick wash, managed to lift her mood and wake her up. The mind fog was lifting again, and Mel knew it was because she had needed to take herself away from the intensity of the situation for such self-care.

She sat down at her dressing table and applied some cosmetics to erase the tiredness from her face. This was more about doing something else than vanity for Mel, and the act made her mind slip into that void where she stored information and she began to see the evening unfold again.

The night before had been so intense, from the minute her guests arrived, the observant Mel had been on edge. There had always been something wrong, she just hadn't seen it, distracted as she was by the presence of her old friends, but also by the thought of seeing Derrin again.

Derrin was the one constant in the last few hours, with his stoic dedication to finding the thief and murderer, but also because there was no one in the world she trusted more. And this faith, she realised, was not misplaced. Derrin was as true as he appeared and no matter what happened between them, she didn't regret him being back in her life, though part of her hoped for more of that, and not less, and a bit more consistency in their meetings.

There it is again, Mel thought. *I'm distracted because of the confusing feelings I have for Derrin.*

Their unfinished business was still burning in the background. All thoughts of him in any way other than a professional one, for now, must be shelved. Mel took in a breath, then released it slowly. She could do this, she hadn't lost her edge, what she had been short of was time alone to regain some clarity.

Back to last night.

The guests had all arrived in a particular order, none of which, Mel thought, was even slightly relevant. What they did when they arrived, however, could be.

Recalling each account of the activities on that night Mel ran them side by side.

Michael and Mabel's observations of Eleanor and Charles, and Charles' behaviour all correlated, with the slight variation of some detail. All of which Mel would expect, because different people observed different things and she knew from experience that no two witnesses ever give the exact same account – unless their stories are contrived and they have worked together on the detail. The truth was, some people were more observant than others, and contributing factors could water down detail in accounts. For example, was the witness's attention taken elsewhere and did they look away, missing something vital?

Mel was interested in Michael's take on Eleanor and Charles's relationship. He had observed a problem between them right away. Mabel, on the other hand, had claimed to be surprised as Charles had never given away his dark side in front of her or Clara. But was it the truth? Michael said he had planned to reach out to help Eleanor, but insisted he hadn't sent the note that had caused the disagreement between him and Charles. If this was so, the question of who had remained. There was only one conclusion: someone else must have observed Charles's behaviour that night, or earlier perhaps, and had reached out, offering help. But which of them was it? No one so far had offered that information.

Mel stored this point for later analysis.

But lingering with Michael, she now studied his behaviour throughout the evening. He had been flippant at times about his return to England, but there wasn't a single moment when she had thought he was lying. Mel had sensed a deep sadness and had connected this with the death of Michael's father in India. They hadn't asked what had happened to his mother, because Mel had heard from Michael soon after his move to New Delhi. She already knew that his mother had caught malaria, and had passed away within months of their arrival. Mel remembered now that although she had replied, offering her condolences, she had never heard from Michael again. She had assumed that he wanted to cut ties with his past and move on, and therefore hadn't pursued their friendship further. It had stung at the time, as she had been fond of him. But she had done what she thought best by respecting his wishes.

Life, and the war, got in the way, and Mel experienced a little guilt at not thinking very much about Michael thereafter. She wasn't much of a friend to him, and should have tried to stay in touch. But her own losses, and trauma, had made her connection with the past so fragile, and if she was honest, difficult, because it reminded her of everything she had lost too. And that was a pain that wouldn't go away at the best of times.

Mel brought her thoughts back to now: there was sadness all around Michael, and a deep loneliness, that she believed he had been carrying for some time. Not specific to his father's death, but perhaps compounded by it. In fact, Mel had never seen anyone who carried such a feeling of isolation around them. Michael did his best to hide it, but Mel had observed it, banked it in her mind for later analysis, and only now realised what she had been perceiving. She thought now that he was the only one among them that had come to the weekend with the sole purpose of finding friends to ease his seclusion.

With her mind clearing again, Mel turned her thoughts to Clara. She saw her now at the dinner table, casting the occasional glance at Michael as she tried to sparkle and be witty, all of which to the casual eye might appear to be natural, but was, in fact, forced. She was struggling to be what she thought everyone expected, and under the façade, Clara was nothing more than an unhappy woman who saw herself as a future spinster.

Not that being a spinster is such a bad thing, Mel thought, remembering a favourite aunt who always seemed happier than everyone else, yet was cursed with the 'spinster' slur because she had never wanted to marry. She had told Mel once that she had chosen her own life. Mel had always admired Aunt Belle's commitment to what she believed, and she knew that she had not gone to her grave in despair.

'Stick to your guns, Melinda,' Aunt Belle had often said. 'You can't regret, only move forward.'

Mel saw something of Belle in Clara, but Clara's trajectory was not by choice as she wanted to change her apparent destiny. Perhaps then Michael was going to be, as Eleanor had suggested earlier, a chance at a future. A chance, Mel thought, that was possibly blown the minute Clara started to crack and show her true colours. Michael had pulled her up for the hate she had spewed in Mel's direction, defending her from the attack. She was sure that in Clara's eyes, that was a betrayal and all Mel's fault as well.

Mel closed her eyes, blocking out the image of herself in the dressing-table mirror.

She replayed the onslaught, seeing Clara wincing as Michael spoke up. She had known she was appearing unreasonable, and in a very bad light, but had backed herself into a corner and was trapped there. All she could do was fight her way out. Mel was sympathetic to Clara's plight but still couldn't fathom how she had never picked up on her hatred for the Greenways. Was it something that stemmed from Clara's parents, perhaps? Mel couldn't recall any time when she had been invited to the Taylor-Smith home, though Eleanor and Susan were often there. Why hadn't she ever questioned that before?

A lot of what Clara had expressed earlier now sank home for Mel, and she realised she had always felt that bite of jealousy from Susan, but never Clara. But now she saw why. Clara had given the bullets, and Sue had fired them. Often with those characteristic snide barbs that said one thing and meant another. A double-edged sword that gave compliments while taking the other person down. Mel had never let Susan get to her though, for as long as she'd had Clara and Eleanor, it didn't seem to matter. She was tougher than that anyway, and confident enough not to feel the sting of those barbs.

Where any of them ever my friend? she wondered.

She stored Susan away now too because, despite the references to her bad behaviour earlier towards Mabel, Mel couldn't see how Sue had any connection to this game. She wasn't here, and had not reached out, and Mel hadn't given it a second thought, which confirmed that she knew all along Sue wasn't a friend and never had been.

Eleanor was though, and Mel still had a big question mark where she sat in all that had happened. As she had said earlier to Derrin, she wondered if Frank and Eleanor had a relationship beyond the outward appearance, but she had sensed nothing coming from Eleanor in that regard, even if Frank may have an interest in her. It wasn't an impossibility, though she was sure that after Charles, Eleanor's parents would be disappointed, unless Eleanor told them the truth about his behaviour.

Mel revisited the moments in the study. As she brought the tableau to the forefront in her mind, the carpet in the room became the checked base of her analysis chessboard. She super-imposed the suspects and saw them again in their respective positions in the study.

As she had observed earlier, Eleanor was the queen, Frank a knight – yes she saw him glaring at Charles's back, an expression of disgust and anger barely disguised in a small smirk. Clara was on the sofa, looking at Charles in shock. Mabel was beside her, eyes wide; a quiet terror evident at what she too was observing. This was perhaps the first moment they became aware of Charles's true nature. But the question that popped into Mel's mind was, were they both pawns, or was Clara the queen for the opposing team, and Mabel her stoic knight? *And who*, she wondered, *was playing black to the other's white?* All of it niggled while Mel processed the information this observation gave her.

Her mind's gaze fell now on Michael. His hand was pulling back away from the brandy glass. Was there something subtle on his fingers? Was she really remembering that or just imagining it? She banked it, determined to examine Michael's hands later when she went downstairs.

Mel shook her head and with it the characters in this montage all moved. Clara sat back on the sofa, her hand under her chin, thoughtful. Charles moved behind Michael's chair. Eleanor leaned in to talk to Michael. Charles's jealousy reared its ugly head: his eyes were on Eleanor.

Was this the moment, Mel wondered, when he rammed the knife home?

Mel felt a movement to the left, she turned the mental image slightly, and saw Mabel looking towards the window, her face for once completely blank. She gave an imperceptible nod. *Curious.* Mel's mind tried to see what the girl was looking at, but only came up with the blank window frame against the dark night. Why hadn't she been her normal observant self? Of course, the chloroform contamination…

This was the game as she knew it so far. But what did it tell her about the next moves?

Mel opened her eyes. The images were growing clearer, the culprit was in sight but remained a blurred shadow in the backdrop of Avonby hallway.

There.

Mel came back to herself. She was on the cusp of revelation, but there was more to this scenario that required her other senses. She had to revisit the study and look around with her memory of last night to the fore. Then perhaps those other senses might kick in and take over. The smells, sounds and touch of various textures could trigger a memory, but Mel didn't know what those might be until they occurred. She did know though, that the answer was in her grasp, she just had to do some further, quiet, searching, that could only be done by following the trail that her mind had just presented her with. For that, she needed no one but herself, and the breadcrumbs that the witnesses had already given. For this reason, she was not yet ready to share her suspicions until she had done what was needed to validate them. Not even with Derrin.

23

THE SMELL OF BAKING BREAD WAFTED UP from the kitchen as Mel arrived back in the hallway.

'We'll have to feed the suspects again soon,' Derrin observed as though the aroma was tantalising him too.

'It would be the humane thing to do,' Mel said.

'We've had another round of bathroom visits, which I supervised, and Mr Williams has taken over from Toby.'

Toby was now down in the kitchen, helping with the preparations for lunch.

'You look thoughtful,' Derrin said. 'Have you had a breakthrough?'

Mel smiled.

'You're very intuitive,' she said.

'Well, I'd be surprised if you hadn't,' Derrin said. 'What do you need now to bring this all together?'

'A final talk with Clara,' she said.

Derrin gave her a look of surprise at this. 'You think…?'

'I'll tell you my thoughts soon. There are still some pieces that aren't quite working for me.'

In the study, they found Clara sitting by the window, looking outside as the day was fully blossoming and lunchtime approached. Clara looked tired, and the anger and hatred she had expressed earlier had deflated. She didn't look around as Mel and Derrin entered the room.

'Where is the painting?' Mel asked, her voice little more than a whisper.

'*How would I know*?' Clara said, her voice like ice.

'Mabel told us she saw you leaving the study with it,' Derrin said.

Clara turned to look at them then, her eyes wide with surprise.

'I don't understand why Mabel would say that,' she said. 'You must be lying.'

One of the issues they had in this situation would be the chaos caused by different people accusing others of the crime. Mel had suspected that this might happen more as time ran out. Now she saw genuine confusion and doubt in Clara's eyes. The riddle shape sharpened and she could see the light, the endgame, approaching like a train hurrying through the longest tunnel to its final destination.

'Mabel wouldn't have said that,' Clara said again and looked from one to the other of them in search of confirmation that they were mistaken. 'She's loyal to me. And it's not true.'

'Here's the thing,' Derrin said. 'Mel doesn't care who stole the painting. We just want it returned.'

'Are you still saying that you won't press charges?' Clara asked.

'All I want is the Turner back in its frame before my cousin's return.'

'I wish I could help you,' Clara said. 'But I really can't.'

Mel didn't believe her on that score because Clara wanted her to suffer. This, after all the vitriol she had spoken earlier, could be a form of revenge.

'You could help me…' Mel said. 'I know you have answers.'

'I have no clue where your wretched Turner is! I didn't come back to the study until you sent for us. And this is the last time I'm going to say that to you.'

Mel kept her face steady, but she did believe that Clara meant what she said. A belief in one's words was the closest someone could get to appearing truthful, even if they weren't telling the truth. It was something that Mel had studied closely, a process she could mimic, given the need. She didn't believe that Clara would understand how to do that though, which was what led her to the conclusion that Clara wasn't the thief. Nor was she the accomplice to one. Mabel could have been mistaken, or perhaps lying to cover for someone else entirely.

Mel saw Mabel again, looking out into the darkness… Ah!

The picture she had just seen in her mind revealed a huge chunk of information to Mel that she would have to examine further and find some real evidence to back up. As Mel came back to the present she saw the curious expression on Clara's face and was concerned that she had been observed sinking into herself to process what she knew. Such moments did not give away anything she thought, just that she was in a deeper state on consciousness than most people ever went to.

'What was that?' she asked. 'Are you ill?'

'She's fine,' Derrin said, but didn't explain Mel's method.

'Can you please go into the hallway,' Mel said to Clara. 'I need this space to myself.'

Taking her cue, Derrin took Clara outside and closed the door.

As soon as they had gone, Mel took up Mabel's position from the night before and looked outside at the now visible lawns of Avonby's beautiful gardens, which were framed by a mature row of leylandii. The evergreens were still plush and full, and afforded the house some privacy, but were, Mel thought, also a great place to hide in the dark and be unobserved. She stared at them, then stored what she saw for later investigation: another piece dropping into a place when her thoughts could be confirmed.

She hadn't forgotten that there was likely to be an accomplice outside. Nor that this person could be dangerous, as they'd had no qualms in destroying her motorbike, or in slashing the inspector's tires. But who that might be was still a mystery.

As she moved to where Clara had been sitting moments earlier, Mel smelt a waft of heady perfume, and recognised that this must be the Coco Chanel scent that Mabel had mentioned. A scent she had smelt subtly before. Another element of the mystery presented itself.

Of course!

She hurried to the door and, finding Derrin in the hallway with Clara now seated on the chaise, she said, 'Do you have the note?'

Derrin withdrew the paper from his pocket and held it out.

Mel took it and raised it to her nose, smelling the subtle aroma. She moved closer to Clara and there was no mistaking that the note smelt of the same fragrance, although much more subtle than the amount Clara was wearing.

Mel sat down opposite Clara.

'You said earlier that you thought Charles was a little possessive. And he had a mean streak,' Mel said. 'You knew that Charles was abusing Eleanor, didn't you?'

Clara folded her hands in her lap.

'It was obvious that something was wrong,' she said. 'She was terrified to be late, always scurrying off and at his or his parents' beck and call. She was at the very least intimidated by him. At the engagement party she was like a deer caught in a hunter's sights.'

'Why didn't you ask her what was happening?' Derrin said.

'One doesn't just come out with these things. I needed to be sure. The weight loss alone was a cause for concern, but no one else appeared to notice, and so I thought it was just me, trying to see the negative in something that was supposed to be perfect.'

'You thought you were jealous of her?' Mel said.

'I was. A little. But then I saw it wasn't all a bed of roses and Eleanor was, in fact, miserable. It was one of the reasons I suggested we come to see you. I was trying to get her away from Charles, to remind her of happier times. And to see if she would open up and tell me what was going on. That blew apart when *he* insisted on coming. I knew I'd never get her alone unless I let her know I was worried.'

'You sent her this note,' Derrin said.

Clara nodded. 'I wanted her to know she wasn't alone. That I could help her. She's my closest friend. I was worried about her.'

'And how were you planning to help?' Derrin asked.

'Be a shoulder to cry on, I guess?' Clara said. 'Give advice that might encourage her to end the relationship. I don't know. I would do what I could for her.'

'Eleanor must have known it was you all along,' Mel said. 'She knew your handwriting. Do you know why she didn't say to Charles it was you?'

'When Charles jumped to the conclusion that it was Michael and went on a rampage, Elle came to my room. She was crying but relieved that I had realised she was in trouble,' Clara confirmed. 'She let him believe it was Michael, so that she could get away from him.'

Mel could see it now, as the pieces of the conundrum moved closer together. Eleanor and Clara were having their heart to heart, and both were hoping that Michael would punch Charles and teach him the lesson he deserved.

'We knew that Michael could stand up for himself,' Clara explained. 'And you can see, I wasn't alone in my room, and I didn't come downstairs, despite what you may have been told. I was with Eleanor. She'll confirm it.'

'Go back to the drawing room,' Mel said to Clara.

Clara blinked, surprised, but she stood up.

'I'm sorry about what I said earlier,' she said. 'I didn't mean it. Not all of it. I was frustrated. Upset. And you got the brunt of it for keeping us all locked up.'

Mel nodded but didn't respond, and Clara walked away, shoulders slumped, body weary, as though the burden of her hate-filled tirade had drained her.

When the door to the drawing room was closed, Mel turned to Derrin.

'I know who took the painting now,' she said.

'Who?' Derrin asked.

24

'Mr Williams,' Mel said as they entered the kitchen. 'The inspector and I are going outside. I want you to lock the door after us and don't open again until we return, or the police arrive.

'Right you are, Lady Melinda,' Williams said.

Mel pulled her thick coat and boots on as Michael borrowed some wellingtons from the row in the boot room. He removed his dinner jacket too, and replaced it with an outdoor coat that Toby wore when he went to the vegetable garden for Mrs Weston to bring in fresh herbs.

Derrin stowed the pistol in his pocket, and Williams looked away, pretending not to notice.

They opened the door, Derrin looked out first, then both he and Mel left. They heard the bolt draw across the door after Williams closed it.

'Do you want to tell me who we are looking for?'

Mel shook her head. 'You'll see.'

Keeping close to the walls of the house, while searching for evidence of someone else's presence, Mel led Derrin away from the back door.

Earlier, when the telephone lines were back on, Mel had rung the neighbouring farm and had warned the farmer to stay away. She had also asked him to visit Rosa and Joseph and to tell them to remain home and not come to Avonby. For this reason, the gardens and surrounding farmland were still and the usual bustle was absent for a normal working morning. Mel observed that even the common wildlife appeared to be silent, undisturbed as they were by the onslaught of farmworkers, machinery and comings and goings of the vehicles, including Mel's motorbike, that often bothered them. Mel and Derrin fell into this calm as they traversed the exterior of the manor, enjoying being outside after the enforced imprisonment of not only the suspects, but themselves.

As they reached the coal hatch, Mel stopped. Derrin watched but said nothing as he saw her analysing the disturbed ground beside the trapdoor. The entrance was always locked tight unless there was a coal delivery, and as they'd had one the previous week, and the cellar was full, they were not expecting another until closer to Christmas.

Mel looked around the access, careful not to disturb any evidence. She didn't need to point out the shoe print to Derrin as he had already seen it. The size and detail of the print, Mel knew, did not belong to anyone who worked at Avonby. Someone else had been there recently, and by the smearing on the hatch handles, they had tried to get in without success.

'Come on,' Mel said.

They moved past the cellar doorway, still hugging the house, and Mel led them off towards the garage and the parked Rolls-Royce that had belonged to Charles. The tyres were let down, but not slashed, and Mel saw the pieces of her bike, dismantled and scattered, as Toby had described. Mel knew she could fix the bike at least when all this was over, though there were some parts that would need replacing. For now, it wasn't something to worry about, they were looking for something else entirely.

It was good to be outside, and Mel's spirits lifted with the adrenaline rush of a practical search and the examination of the grounds, which was a relief from the intense mental investigation. She was in her element and everything she saw as they walked the perimeter of the house was being stored in her mind for later analysis or became a positive reinforcement of what she already suspected.

As they approached the corner that would lead to the front lawns, Mel stopped. She tilted her head towards the start of the row of leylandiis and then curved away from the house again, and went around the opposite side of the tall, thick evergreens. Derrin followed.

Halfway around the perimeter, Mel saw a bare patch in the thick growth. She showed Derrin. The place had the perfect vantage point to observe the study. The same shoe prints they had seen by the cellar now marked the ground, showing that someone had occupied this spot for a long time. Watching, no doubt, all the proceedings that had taken place in that room during the first hours after the painting was stolen.

'We were a goldfish bowl in the dark, even with just candlelight. The accomplice couldn't have failed to see us, even though we couldn't see them,' Derrin said.

Mel nodded.

They moved on, silent and slow, until they reached the bend in the trees that would take them around the other side of the lawn.

Ahead Mel paused. She held out her hand to stop Derrin moving. She had heard the subtle snap of twigs under a stealthy foot. The accomplice was, as she suspected, still lurking. Perhaps even getting some messages or signs from the insider in the drawing room.

Mel glanced at Derrin. The person was just a few feet away. Mel nodded her head to Derrin, and he swooped around the corner, taking down the suspect even before they turned to see him there and realised they had been tracked.

There was a struggle, but Derrin overwhelmed the hooded culprit, twisting their arm behind their back before pulling them back to their feet. Then he marched the accomplice back to the house, with Mel in tow.

Mel pounded on the back door, drawing Williams back to let them in.

They pushed the criminal inside and dragged them, struggling, through the boot room and up the service stairs to the hallway with Mrs Weston, Williams, Daisy and Ruby gaping open-mouthed as they did.

In the hallway, Mel yanked the balaclava from the accomplice's head. A tumble of blonde hair fell over the person's shoulders and that was when Mel and Derrin confirmed that the mastermind behind the theft was a woman.

'Hello Susan,' Mel said, her voice calm.

Susan gave a silent glare, then her lips curled up into a crooked sneer that attempted to be a smile.

Because Mel had already guessed which of the suspects had stolen the painting, this piece of the puzzle made a great deal of sense. She had already known it was Susan, but not why she had orchestrated the theft in the first place.

'Care to elaborate?' Mel asked now.

'I have nothing to say to you,' Susan said.

Mr Williams had followed them upstairs and was now standing by the front door, shocked by what he saw.

'Let's go and out your partner in crime,' Mel said.

She grabbed Susan's arm and pulled her towards the drawing-room. It was time to put an end to the mystery of the missing painting and learn the dark truth behind this heist.

* * *

As they opened the drawing-room door, Eleanor was the first to look their way. She gasped when she saw Susan being held firmly between Derrin and Mel.

'Sue! What are you doing here?' she said.

Mel and Derrin brought Susan into the room and Mr Williams followed, closing the door behind them. The butler rested his back against the door, making it clear that no one would leave, nor would anyone come in until Mel and Derrin had finished what needed to be done.

'I must admit,' Mel said, 'that this outcome should have taken me by surprise, but after the revelations of this evening, it doesn't.'

Eleanor was sitting forward on the sofa. She looked stressed and afraid. Clara's expression showed a silent acceptance; Frank looked on with open curiosity and Mabel began to chew her thumbnail as though the sight of Susan was terrifying and reminded her of the ordeal she experienced at the woman's hands. Michael was the only one in the room that had a gleam of pride as he looked at Mel.

'There have been an awful lot of convoluted explanations these last few hours. Red herrings thrown everywhere, fingers pointed in different directions, and the best smoke and mirrors I've ever seen,' Mel said.

'Go on, old bean,' Michael said. 'Who is the culprit? We are all dying to know.'

* * *

After going to her room to think, Mel had begun to put together the missing fragments. By then, she already suspected who the liar was, but the evidence had been buried behind half-truths and bits of stories that when you laid them all down, side by side, they cross referenced and slotted together in a perfect jigsaw. But there were still so many fragments missing that the gaps had been distracting, blinding her, at times, to the obvious.

Refreshed and changed, Mel had reached the bottom step of the service stairs, having traversed them from the first floor. On one side was the kitchen, on the other the servants' quarters, and just between both was the door to the cellar.

Ignoring the bustle in the kitchen, and a hovering Mr Williams, Mel had taken the keys for the cellar and gone down once again into the coal storage area. Many thoughts were shifting through her mind of how she and Derrin had been downstairs the night before when someone else had come down. They had thought it was one of the servants, but now Mel wasn't so sure. She just needed another look, and a moment below to reimagine what she had observed and seen.

Once in the cellar, Mel saw that the trapdoor was closed and locked from the inside. But she could see that the pile of coal had been disturbed and now knew why: someone had climbed it.

Part one was in place, and Mel saw that person moving on her chessboard, falling into position below the hatch.

There was a struggle to pull back the heavy bolt, but, having failed, the culprit returned upstairs, just seconds before Derrin and Mel had come from the wine cellar, close on their heels.

Mel had returned to the kitchen. Those crucial moments, when she and Derrin had loitered in the wine store, meant that the culprit had not been seen. She now recalled how the coal pile was still slipping as they exited the storage area and headed for the stairs. It was one of those details that she had not, at the time, needed to focus on, but had subliminally retained.

'Mr Williams?' she had asked as she reached the kitchen. 'Did you see anyone go down in the cellar last night?'

Williams shook his head, and Mrs Weston confirmed she hadn't seen anyone either. The perpetrator might have remained a mystery, except for one thing: the stain on Clara's dress.

* * *

'As I went upstairs,' Mel explained now. 'I glanced at the coat and umbrella stand. That's when the final pieces came together.'

Mel looked around the room, noticing the subtle changes in demeanour of the suspects as they watched her. She saw the main suspect attempting to keep their face passive, but there were tells which gave her away.

'Mabel, *you* attempted to open the hatch but couldn't manage it,' Mel said. 'You didn't bank on the bolt being jammed closed by the cold. Or how high above the coal pile the hatch is, making it impossible for someone of your height and build to have the strength to force the bolt open. And it left your accomplice, Susan, outside in the cold, unable to take away the stolen painting before it was discovered missing.'

The collective heads turned to look at Mabel and then at Susan.

'It doesn't make sense,' said Clara coming once again to the girl's defence. 'Susan was awful to her. So why would she help her? Tell them you didn't do it, Mabel!'

Mabel continued to chew her thumbnail, as silent as Susan. But the guilt was written all over her face, because she knew she had been caught and there was nothing she could do to deny it.

'Mmm. Let's talk about that,' Mel said. 'You said that every time you were over at Susan's, she bullied Mabel. She pinched her, yelled at her, slapped her even. And you felt compelled to intervene. As ultimately, Clara, you're a nice person.'

Clara flushed with guilt at this comment, knowing she hadn't been so nice to Mel earlier.

'Your feelings about me aside,' Mel said a small smile on her face.

'You're saying she orchestrated all that for my benefit?' Clara said.

Derrin nodded, 'She did. And she set up this whole robbery too.'

'It's absurd,' Clara said. 'She didn't even know about the Turner, how could she? And Mabel came to stay with me months ago. Before we'd even had contact with you.'

'I'll come to that,' said Mel. 'But cast your mind back, Clara, to when Susan first mentioned to you that I was now residing at Avonby. Recount for us, if you will, how that came about.'

* * *

Two months earlier

'You're telling me Mel Greenway is now Lady?' Clara said. 'How… amazing. How did that happen?'

'Someone died, I suppose. That's how these things occur, isn't it?' Susan said. 'More tea?'

Susan picked up the teapot and poured the brown liquid into Clara's cup, smiling. Clara ignored the fact that she hadn't added the milk first. Very uncouth, but Susan didn't seem to care about those things in front of her, even though Clara knew she would never slip up like that in different company.

'I forgive you by the way.'

'Forgive me?' Clara said. 'What for?'

'For stealing my personal maid. She was a gem in so many ways.'

'Look, Sue, I think you and her were a clash of personalities. You seem to be getting on so well now with the new girl…'

'Indeed. She has some talent and isn't as… *annoying*… as Mabel was.'

Clara sipped her tea feeling even more guilty. She had been avoiding Susan since poaching Mabel, but also because of her terrible habit of insisting on introductions. Like the Mountbatten one at the theatre. Clara had found that one hugely embarrassing, because Susan didn't seem to have any boundaries when it came to asking blatant questions. Clara had zoned out while Susan had grilled Lord Mountbatten, unaware that she had learnt at that point that Michael Chase's father had died and he was planning to return to London.

Clara hadn't listened to the details that Susan coaxed out of the man, putting it down to some awful fascination which she couldn't quite fathom. Instead, Clara had looked around, awkward, trying to find someone else she knew to escape to and had, at the first opportunity, gone to speak to someone else she knew to get out of the situation.

'You should really connect with Melinda,' Susan was saying. 'She lives in a stunning manor house now, with acres and acres of land.'

'How do you know all this?' Clara said, curious, but also irritated that Susan knew all the gossip before anyone else.

Susan's eyes seemed to sharpen and focus on Clara as if she had been seeing her for the very first time.

'You really have no clue what is going on in society, do you?'

'I know what I need to,' Clara sniffed, biting back a retort.

* * *

'I guess I just thought she was nosy,' Clara said. 'She does always seem to know everything. Some of the rumours, I'll admit, I quite liked to hear.'

'You never said what you were doing at Euston the day Michael arrived though,' Derrin said.

'I was supposed to meet Sue at the tea room, but just before I saw

Michael, a boy came and gave me a note from her. She cancelled on me.'

Mel looked now at Susan. 'So you got all this information from Lord Mountbatten? You knew exactly when and how Michael was arriving?'

'Not quite,' Susan shrugged.

Mel suspected then that Susan had her own sources. But the woman was unwilling to give anything else away at that time.

'Clara, you should know that Susan used you. She set you up to be at the station, knowing you'd spot Michael. I suspect she was nearby, watching the proceedings and making sure you did "accidentally" meet.'

'But why?' Clara said addressing this now to Susan.

'I knew you'd invite him to come here with you, you were desperate for a boyfriend,' Susan said.

'And the more people here, the better the opportunity for Mabel to steal the painting for her, and more suspects to look at if she got caught,' Derrin said. 'But I suppose you didn't expect Charles's murder did you?'

Susan shrugged, 'You're not pinning that on me, I didn't even know the fellow. Eleanor never introduced us…'

'As you can see, you have been strung along,' Derrin told Clara now. 'Mabel and Susan set the scene and your natural empathy did the rest. You felt for Michael as he arrived home, grieving. Just as you had to rescue Mabel, didn't you?'

Clara nodded. 'I didn't suspect. Even for a minute.'

'Got ya,' said Mabel, giving her a wink and showing the dark side that Mel had always suspected was hidden under that fake-nervous exterior.

Mel grew thoughtful. Charles's murder was still something they would have to solve, but the thought of outing anyone for it left a bad taste in her mouth. She thought she knew who it was, but just needed some further affirmation before she would even consider revealing the person. She shouldn't condone murder, but the man was a dreadful person, and there was no way around that. She would be relieved to hand that over to Derrin and his officers soon, so that the onus as to if the person responsible was to be arrested or not wouldn't be on her.

Mel turned her mind back to the painting and the thief, because there were still so many questions she wanted answers to.

'Mabel. You have a chance now to make things right. Will you tell us where you hid the painting?' said Mel.

Mabel stopped chewing her thumbnail and looked Mel square in the eye. Mel saw then that the girl would never give her the answer. She was as hard and as ruthless as Susan.

'You're making a big mistake,' Derrin said.

Eleanor moved to sit next to Clara, and took her friend's hand in hers, showing quiet solidarity. Clara looked away from Mabel. She couldn't hide her shock and disappointment. Her sweet, shy and nervous maid was a ruthless and conniving bandit. What was the world coming to?

'So, who murdered Charles?' Michael chipped in.

'Not now,' Mel said. 'There are so many other questions yet to be answered. And, if I'm not mistaken, that's the doorbell, isn't it, Mr Williams?'

Williams nodded. He opened the drawing-room door and looked down the hallway as Toby opened the door to several constables.

'Good timing,' said Derrin.

Williams stepped aside as the constables came in. Mel recognised the young constable, Jennings, among them, recalling how he had worked with Derrin during the crime that had occurred on the Avonby estate some months earlier. Derrin handed Susan over to him and another officer cuffed her and Mabel.

Surrounded by constables, the two thieves were led away.

25

'Now what?' said Michael as Derrin came back, followed by Constable Jennings.

Derrin had supervised Susan and Mabel being chained up in the paddy wagon.

'We've sent for the coroner to take away Charles's body, but there still remains the question of who killed him,' Derrin said.

'Oh, no more! *Please*!' said Eleanor. 'Haven't we suffered enough?'

'I agree Miss Parkinson. So, I'm going to suggest you all take up residence in the Mermaid Inn,' Derrin said. 'Don't leave the village until this is resolved. Jennings is going to drive you there when you've gathered your possessions from the guest rooms upstairs.'

'You're letting us go? Just like that?' said Clara. 'What about your painting?'

Mel smiled. 'That's already in my custody.'

'Did Mabel tell you where it was?' Eleanor said.

'In a manner of speaking, though no, she didn't own up, much to her detriment. A good liar always mixes in fact with the deceits. Come with me, I'll show you.'

Mel walked from the drawing room followed by Derrin, Clara, Eleanor and Frank, with Mr Williams bringing up the rear.

'As she already admitted, Mabel heard us coming from the study last night,' Mel said.

She reached the top of the service stairs and pointed downwards.

'She was lurking there, not by the coat stand at that point. By then, the lights had gone off, a factor that bought into her plans by sheer fluke.'

Mel described how Mabel saw the guests going upstairs, and her and the inspector going to see the fuse box.

'While we were gone, she hurried back into the study and cut the picture from the frame, smashing the glasses and a bottle that we'd left on the mantlepiece in her haste. The problem is, we came back too quickly. That was when she hid in the coats to avoid being seen while we were milling around.'

'But she did come upstairs to me,' said Clara. 'How did she have time to steal and hide the painting?'

'Well, by your own admission, she was at least fifteen to twenty minutes, because Eleanor had come to see you in that time, hadn't she? Perhaps it could have been longer than twenty minutes?' Derrin said.

'We almost caught her in the act a few times. By then, she knew she couldn't get out of the house via the coal cellar, and so she had to find another solution. Perhaps she was planning to go out through one of the doors or windows. When she heard us return, she realised this wouldn't work and that the theft would be discovered any second. Trapped by the front door, all she could do was hide,' Mel explained. 'So she buried herself among the coats on the coat stand.'

'So where did she hide the painting, old girl?' Michael asked.

Mel now went towards the door. She parted the coats, revealing the umbrella stand, which was partially hidden behind them. She reached inside and extracted the rolled-up canvas from among the umbrella and walking sticks that were stored in there.

Clara gasped.

'Well done!' said Michael.

'As she was trapped, this was the only place she was able to hide the painting to make sure it wasn't found on her, or in her possession,' Mel explained.

'It's likely she thought we'd find it and she'd be in the clear. As the attempt had failed, no harm had been done,' Derrin said.

'The problem was, when we searched the house by candlelight it was not obvious among the umbrellas and walking sticks,' Mel explained. 'I didn't notice the canvas until I did the walk through, recreating what Mabel might have done, and examined where she had said she had hidden. I saw then the coal dust fingerprint on the wall near the coat stand.'

'Odd that she told you she was by the coat stand. Almost an admission?' Michael said.

'At that point she was willing to throw Clara to the lions to get the heat off herself,' Derrin said. 'If we did find the painting, she could say Clara must have put it there. Would probably have claimed once again she didn't want to betray her, as she had earlier.'

'What gave her away?' Clara asked.

Mel glanced her way, seeing the vulnerability that was clear on Clara's face. She hadn't appreciated being duped, and perhaps, because she had felt as though she had rescued Mabel, the insult was even worse.

'When Mabel turned the blame in Clara's direction we were both wary, as we had believed Clara's account of how Mabel came to work for her,' Mel continued. 'And by then, I had worked out Mabel's tells and knew she was lying.'

'You're a genius, old girl,' said Michael. 'You two make a very good team.'

'I appreciate your confidence but we are at a loss over Charles's murder,' Mel lied as she glanced at Eleanor. 'I'm sorry.'

'Oh, but the brute deserved it,' Clara said. '*What?* It's what we *all* think!'

They all felt silent at this and Mel tried not to look too hard at Clara, Eleanor, Michael and Frank, knowing that such obvious scrutiny might give away her suspicions.

At that moment, Constable Jennings came back inside the house.

'Is that the missing painting?' he asked, his eyes round as he looked at the canvas in Mel's hands.

'Yes, and I'm not going to let it out of my sight until it's back on the wall where it belongs,' Mel said.

'Jennings, if you can take these people to the Inn now, that would be appreciated. I've already asked Nancy and Ruby to help the ladies pack and Toby and Mr Williams will be on hand to help move the luggage,' said Derrin.

The suspects, which Mel couldn't stop herself from still referring to them as, dispersed to their collective rooms to supervise the packing of their belongings. Clara and Eleanor went together followed by Michael, who remained cheery, even though Mel knew that was a front he put up in adversity.

'Frank?' Derrin said as he approached the service stairs to go down to the servant's quarters to collect his few possessions. 'Have you anything to add about Mr Charles?'

Frank shook his head, 'I can't tell you anything more, I think you know it all now.' Frank turned to leave and then paused. 'What about the Rolls-Royce? I suppose I can take that back to Mr Charles's family?'

'The tyres were deflated and so until that's sorted out it will stay here,' Derrin said. 'Plus, our team would like to look it over. We want to make sure that nothing is missed. You'll go to the inn too, and stay there with everyone else until the station releases you.'

Frank nodded, 'Only a guilty man would run.'

A short time later, Eleanor, Frank, Clara and Michael climbed into Jennings' car. The boot was filled with their collective cases and bags, supervised by Williams.

As the car drove away, Mel watched. She was riddled with conflicting emotions. What should have been a fun reunion had turned into an endless night. She was relieved to see them go, but also bruised and battered by the intensity of the last few hours.

Now she sank down into the chaise in the hallway and put her head in her hands. She let go of all the stress and anxiety as the adrenaline rush that had kept her going the last few hours was leaving her body along with her remaining strength.

'You're exhausted,' Derrin said.

'So are you.' Mel said.

'I am,' he agreed.

Another constable came in to the hallway to announce that the 'meat wagon' had arrived.

Mel got to her feet, pushing through the tiredness and followed him and Derrin out. In the hallway, she unlocked the cloakroom door, turned the light on, and stepped back to allow the CID to enter. She knew they would want to search the house too, and possibly take fingerprints and other evidence in relation to the case. Out of respect, she felt she needed to wait by the door until Charles was covered up, and taken out on a gurney.

While Derrin supervised the removal to the mortuary van outside, and the careful wrapping of Clara's dress. Mel turned back to the room and glanced in, taking in the space where Charles's corpse had been placed. As she reached for the light switch, a flicker of something under the shoe rack caught her attention. Mel paused. Keeping her eyes firmly on the location, she moved into the small room and bent down. Underneath the rack was a small vial.

Mel glanced back at the door and saw that she was still alone and hadn't been observed. She toyed with the idea of removing the object and disposing of it. For possibly the fingerprints of the murderer were on it. Mel already suspected who was responsible, but she also didn't want to know for certain. She didn't want to see that person hung for the death of Charles. They didn't deserve it.

Taking a handkerchief from the pocket of her slacks, Mel scooped up the vial and put it away. As she stood, she found Derrin standing by the door. Mel flushed with guilt. What if Derrin thought she had poisoned Charles and was now getting rid of the evidence?

'Let's get out of here while they do their work,' he said. Then in a much quieter tone, 'Bring it with you.'

Mel took a deep breath and followed Derrin outside. By now, a mechanic had been brought in and four new tyres had been placed on Derrin's car. He opened the passenger door for Mel and she climbed inside, careful not to crush the vial in her pocket.

Derrin closed the door then went back to talk to the constables, the detectives from CID and a sergeant who had just arrived. Mel couldn't hear what was said until Derrin turned back and headed towards the car.

'Please be careful of Lord and Lady Greenway's property.'

Without further comment, Derrin got into the driver's seat, started the engine and drove away from the house.

It wasn't long before Mel realised where they were heading. And in the village, just beyond the boundaries of Avonby, Derrin pulled the Jowett Javelin up in front of the cottage he had rented, then bought, since he moving into the area.

They went inside, and for a minute Mel wondered what his intentions were, but as he pulled off his crumpled Tuxedo jacket and placed it over the back of the sofa, she could see the same exhaustion that had overwhelmed her earlier now take over Derrin.

'I know we have a lot of talking to do,' he said, 'but can we just get some sleep first?'

Mel was swept with an overwhelming relief at the suggestion. It seemed a lifetime ago when they were going to have a 'personal' conversation about their relationship, only to be swept away on this hellbent mystery. Anything they might have said earlier was now irrelevant. They had worked together throughout this situation so well that Mel was in no doubt that they did have the same values, the same inner strength and that more importantly, he respected her as much as she respected him.

'Give me the vial,' he said now.

Mel took the handkerchief from her pocket and handed it to him. He placed it on the coffee table.

'We'll talk about it later when we've rested and can reflect,' Derrin said.

Then taking her hand, he led her up the familiar small staircase, and stripping off down to their underwear, they slipped under the covers of his small but comfortable bed.

Derrin turned Mel and pulled her into a spoon, then promptly fell into a much-needed sleep.

Mel relaxed into the soft pillow. Derrin's arm around her waist made her feel safe and, content, she soon drifted off, shutting out the stress of the last few hours and all thoughts of how telling it was that he'd brought her away from it all, to get the rest she deserved.

26

MEL AWOKE TO FIND HERSELF IN THE dark and, for a second, she wasn't sure where she was. She felt punch drunk, and as if she hadn't slept enough. Then she noticed she was alone. Even though she had slept so deeply, she hadn't moved from the original position she had been in when she and Derrin had fallen asleep.

She sat up and got out of the bed.

Derrin's spare robe hung on the back of the door and she pulled it on, then wandered downstairs to see where he was.

She followed the trail of small lamps that led her through the hallway and into the cosy lounge. From there she could hear Derrin was in the kitchen.

She also noticed that the vial was no longer on the coffee table.

There was a waft of hot food cooking on the stove, and Mel's stomach groaned, reminding her that she hadn't eaten since that morning and despite Mrs Weston's best efforts, hadn't stayed to eat the soup and fresh bread that had been prepared for them. She felt guilty for a minute and paused in the hallway, thinking she should return to Avonby as soon as possible and make sure everything was well.

'I'm in here,' Derrin called.

The thought of bailing on him vanished, and Mel opened the kitchen door and went inside.

There she found the small table already laid, and Derrin dishing out two bowls of chicken stew. On the table was a loaf of fresh bread and a butter dish. He must have been out to buy the bread while she slept, and Mel was quite touched by the effort he'd made to make sure he had food to give her when she woke.

'Help yourself,' he said.

Mel sat down and it was only then that her eyes fell on the vial, still wrapped in her handkerchief, on the work surface near the oven.

'I had a look. It's empty, but there is a strong smell of almonds, so I think it's fair to say the arsenic was in that,' Derrin said, noticing her study of the vial.

He placed the bowls down on the table and sat next to her.

'I thought you might need this. I know I do!'

He tucked in and Mel cut a slice of the bread and began to butter it. Then she tasted the stew, mixing it with a bite of the bread. It was delicious. Was there nothing he couldn't do?

After they were replete, Mel leaned back in her chair. Her body was rested but she still ached from lack of a full night's sleep. Derrin stood and began to clear the table, refusing her offer of help.

He took a bottle of his favourite cognac from the cupboard along with two glasses, in which he poured a generous measure.

'We have to talk,' he said.

Mel pushed her wayward hair from her eyes and tucked it behind her ears. She had completely lost where they were before this happened, and had hoped he would too, but now she wondered if a gavel was poised to slam down on their relationship.

'You did a great job,' he said. 'Though as you might imagine this is far from over.'

Mel nodded.

'I rang the station: Mabel and Susan are both locked up in separate cells, waiting to be interviewed. Susan hasn't said a word since we took her in. Mabel is playing the downtrodden victim again.'

'Well, it almost worked for her last time,' Mel said.

She glanced again at the vial.

'What are we going to do about that?' she asked.

'I don't know yet. It's an insurance policy for now,' Derrin said.

'Insurance?'

Derrin didn't elaborate but she saw him lapse into thought, and wondered if this was what she did to him when she knew something he didn't, but wasn't ready to reveal. She let it go.

'Are you going back tonight to do the interviews?' she asked.

'No. I'm going to let them stew,' he said. 'Then, tomorrow, you and I will go in hard.'

'Both of us?'

Derrin nodded, 'Not officially, but I do need your help, you know that.'

'Okay. I'm willing.'

Derrin took her hand and lifted it to his lips. 'As for us…'

Mel smiled. 'We are… *complicated*,' she finished for him.

'It wasn't what I was going to say, but it'll do for now.'

Mel stood and came to him, sitting on his knee. She took his face in her hands and drew his lips to hers because it felt like the right response. They kissed for a long time and all guilt of this moment slipped away. They had been through so much and all she wanted right now was his touch. She wanted to forget the theft, and the murder, and above all the opinions some of her former friends had of her.

Derrin lifted her from his legs, and positioned her on the table top, legs either side of his thighs as he pulled her closer. His mouth travelling from her lips, to her throat and down over the rim of her breast.

'I feel… untidy,' he said.

'Should we have a bath?' Mel suggested, feeling like she need to wash too.

'Oh yes, and then I'm going to lay you down and make a great deal of love to you.'

Mel fought the girlie giggle that rose to her throat. Derrin brought out so many different sides to her. In the past she would have hidden this lighter side, this young woman that still wanted to be loved, admired and made love to. But now she felt that there was no need for such mystery. He didn't, after all, hide himself from her, did he?

She pushed away the urge to analyse this thing they had between them. Passion, yes. Respect, certainly. But was there any kind of need for each other? Did she lose her independence by letting go sometimes? Mel didn't think so. In the world she lived in, sometimes you could have it all. The problems came when you didn't believe that and thought you didn't deserve to be happy.

Mel pushed away this dark idea as she picked up their glasses and followed Derrin upstairs.

In the bathroom, he turned the hot tap on and added some bath salts to the water. The water filled the bath halfway before Derrin added the cold. When it was ready, Mel slipped out of the robe and her underwear and into the water on one end and he took the other.

There followed a languid session of mutual cleansing. Derrin turned Mel around to be between his legs as he lathered a sponge and ran it over her back. Then he pulled her back to rest on him, as the water sloshed around them. Despite the hour, Mel didn't let her anxiety about Avonby interfere with the time she was spending with Derrin. She was relaxed, secure and experiencing a feeling of elation at just being there.

When they had bathed enough, Derrin took the towel-clad Mel back into his room.

They didn't speak as they reached for each other: there were no words necessary. True to his word, Derrin took his time, bringing Mel to an exquisite orgasm before allowing his own pleasure. After which, they both fell back to sleep until the early hours of the morning.

27

ON ARRIVAL BACK AT THE HOUSE AT six that morning, Mel had hurried to her room to change, before taking up her morning duties, behaving as if she hadn't been absent all night. The first thing she did was check the house wasn't in total disarray after the forensic search, and she instructed Daisy and Ruby to get on with straightening the rooms that weren't already dealt with after the police had left, in particular, the drawing room and Jonathan's study, which was marked with dust from the fingerprint kits.

Then she went to the garage and began to put her motorbike back together, which took the best part of the morning.

As she finished, a framer from York arrived and Mel left the man in Avonby's workshop while he reframed the Turner under Mr Williams's supervision, because although she trusted the man, she wasn't taking any chances.

The damage to the painting itself was irreparable, and so the new frame would need to be smaller than the original, but not by much, and she doubted anyone would really notice.

Derrin had said he would send for her before he began the interviews at 1 p.m. and as promised Constable Jennings arrived at midday to take her to the station.

She had yet to have the awkward conversation with Jonathan about the attempted theft and the murder, and she wanted at least to have some information of the potential prosecutions before she did.

'I don't suppose the inspector has got a confession from them?' she asked Jennings as she got into the passenger seat beside him.

'I'm afraid not, Lady Melinda. They've been tight-lipped ever since we took them in. That might change o'course, as they get to see their appointed lawyer and he tells 'em they are bang to rights. At that point, the likes of them would usually angle for a plea bargain.'

They arrived at the station and after parking the car at the front, Jennings took Mel straight inside and into the back office where Derrin was waiting.

'I've squared your presence as a consultant with the brigadier,' Derrin said once they were alone.

'How did you manage that? Isn't it a conflict of interest?'

'That would depend on if we are going to prosecute them for the attempted theft or not. I have to say, they wouldn't get much time, even if we do, and Susan has brought in an expensive lawyer who has been in with her all morning,' Derrin explained.

'So, you're saying they are going to get away with it?' Mel was shocked by this revelation.

'I don't want them to, and I'll do my best to make sure they get some form of punishment. But I want to offer a deal, in exchange for information.'

At this point, all Mel wanted to know was why they had done it in the first place. As Eleanor and Clara had confirmed, Susan wasn't short of money, so it couldn't be for that reason.

'I'm open to it. But I want to know all the details of how they planned this, and why.'

'Okay. I'm going to start with Mabel to see if she'll crack. Then we'll go in with whatever she tells us to leverage some cooperation off Susan.'

Derrin took Mel to the observation room and through the two-way mirror she could see Mabel was already there under the supervision of Constable Jennings.

As Mel took a seat to watch the interview, Mabel glanced at the mirror as if she knew that she was being watched. Derrin came in and sat down opposite her, and placed a pad of paper down in front of her.

'So, Mabel. Can you tell us about the conversation you first had with Susan Erskine, regarding Lord Jonathan Greenway's artwork?' Derrin said.

Mabel didn't answer.

'How long have you been plotting with Susan Erskine to steal the Turner?'

Mabel looked at the mirror again.

'Let me start with something simpler,' Derrin said. 'How long have you been working for Miss Erskine?'

Mabel took a deep breath, then closed her mouth, indicating that she had no intention of speaking to Derrin.

'Well, perhaps I can refresh your memory?' Derrin said. 'Miss Erskine says you've been working for her for several years. Since her fortunes changed during the war.'

Mabel hid her surprise.

'She wouldn't tell you nuffink,' she said folding her arms across her chest.

'Are you so sure?' Derrin said. 'Only she spent a lot of time with her fancy London lawyer today, who has been giving her some solid advice. I believe you've seen the appointed defence counsel?'

Mabel looked thoughtful. Then narrowed her eyes.

'I'll be looked after,' she said, but she didn't sound convinced.

'I'm going to talk to her again now, and I expect to be making a deal. Though someone will have to pay for the crime, and your fingerprints are all over the painting and the utility knife.'

Derrin stood up and picked up the pad, having written not one word on it so far, and turned away. He had only taken one step towards the door when Mabel cracked.

'Yeah. I worked for her a long time,' Mabel said.

Derrin stopped, his hand on the door knob. 'You better not waste my time.'

'I don't know much…'

'Then tell me what you do know,' Derrin said.

* * *

London, 1942

Mabel was happy to do the hair of Mrs Elizabeth Wren's friend, even though she knew that Miss Susan Erskine wasn't anyone of note. Now she brushed and styled the lovely long blonde locks, swooping them up onto the woman's head into a sophisticated chignon.

Mabel had been working for the very young Mrs Wren for a few months. She was from a good family, even though the war meant she was less choosy about her friends. Miss Erskine being a point in case, with her cheap shoes and gravy-browning tanned legs: the smudged seamline drawn in eyebrow pencil at the back was a dead giveaway.

Mabel had watched how the woman, who must be a year or two older than herself, had latched on to Mrs Wren, sycophantising her way into the inner circle of friends. She was a piece of work, but her boldness was something to admire. Miss Erskine displayed an amazing amount of self-confidence, the like of which Mabel had never seen before. She was a force to be reckoned with and definitely no one's fool.

Susan Erkskine relaxed under her administrations, only opening her eyes when Mabel finished.

'You've done a brilliant job!' she said when she saw the up-do in the mirror. 'I'd have you come work for me, if I could.'

Mabel hadn't taken much notice of this half-offered job, knowing that the woman didn't have two pennies to rub together, so she definitely wasn't going to be able to afford a full-time personal maid. But she took the compliment and gave Miss Erskine a smile of thanks.

'Don't you dare think of poaching her Sue,' Mrs Wren said laughing because she knew, just as well as everyone else in the room, that she couldn't.

'Where are you ladies off to tonight?' Mabel asked shyly. 'I have some nice red lipstick in me bag if it's somewhere special.'

'Oh yes, Mabel! Red lips for everyone. Promise not to tell?' Mrs Wren said.

Mabel nodded, 'You know I always keep your secrets, Miss,' she said as she brought out the half-used stick of lipstick.

'We're going to a speak-easy,' Mrs Wren confided.

'Really, Miss? I always wanted to go to one of those places. Will you tell me all about it tomorrow?'

'Of course!' Mrs Wren had agreed, and the women, all wearing the red lipstick and beautified within the little realms of access to decent cosmetics, all left feeling prettier.

Several weeks later, Miss Susan came calling again. This time she arrived when Mrs Wren wasn't home. She was driving a brand-new swanky car too, and she asked the butler to fetch Mabel.

'Come for a drive with me,' Miss Susan said.

Mabel had never been asked to go anywhere in a car before, so, with Mrs Wren not due back for many hours, she agreed to go. She didn't fail to notice the expensive clothing Miss Susan was wearing either. The mink coat, over a sophisticated tweed two-piece. She had on proper silk stockings, and shiny patent leather shoes which had silk bows on the back, which Mabel spotted as Miss Susan led her to the car. All the while, Susan messed with the perfect string of pearls that were so long she had to put a fashionable knot in them. Fashionable, that was, in the 1920s, Mabel observed. But expensive clothing and jewellery never dated, and Miss Susan wore it all well with her slender figure.

The drive took them across London from Mrs Wren's Hampstead home, and into Greenwich where she pulled in at a three-storey terraced house, huge compared to Mrs Wren's place, and Mabel then learnt that Miss Susan had come into some money. Not only was she thriving compared to everyone else during the war, but she looked happier than the last time Mabel had seen her.

'I moved out of my mother's place,' she explained. 'I have a housekeeper, a scullery maid and a butler now. All I need now is someone who knows how to dress a lady. You're that person Mabel.'

She made Mabel an offer she found hard to refuse, doubling her salary with a promise of bonuses and good working hours. Mabel went back to Mrs Wren's and gave in her notice immediately. She just had a good feeling about Miss Susan, who was going places for sure, and hardly appeared to be affected by the awfulness of the war.

At that point only half of Miss Susan's house was used: Miss Susan's bedroom; a few rooms in the servant's quarters – one which Mabel was given; the kitchen; and the small drawing room. All other rooms were kept locked and Mabel never saw inside them or even knew if they were furnished. She also knew better than to ask, besides, it didn't matter to her.

Miss Susan didn't entertain at all, but she went out a lot. Although she had money most of the time, there were occasions when the situation became tighter than usual, and she would be cautious about the household spending. She always made sure that salaries were paid during these times, and cuts that were made impacted Miss Susan only.

After a few months of working for her, Mabel began to wonder if Miss Susan had a man friend – probably a married one who was taking care of things but sometimes lapsed on the money side of things. She wouldn't be the first to live that way.

Things began to look up as the new year came, and Miss Susan was happier, and wealthier than ever. Then a few months in, things took a turn for the worst and Mabel found her own job in jeopardy for the first time because Susan couldn't pay them.

'I'll stick by you. We've been through worse, ain't we?' Mabel had said, declaring her loyalty, but something was badly wrong, and Miss Susan was worried. A few times, Mabel found her crying in the bedroom.

'Oh, Miss! Whatever's wrong?' Mabel asked on one such occasion.

'He's disappeared, Mabel,' she confided eventually. 'No one knows where.'

And Mabel had her suspicions confirmed that a man kept Miss Susan, even though she never brought him home.

After that Mabel was watchful of Miss Susan, making sure she was all right. She really liked her, despite her first impression of the woman. Miss Susan's beau, she assumed, had been away to war and was now missing in action. But she never dared ask Susan if this was the case, at that point she didn't think it was her place to.

Then, a few weeks later, Miss Susan received a letter, and at that point Mabel learned that Miss Susan's man-friend was confirmed dead. She never told Mabel what happened, but it threw the household into turmoil, and suddenly she was disposing of some of the expensive items she owned to make sure that bills could be paid.

Mabel had noticed the lovely artwork, for example, but the pictures disappeared, one by one, from the walls, and because they were in the war, Mabel was sure they weren't sold by traditional means and perhaps Miss Susan didn't get what they were worth either.

With the influx of the money from the artwork sales though, things did improve, and she caught up on the salaries. After that, Miss Susan started going out more again. She had obviously, in the past, spent time with the now deceased boyfriend on these jaunts, but she was now involved in something else. At times, she'd come back home with a case that Mabel suspected was full of money. Though Miss Susan never revealed anything more to her, the household finances stabilised and Miss Susan stopped selling her prized possessions.

* * *

Derrin sighed when Mabel stopped talking.

'Are you trying to tell me you don't know where this money came from?' Derrin said.

'I thought it was the sale of her pictures. Some of them was pretty special,' Mabel said.

'Get to the point girl.'

Mabel went quiet.

'I was suspicious of what she were doing, so a friend helped me follow her one night. I found out she was running one of them speakeasies. And fings were being sold and bought there that were more than black market hooch,' Mabel said. 'I fink that's where she got her money from.'

'I'm not really that interested in those sorts of crimes,' Derrin pointed out. 'That was the war days, and that stuff is best left there, don't you think?'

'I 'oped you'd say that Inspector. Cos she were only doing what she 'ad to. To survive. Even though, after that fings did take a turn for good.'

'I already know she has money. You still haven't told me about the theft. I want to know when she involved you, and why.'

'It were about a year ago, when Miss Susan finally found out what happened to her love…' Mabel said. Then she began to explain how Susan had taken her into her confidence.

It wasn't a story Derrin had expected, but it did make a lot of sense as to why she had targeted Avonby and the Turner.

It was clear that as a loyal servant Mabel had agreed to hoodwink Miss Clara, and then go and work for her. The plan Susan had was a long-term one, a slow burn, and she was not in a hurry to execute it as she bided her time. It showed a devious mind, nonetheless, and a desperate urge for revenge. Even though Mabel had not understood or known all the details until much later.

* * *

Derrin went into the interview observation room and found Mel waiting to speak to him.

'What do you make of all that?' Derrin said.

'Mabel was only made privy to some of the back story, but I think there's much more to this than we know. So she was an art dealer during the war? Theft? Or purchase? I'm not sure it matters now. She was living a respectable life so it doesn't make sense why she targeted the Turner.'

'I'm sending her back to her cell for now, and we'll get Susan in here. I'm going to throw what I know at Susan and see if she breaks.'

Mel turned her attention back to the interview-room mirror. There was a sensation nagging in the back of her mind after hearing of Susan's dealings in running a speakeasy, and the sale of her treasured artwork.

Where did it all come from in the first place? Mel wondered. *Obviously the boyfriend. But who was he, and how did he get his hands on it all?*

Right then, Susan was brought into the interview room with a man wearing a Saville Row pinstripe suit, who Mel guessed was the expensive lawyer. Mel could only imagine how much the man would earn from this morning in York. And again, the question of Susan's bottomless pit of money rose to the fore.

Susan and the lawyer sat down on one side of the table next to each other, rigid and unspeaking as both turned their heads to look at the mirror.

Derrin re-entered and sat down in the seat he had just left and he began firing questions at Susan, for which her standard reply was 'No comment'.

'It seems that your accomplice Mabel was privy to other crimes…' he said. 'Crimes that involved smuggling, and running illegal clubs that provided drugs as well as black market booze.'

Susan straightened up at the mention of this, and she glanced at her lawyer who began to twitch his perfect tie as though it had come loose. He hadn't known of these misdemeanours, nor did he know that Derrin had no urge to pursue her for crimes committed during the war. A fact that would probably not be popular if it was discovered by Derrin's Brigadier, who was known for chasing people for war crimes.

'Miss Erskine…', the lawyer said, 'perhaps we ought to talk about a plea of some sort?'

Susan gave him a serious glare.

'You have no proof of any of this, Inspector, and who would take the word of some silly little maid against me? I'll deny everything of course,' she said.

'The thing is, Miss Erskine, I have no interest in these crimes and can look the other way quite happily depending on the outcome of the current investigation. With regards to the theft you orchestrated with Mabel, well, Lady Greenway is not looking to press charges if you cooperate and give her some answers.'

'Like you'll let me walk out of here, free as a bird?' Susan said.

Derrin glanced at the mirror.

'That does depend on what you tell us,' he said.

'Miss Erskine, I really think we should talk privately before you make any deals with the inspector,' the lawyer said.

'I pay you. And for now, you can be quiet. You haven't been much use so far. What do you want to know, Inspector?' Susan asked.

'I want to know why you did it,' Derrin said.

Susan sat back in her chair and crossed her arms in her lap. She appeared to be thinking while she gazed down at the table top.

'Do you remember a man called Eric Stafford?' Susan said, looking straight into the mirror, directing her question at Mel and not to Derrin.

28

London, 1942

THE WAR WAS TOUGH ON SUSAN UNTIL she met Eric. It was the same night that Mabel had done her beautiful coiffure, and she was hanging out with that awful Elizabeth Wren, for want of better friends. By then, she had barely seen Clara and Eleanor, and Mel had abandoned them all, taking up a new role in RASC, though Susan had heard on the grapevine that Mel was throwing herself into the job of a mechanic, which she had thought laughable at the time. She'd told Clara about it too, knowing she would be amused, but Clara hadn't cared, distracted as she was chasing a general twice her age, a romance that never quite came off the way Clara had wanted.

All this aside, Susan was a survivor and she had latched onto Elizabeth, who could open some of the right doors for her anyway. It wasn't hard, because the woman was a bore and had so few friends that Susan's interest was welcomed, and Elizabeth was useful and generous.

It had been Susan's idea to liven things up and go to the speakeasy. She had heard about it from a girl at work and there had been talk of booze, cigarettes and possibly some soldiers to flirt with for a pair of some much-desired stockings.

'Just flirt?' Elizabeth had asked.

'Maybe a kiss or two,' Susan said. 'They are so randy, they will go for anything.'

As Elizabeth's husband was away in the RAF, Susan didn't find it too challenging to persuade the girl to go out for a little fun. They were times that meant woman had more freedom, and Susan thought Elizabeth was well aware that on her husband's return that wouldn't be the same.

Elizabeth's chauffeur drove them to a house in Surrey on a street that had been recently bombed and therefore abandoned, but for this one stand-out house.

'This can't be it,' Elizabeth said.

'It is,' said Susan. 'You'll see as soon as we get inside. Do you have the entrance fee?'

Elizabeth did, and Susan took the money, saying she would pay it to save Elizabeth any embarrassment. Susan went inside first, then she came out and indicated Elizabeth should come in. She had of course, pocketed the money, as there was no charge for women, because the person who ran the club was trying to make sure there were enough of them available to keep the sailors and soldiers on leave happy.

They were getting drinks when Susan thought she spotted Mel in the distance. But the thought of talking to her soon went out of her head when Eric Stafford sidled up and offered to buy her a drink. She was taken with Eric right away and they spent the entire night together. All the while, Susan watched Elizabeth, drinking and flirting, and banked what she knew about her behaviour for future usage.

The night went fast, and then some incident occurred and Stafford got her and Elizabeth out and into their car before going back inside to sort it out. She didn't exchange contact details with him, but he promised to be in touch even as they heard police sirens in the distance. The chauffeur set off at rapid speed, diving down a side street to avoid the oncoming deluge of police cars coming to raid the club.

The next day, Susan received a gift which was delivered by a scruffy little scrote, who her mother was horrified to answer the door to. Even so, when Susan came to the door to receive the parcel, she tipped the boy. No one ever sent her presents and she was pleased. She was partly expecting it to be a gift from Elizabeth to guarantee her silence of what she might have seen the night before.

To her surprise, the box contained some expensive chocolate and a card signed from Eric. Susan didn't know how he had found out where she lived, but she was hugely flattered by the effort made.

She and Eric soon became an item and Susan learned the privileges of being Stafford's girl, and as time went on, that he had been the owner of the speakeasy, and his finger was in many pies. He bought the house for her, putting it in her name, and to seal the deal, Eric and Susan married in a private wedding that Eric's money paid to keep under wraps.

'But why do we have to keep it secret?' Susan had asked.

'I'm just protecting you, girl,' he said. 'I deal with some heavy people. I keep my private life that way.'

As a result, Eric never came openly to the house, and entered only late at night and under full cover of dark once all serving staff were asleep.

There were rooms in the house that Eric stored things in. Rooms that Susan didn't even have keys for, but when he had first moved her in, he'd taken some pieces of art out of one of the rooms and had it hung on the walls to please her.

Because of what Eric did, sometimes money was scarce. If one of his clubs were raided, Eric would lose money and often found himself in a position where he had to pay for the booze the cops had confiscated. Then other times, they were rolling in cash. There was a safe that he put in the wall behind one of the pictures, and only Susan knew about it. She had the combination, and drew on the funds when she needed them. When times got bad, Eric would shift one of the paintings away, selling it on the black market, which, Susan soon figured out, meant that the pictures hadn't been acquired in the most legitimate way in the first place.

They were happy though, and there were more up times than down, and Susan and Eric were strong. He loved her, would do anything for her. She had never been so happy or so secure… until the night he disappeared and didn't come back.

By then Susan knew some of his gang. They knew she was his girl, and a few also knew about the wedding. Because of the nature of his business, Eric had left one of them with the task of letting Susan know if there was ever a problem.

His name was Petey, and he had been one of Eric's most trusted men.

When Susan turned up at the latest speakeasy, Petey took her aside immediately.

'Cops raided us last night,' he told her. 'Eric was taken.'

He handed her an envelope, which Eric had left in his care should anything happen to him.

'Where are they keeping him?' she had asked.

Petey didn't know, and when he tried to find out over the next few weeks, he came up with a dead end. Eric was not being held in any police station, the suspicion was he had been taken to a secret holding place by the military.

'The word is, he might be tried as a traitor,' Petey said.

Treachery. Eric had never given away anything that suggested this was true. Susan didn't believe he was a traitor, no matter what.

'But why would they think that?' Susan said.

Petey was cagey in his answer, and nocommittal, so Susan began to question whether this could possibly be the case. She was no stuffed shirt and was happy to earn from the Eric's dealings, but treachery was a different thing, and, if proven, punishable by death.

She was in no position to canvas for his release: the wedding, even though legal in the eyes of the church, had never been advertised, bans never read. All she could do was hope that he would be released eventually.

She took on all his operations then, and because some of his men knew about her, they accepted her input, believing it was coming from Eric. And also, because she knew everything he was in to: Eric's letter had revealed a lot. Who worked for him, what he had on them and where a lot of his assets were kept. Even the art dealers he dealt with. Susan got Eric's men to do some of the dirty work in his name, and those who needed to be squeezed were and she found her capital increasing tenfold.

Following the advice Eric had left her, Susan spread the rumour that he wasn't imprisoned but merely hiding out. And so, every order she gave was taken as coming from him. It ensured that no one messed with his men, or tried to come after her for fear of serious reprisal. Susan was shocked to discover how much clout Eric had, he was never anything but gentle with her, but she now learnt that there was a much darker side to him. A side that struck terror into the hearts of other criminals. He was something akin to being a mobster, none of which bothered Susan in the least because he'd left her well provided for.

As the war came to an end though, the police force was starting to take much more note of the gang's activities. The speakeasies closed, and in their place Susan opened a legitimate club. She never told her friends how she earned her money, nor that she turned a blind eye to some of the dealings that happened in the club in those early days. What they didn't know couldn't hurt them.

Even so, Susan never gave up her search for information on what had happened to Eric. It wasn't until after the war, and many bribes later, that she discovered he was dead. He'd been shot as a traitor. The idea that he could betray his country was unfathomable, and she didn't believe it. She thought there had been a mistake. There had to be. That wasn't the Eric she knew.

* * *

'When money changed hands, I had access to official documents, one of which hadn't been redacted and revealed the names of the two people that brought Eric down. You, Inspector Bradley, and Lady Melinda Greenway,' Susan said.

'You orchestrated this crime for revenge,' Derrin said. 'But what revenge did you hope to get? And how did you know about the Turner in the first place?'

Susan crossed her arms over her chest.

'When Eric vanished, I found myself in a situation where I had to sell the artwork. Using the contacts he'd left in his letter, I met with the first art dealer, who was a captain. He told me the painting wasn't worth much, but he would take it off my hands. He had lied and had done me out of a significant amount of money. It was the last time I dealt with him, but I did my homework after that and found the true value of the goods I had in my hands. Later, with the contacts I've kept, I heard about the painting being brought here.'

Derrin frowned. 'Who was the captain?'

Susan smiled. 'Captain Jonathan Greenway. I later learnt he was also Mel's second cousin, and now the heir of Avonby. My spy in the gentlemen's club he frequents revealed he still had the Turner. It's surprising how loose some mouths get when fed a heavy dram of whisky.'

'Jonathan was dealing in illegal artwork?' Derrin said. He gave a sideways glance at the mirror. 'What about your other contacts?'

'I won't be revealing any other names,' said Susan. 'But I had very good reason to target him. And, in the process I'd also get revenge on Mel. I didn't realise that you were still *involved* with her though. That was a real eye-opener.'

'Do we have a deal now, Inspector?' said the fancy lawyer trying to work a little for his fee.

'Not yet,' said Derrin. 'It all depends if Lady Melinda is satisfied with this explanation. But I will tell you this, Miss Erskine… or is it Mrs Stafford…? Eric *was* a conspirator. He drugged a solider in his club. His intention was to torture the young man for information on plans that were being discussed to end the war. Stafford had every intention of selling this on to the enemy.'

'I don't believe it,' Susan said. 'He loved his country!'

'Stafford loved money more. And he had been promised a significant amount to betray us. You should know he confessed.'

'Under duress! You must have tortured him first!'

'I'm not saying everything we did in those days was right. But I have never doubted what I witnessed, what Mel saw. Stafford was a traitor. He died after being tried, just as the law dictated,' Derrin said.

Susan listened while Derrin told her all the things he'd learnt about Stafford. After a while she stopped denying what he said and stayed silent, realising that the man she once loved had been lying to her all along. She had refused to see it, but when confronted with the facts, she could no longer ignore the truth. No one who had been through those terrible years in London would ever want to know such things about a loved one, but Derrin couldn't leave her under any misconception.

Afterwards, he went back to the observation room and he found a very tired Mel still there.

'That must have been hard for her to hear,' Mel said.

'Must have been difficult for you too. The things she said about Jonathan being an art dealer? She could have been lying. But I don't think she was.'

'What are you going to do about it?' Mel asked.

'Nothing. It's a petty thing, and she and her husband did far worse and I am not going to pursue her on that either. What's the point? It won't change any of it, and I think Susan has probably suffered enough,' Derrin said.

'You're a good man,' Mel said. 'I'm not sure if I would take the same stance in your position.'

'If I open that bag of worms, I'll be prosecuting a lot of senior officials as well.'

Mel let that information sink in.

'One last thing, are you happy to let her off with the attempted theft?'

Mel nodded. 'I don't think we want to drag Jonathan through the courts and have that slur come out, do we?'

'That's what I thought. I'll get a deal drafted up with her lawyer.'

'I better go home,' Mel said. 'But, will I see you later?'

Derrin nodded, but he kept his distance, after all it wouldn't be very professional to take her in his arms in the middle of the station, even though he wanted to.

***

As Derrin was writing up his report, Susan requested a meeting. By then she had dismissed her lawyer and had been left to wait in the holding cells of the York police station for several hours. Derrin had as yet not made good on releasing her or Mabel. There was still one very burning question in his mind, and he knew that Susan would have the answer to it, but he hadn't wanted to involve Mel, because he felt she had been through enough in the last 24 hours.

'You said you wanted the truth and I gave it you,' Susan said as Derrin arrived at her cell. 'Why am I still here, and what has happened to Mabel?'

'There's one more thing I want to discuss with you, and if you can answer this question truthfully, I know Lady Melinda will agree to drop all charges against you,' Derrin said, even though Mel already had.

'And what of Mabel?' Susan said.

'Mabel too, but you are never to come near Avonby, Lord Greenway or Mel ever again.'

'I wouldn't want to after this. What do you want to know?' Susan asked.

'From your vantage point in the garden, you must have been able to see everything that went on in the study,' Derrin said.

Susan nodded.

'Tell me about Charles. Did you see his movements that night?'

'Do you mean what he did to Michael?'

'Yes,' Derrin said.

Susan confirmed that Charles chloroformed and stabbed Michael. The details were so close to what they suspected that Derrin knew she was telling the truth. She had, after all, no access to anyone else from that night as she had been outside all the time. And since being arrested, she and Mabel had been denied contact, for fear that one or the other would contrive a story. Therefore, Derrin knew she was telling the truth.

'He was behaving very erratically after that. Eleanor looked worried and Clara and Mabel were startled by his behaviour. I was close to the window, looking in from behind the large oak, a few feet from the house at one point. I was trying to get Mabel's attention, but all eyes were on Charles. Even mine, after a while, I suppose.'

'And what happened in the room after Charles was taken to be interviewed? Did you see anyone touch the brandy glasses, or decanter?' he asked.

'What outcome are you looking for, Inspector?' Susan said.

'You're very astute, Miss Erskine. Obviously one that doesn't end in someone being arrested for his murder.'

Susan nodded then she began to speak. She described a scenario where Charles had the arsenic vial in his pocket. Derrin remained silent while Susan spoke.

'You'll sign a statement to that fact?'

'Yes indeed. And you? You'll release me and Mabel?'

'That's a promise.'

* * *

Derrin was surprised when Mel opened the front door. It was early evening when he arrived at Avonby, just before supper.

'I hoped you'd arrive soon. Eat with me?' she said.

'I'd love that.'

Mel used the bellpull in the drawing room, and after delivering instructions to Williams for when she and the inspector would have supper, she poured them both a martini and sat down on the sofa beside him.

'I have a statement from Susan,' he said, getting to the point. 'She told me that Charles put the poison in the glasses and decanter himself. That then he drank from one of them. She claims he committed suicide.'

'And you believed her?' Mel said.

'She's signed a statement which I've accepted. It does wrap up the death in a very neat bow.'

Mel sipped her drink and was thoughtful. 'I wonder if I can live with this, knowing full well that he didn't kill himself, and who the real poisoner is.'

Derrin mirrored her, taking a gulp, rather than a sip, from the martini glass.

'And who is the real poisoner?' Derrin said.

Mel gave a small smile, 'If I tell you that it will put you in a very awkward position, professionally, won't it? Besides, I think you already know, just as I do.'

Derrin gave a small nod, and neither of them voiced what was forefront in their minds, that Clara had administered the poison, having been desperate to save her friend from the man's clutches. When Charles died, Clara, on the pretext of helping him, placed the vial on Charles's body while she was turning him into the recovery position.

But was the intent to kill? Mel wondered. *Probably not.*

The arsenic in the drink was the type used by ladies as a beauty enhancement. Mel liked to believe that Clara had merely wanted to make Charles ill, and then she might have been able to talk to Eleanor and persuade her to call off the wedding, for Mel remembered well the look of total shock when she announced that Charles was dead, and the colour had drained completely from Clara's face. Recalling her expression after time had percolated the memory inside her mind, Mel had known then that the death was really manslaughter, and not murder, reinforced, as it was, with every piece of evidence they had revealed since. Clara was a protective sort, her misguided saving of Mabel was the first indication, but so much that followed in those next hours proved how much she continued to be.

It was a juxtaposition that even now felt challenging, when Clara had heaped so much hate on Mel. But then Mel was not someone who would ever need saving, and perhaps that was why, with Clara's personality, they could never quite meet in the middle.

One thing was for sure, Mel's friendships from the past must, from now on, remain in the past, with Derrin being the only exception.

'There is another issue, of course,' Mel said. 'What will you tell Charles's parents? They will want a reason for their son's suicide.'

'According to the accounts we've had of Charles's behaviour, it won't be too difficult to convince them that his issues were severe enough to have led to this,' Derrin said.

'You've thought of everything then,' Mel said.

Epilogue

After supervising the restoration of the Turner and its return to its position over the fireplace in Jonathan's study, Mel walked the halls of Avonby, opening and examining every room in the house, to ensure that the standard of cleanliness and perfection would meet the ideals of Laura and Jonathan. They were due to return any time, and Mel had given a bitesize brief to Jonathan of what had happened, leaving out some significant pieces of information she had learnt about the origins of his acquisition of the Turner, and of his association with Susan during the war.

'Luckily the burglar was disturbed and never got away with the painting,' Mel told him. 'Inspector Bradley believes it was just an opportunist, someone who had sneaked into the house during the day unseen, and hid inside, waiting for an opportunity.'

Mel, Jonathan and Derrin had decided that Charles's death should be kept from Laura, as they all felt nothing would be gained from her learning that the thief, trapped inside and unable to escape, committed suicide instead of the scandal of being caught.

Having briefed the Avonby household never to mention the incident again, Mel and Derrin had continued their discussions with His Lordship, who was deliberately keeping Lady Laura away to give them the opportunity. As that night had been traumatic for all of them, the occupants of Avonby were more than willing to clear away the evidence and move on.

Mel knew she could rely on them, as they had come to rely on her.

Since Susan's statement had been made official, Mel had gone to the Mermaid Inn with Derrin, taking Charles's Rolls-Royce to give back to Frank. The meeting they had with each of the suspects, releasing them from their confinement and giving them a redacted version of what had gone on, was met with different responses. Eleanor was relieved to have any explanation, and Charles's apparent suicide meant an easier explanation for his parents to digest than them learning about his awful behaviour and subsequent murder. It was clear when Frank offered Eleanor a ride back to London, that much had occurred between the chauffeur and his boss's former fiancée during their stay at the Mermaid Inn and their tentative friendship looked set to blossom in another direction.

'I'm glad it's all resolved, old girl,' Michael said to Mel after she briefed him of the findings. 'I was impressed with how you handled yourself. And, well it's obvious how you feel about the Inspector, but if things don't work out there, you'll know where to find me.'

Mel had given a brief smile to Michael's comments but she knew there would never be anything between them, whatever went on between her and Derrin.

As for Clara, without a personal maid, she accepted a ride back with Eleanor and Frank, hoping she would never see Mabel or Susan again. And, Mel noted, with a huge amount of relief in her part on the news of Charles's death being declared suicide.

Mel, however, was left deflated when they had gone. She hoped she had made the right decision in letting Charles's killer go. Clara had shown no signs of being dangerous to anyone else, and she hoped that her assessment of the situation was correct. Only time would tell.

But for now, life at Avonby was perfect again. Mel and Derrin were reconnected, and it was, most certainly more than before, and with the Brigadier's permission, she was also going to be brought in as a consultant to work with him. Something that Mel was excited about, for she wanted to use those skills she had for the greater good. And nothing, not even her work at Avonby, gave her greater satisfaction than solving mysteries.

Acknowledgements

Massive thanks to my agent Camilla Shestopal, Editor Maxim Jakubowski, Jamie Hodder-Williams, Polly Halsey and the amazing team at Bedford Square. And to my husband David.

Keep reading for an excerpt of
Samantha Lee Howe's *The Bride in Funeral Clothing*

Prologue & Chapter 1

Mel Greenway Investigates: Book 3

PROLOGUE

LORELIE COURTNEY RAN HER FINGERS OVER THE antique lace of her wedding gown. The dress was perfect and fitted, as the saying went, like a glove. She'd had it altered from her grandmother's original design, which had been rather archaic, and not at all the fashion. Now the floor length dress was a modern calf length, with a neckline lower than her grandmother would have worn and the full sleeves had been cut down to three-quarters. She had bought a new much shorter veil, and the bulky Victorian paste jewellery her grandmother had passed down was going to remain in its box, unused, as Lorelie preferred more delicate, less ostentatious, ornaments that didn't drown her slender neck.

A far cry from funeral weeds, she thought as she examined the dress with a critical, but happy eye because even thought of the bad times couldn't bring her down today. Who would have thought that old yellow rag would wash up to white again, and could be moulded into this very splendid design?

Glancing at the fireplace, Lorelie noted the time on the small carriage clock. Her mother had loved the ornate timepiece above anything else: a reminder of her father's death. George Courtney had worked for the London, Midland and Scottish Railway when an engine caught fire, and George had received burns to over 90 per cent of his body. The injuries were fatal, and although he had lingered for a week or more, he never regained consciousness. A point Lorelie's mother, Emilia Courtney, had, deep-down, been grateful for.

But the railway officials hailed George a hero, and the clock was engraved and presented to her mother for posterity. It hadn't helped Emilia, who had become ill with an undiagnosed frailty soon after. Despite bringing in a fancy doctor from York, nothing helped. After a year-long deterioration, she followed her husband to an early grave.

The Avonby village locals had been sympathetic to the newly orphaned Lorelie at the age of 18 and rallied to make the transition easier. That was when Lorelie made some real friends. The general consensus was that Emilia had been pining for George, but Lorelie wasn't so sure. Even now, she wondered if the stress of living with her father had taken the life from her, and once he was gone, Emilia had nothing left: not even the will to live.

Too much black, Lorelie thought, recalling the misery the last few years had brought. So many losses. So much fear and pain. The war had changed everything for her and the villagers of Avonby. Even as she held the dress up for one final look, she could hardly imagine taking the plunge to wear white after so long. But then again, she must, it was her wedding.

Lorelie thought now of her fiancé, John. He was an upstanding young man, considerate, kind: all the attributes she wanted in a husband, and she loved him, more than perhaps anyone, even he, knew.

A dark cloud shadowed her mood as memories of the last two years and the strain she had been under, flooded back to blot the rush of happiness she had just been enjoying.

I deserve this, she thought pushing the anxiety away. *And nothing is going to spoil my day!*

Lorelie left the small sitting room and, taking the dress with her, opened the door to the kitchen. The glass of wine she had been saving all evening was still on the table, left there when her maid of honour Sandra had left. She picked it up now and, careful not to spill it, or to damage her dress, she walked up the stairs to her room.

She placed the glass by her bed and hung the dress on the outside of the door to her wardrobe giving it one last brush with her hand. Then she took off her robe and climbed into bed.

She sat looking at the room as the light from the lamp cast warm shadows over her few possessions. She picked up the glass. Sipping the wine, determined to finish the glass in the hope that it would relax her enough to sleep as Sandra had said it would.

This would be the last time she would sleep alone, and the thought brought back that light-hearted romantic feeling that she had when thinking of her future with John and what would happen in the marital bed that was beyond the few kisses they had so far shared. Though even now, a small voice inside her head questioned if she was sure she was doing the right thing.

Lorelie quelled her internal noise, shutting the door that tried to leak suspicion into her mind. *I am.*

John was a good man. Nothing like some others she had come across. She wouldn't have let him into her life if she had any doubt that his behaviour might change. No, it wasn't there. Not a mean streak in his tall, broad shouldered, handsome frame.

Lorelie yawned. Her heart full of excitement but tiredness from the wedding preparations was finally catching up. She took a further sip of the wine, then placed the half full glass back down on the bedside table, before turning the lamp off.

Lorelie lay down and closed her eyes. Before long, she was floating in a vision of the expected day, her dream full of church, bigger and more impressive than it was. There were beautiful flowers all along the aisle. Lorelie began to walk towards John standing at the end, though it seemed that she never quite made it to the altar. She sank down, deeper, and the dream became something else. A thought that looped through her, causing more anxiety.

She thought she heard something. A sound like breaking glass. She opened her eyes briefly, the dreams still floating in her mind. She reached for the wine glass, half sat, swigging more. Before collapsing back down, sweat dripping from her forehead, as though she had a fever.

The tiredness swooped back and she began to fall again, a swirl of thoughts, fears and phobias whirled into one. She tossed and turned in her fever dream, tormented by demons long gone.

A hand clamped hard over Lorelie's mouth and nose, pulling her from her tortured sleep. In shock, Lorelie tried to yelp but large fingers blocked not only the sound, but her airways. Lungs heaving for breath, head bursting with the pain, she struggled against her captor.

Oxygen deprived and confused, she was pulled from her bed. Her half dazed mind heard the glass tip over beside the bed, as it screamed one last thought before the lack of air took its toll; *I didn't hear him!* Then, Lorelie slipped into oblivion.

In the dark, the bulky figure wrapped Lorelie up in the bedsheet, then hefted her body up and over one broad shoulder, carrying her from the room. As the man passed the wardrobe, he brushed against the wedding dress, knocking it sideways. The dress rocked and the soft fabric slipped free and fell, pooling on the floor in a crumpled heap.

1

THE QUIET COUNTRY ROAD WAS DISTURBED BY a loud roar as Lady Melinda Greenway turned her motorbike into the sleepy village of Avonby. It was seven in the morning, and Mel was heading to the small bakery where she had ordered a cake as a birthday surprise for Avonby Hall's dedicated cook, Mrs Weston. Mel had been planning a secret party for Mrs Weston for a few months. She was conscious of how little time the cook spent on herself, focused as she was on taking care of everyone else. The treat was long overdue and Mel had managed to keep the whole thing under wraps, which was something of a miracle in the gossip mill of the estate.

Mel passed a row of houses, which included Inspector Derrin Bradley's cottage, but her mind wasn't on Derrin, or their confusing relationship, that day. Instead, she kept her focus on the road, driving past the local tavern, The Mermaid Inn, and carrying on to the bakery, before pulling the noisy motorbike to the kerb at the front of the shop.

The bakery wasn't due to open for another half an hour, but Mel had arranged to come early to avoid being seen.

Turning the engine off, Mel pressed the kickstand down with her foot, before removing her helmet, which she hung by the straps on the arm of the bike. Climbing off, she reached into the box that was secured on the back, and took out the tray of eggs she had brought from the estate.

The door opened as she walked towards the shop and there was a faint ring of the bell as Mel came face to face with the shop owner, Margery Ackroyd, a woman in her 40s who had taken the business over when her husband Arthur was drafted. Arthur never came back from the war, declared missing in action, but Margery had sustained the shop throughout, since she had always been the main baker anyway. She had managed to adapt recipes even during the shortages, and the village respected and appreciated her. She was an astute business woman and appeared to be content even though she worked the bakery with only the help of a local girl. Mel knew she was training the young woman to take on more of the baking as well serving over the counter. She had no children of her own and rumour had it that she took a motherly interest in her apprentice.

Mel held out the eggs, 'I thought you could use these.'

'Come in,' Margery said taking the tray. 'And thank you! These are *very* welcome!'

Margery closed the door behind them, setting off the sharp ring once more. Then placed the eggs on the counter next to a cake box, which she proceeded to open.

'There it is,' Margery said.

Inside the box was a beautiful round cake, covered with yellow icing and decorated with small purple, edible flowers, with *Happy Birthday* piped in purple icing across the top.

'It's wonderful!' Mel said. 'How much do I owe you?'

Margery shook her head, 'Nothing. Mrs Weston deserves this. She's always been a kind soul. During the war she let me have her personal rations of flour, you know? She said it was more important that I could continue to offer my bread to the village.'

'It doesn't surprise me,' Mel said.

A wailing sound echoed in the distance and grew louder as a police car sped by the shop, lights flashing and mechanical siren rising and falling with a sonorous scream. Both women turned to look through the window.

'Good heavens!' Margery said. 'What's all this?'

Mel knew this sleepy village barely ever had any such disturbance, and so she was aware that something bad must have happened.

'I'll go and see,' she said as the car came to a halt down the street.

Mel opened the door and looked out. On the opposite side to Derrin's cottage two police officers got out of the car and started talking to a woman standing by the garden gate of one of the other cottages. She was gesturing wildly, pointing at the house, and to an upstairs window.

Drawn by the noise, Derrin emerged and crossed the road to speak to the uniformed officers. He wasn't wearing his coat, but was dressed in his smart work trousers, shirt and braces, though he hadn't put a tie on yet.

'Inspector Bradley is there now,' Mel said to Margery who had come to look.

'That's the Courtney cottage,' Margery said.

'Who is that talking to the police?' Mel asked.

'Sandra Ainley. She's Lorelie Courtney's maid of honour. She's supposed to pick up the wedding cake this morning. Lorelie's wedding is this afternoon. I wonder what's wrong?'

Mel watched as Derrin went into the cottage with Sandra. He didn't emerge until sometime later and by then several villagers had come outside of their homes to watch the proceedings.

A small queue of people started to form outside the shop as it was almost opening time, but all eyes were watching the street and the police.

A police constable took up point at the gate as a cordon was put in place and this fact made Mel's stomach lurch. Her first thought had been a break in, but now it was looking far more serious.

'I'll be back,' she said slipping out of the shop, and leaving the cake behind on the counter.

Mel walked towards the cottage and stopped just short of the barrier. The cottage was a small two up, two down, and Mel examined everything she could see from where she was. The exterior of the house looked normal, but the gate where the constable stood, was hanging off its hinges as though a violent gust of wind had smashed it against the low, stone, garden wall.

Mel heard the raised and panicked voice of Sandra coming from inside, her thick Yorkshire accent blurred as she spoke. Derrin emerged from the house with the woman, and Mel saw Sandra was wearing a pastel dress, too dressy for this early in the morning and assumed it must be her maid of honour outfit.

'She's not just *left*,' she said, agitated. 'You saw that window!'

'Please be calm Miss Ainley,' Derrin said. Then he saw Mel standing on the pavement, next to the cordon. 'Wait here. And as I said, don't touch anything.'

Derrin left Sandra and went to the garden gate and passed the constable.

'Come with me,' he said to Mel.

They headed across the road to his cottage.

'What's happened?' Mel asked when they were far enough away from the spectators to be overheard.

'Lorelie Courtney is missing. She was getting married today but when Miss Ainley arrived to help her, she found the front door ajar, and no sign of the bride. Her first thought was cold feet, but then she found the back door was open, and the kitchen window broken. There are signs of a struggle up in the bedroom.'

'A kidnapping?' Mel asked.

'Or a murder,' Derrin said. 'Hard to tell at this point.'

'No traces of blood inside?' Mel asked.

'None that was obvious, but I haven't looked properly as I'm waiting for CID to arrive before we gather evidence.'

'Can I take a look?'

Derrin glanced over at the cottage and the people milling around. 'Eyes are on us. I can't do anything until after the team does their job.'

Mel nodded. 'Let me know if I can help.'

She left Derrin and walked back to the shop. By then, Margery was in full swing serving her early morning customers. Mel took the cake from the counter top and left before Margery saw her. She didn't want to be asked any questions as she knew everything Derrin had told her was confidential.

Stowing the cake in the box on the back of the bike. Mel placed her helmet back on, then got on the bike, started the engine, and drove out of the village.

Mel's drive home was slower because she was worried about damaging the cake. Instead of going in through the back door of Avonby Hall as she usually did, she pulled the bike up to the front of the house to unload unseen. As usual the butler, Mr Williams, was looking out for her from his post, and as she walked up the steps, cake box in hand, the door to Avonby Hall opened.

'Lady Melinda!' Williams said. Despite Mel's constant requests for him to just call her 'Mel', the butler would never drop his formal address. 'Let me take that for you.'

He took the box, and hurried away to hide the cake as prearranged with Mrs Felman, the housekeeper, in her private quarters; a place that neither Mrs Weston, or any other occupants of Avonby Hall, ever went. The cake would remain there for a few days, until the cook's birthday.

As Mel turned to go back outside, the phone rang in the hallway and Mel, knowing that Williams was preoccupied, went to answer.

'Avonby Hall,' Mel said. 'Who is calling please?'

'Mel! Glad it's you! It's Derrin. I've spoken to the brigadier. I've proposed you as a consultant. Can you come to the station this afternoon to meet him?'

Mel had a surge of excitement at the prospect of this opportunity. Derrin had mentioned some time ago that he wanted to put her forward, but she hadn't believed it would happen. Not because of Derrin's failure to keep a promise, but more because she had so many rejections in the past.

Mel's mind slipped back into one such situation, when she had interviewed for a mechanic job soon after leaving the army. She had arrived at the garage and the head mechanic had merely shaken his head, shocked when he realised that her application, under M. Greenway, was not the man he was expecting.

'Not today, Miss. Not here,' he had said.

'Let me show you what I can,' Mel suggested. 'I'm every bit as good as any of your mechanics.'

'There's no way I'm sending you in that workshop with the men. They'd think I've lost my mind,' he said.

'But the army trained me!'

'Yeah. But you can find a husband now, love. Leave the working to us men,' the mechanic led her to the door and all but pushed her out. After which, Mel heard an eruption of laughter.

Mel had been furious by the assumption that marriage was all women were fit for but there was nothing she could do. This was just one of many incidents she later injured.

Even so, the times were changing. Women were finding a place in the police force, though their roles were often more admin, or victim support. And no real detective work was ever put their way. Derrin had said that the brigadier was more progressive, and now, with the prospect of meeting him looming, she hoped he was right.

'I'll make sure I can. What time?'

'Fifteen hundred hours,' Derrin said, then promptly hung up.

'Who was that?' Lady Laura said from down the hallway.

Mel put down the receiver and turned to see the disdainful face of her second cousin's wife, Lady Laura Greenway.

Laura was frowning as she surveyed Mel's clothing of a male leather jacket, breeches and thick boots. Unsuitable to her eye. Now she ran her hands down her own, expensive day dress of pink satin as if making a comparison between Mel and herself.

'It was…I forgot something in the village, so I must go out again later,' Mel said ignoring the judgement on Laura's face.

'Good morning Mel,' said Lord Jonathan, Mel's second cousin and the recent custodian of Avonby Hall. 'Do you have time to go over the progress of the vegetable farm and the plans for the new barn this morning?'

'Yes, of course,' Mel said, grateful for the interruption from Laura's awkward questions and scrutiny. 'Give me half an hour to stow my bike and change.'

'I'll be in my study,' Jonathan said.

Mel hurried back out of the front door, and, mounting the motorbike once more, she started the engine and drove it around the house to the large garage.

Pulling in, Mel saw the chauffeur, Henry, washing the Rolls Royce.

'Morning Henry. I need a ride into York later. An appointment at three,' Mel said. 'Can you take me?'

'Another shopping trip, Lady Mel?' Henry asked.

Mel gave the astute driver a smile which he followed with a cheeky wink.

'I'll be ready for you at two,' Henry said. 'As it happens, his Lordship has already told me he's not going out today.'

Mel left Henry to finish washing the car and headed to the back door. She felt no guilt at bringing the chauffeur into her small conspiracy because over the past year Mel had done a great deal of bonding with the employees of Avonby Hall. A thought that kept her going during the tough times with her cousin and his wife, Laura, who had made little secret of the fact that she didn't really want Mel living with them, and didn't see her at all as part of the family. Despite this, Laura tolerated her because Jonathan on the other hand had shown a great deal of appreciation for Mel's skills. Mel was useful. Not least because she was trained as a mechanic in the army during the war, but also because of her knowledge of horticulture. From the day she arrived at Avonby, a virtual pauper, homeless, and unable to find work, Mel had worked hard to turn the Avonby estate into a productive and working vegetable farm. The farm now supplied their entire family and employees with fresh produce, but also sold the spare produce in markets in and around South Yorkshire. They had recently completed the building of two huge greenhouses and the estate's old retainer, head gardener Joseph, and his wife, Rosa, were taking great pleasure in growing food all year round in this protected and warm environment. As a result, the finances of the estate had vastly improved, a situation that Laura couldn't really complain about.

For all that this was true, Mel still felt she was walking on eggshells with her cousin's wife. Relying as she was on Jonathan's discretionary support, and meagre allowance, Mel didn't take anything for granted. Even though she was useful, she understood that no one was indispensable, which meant she was always slightly insecure about her position at Avonby. A vulnerability that she knew Laura would exploit at the drop of a hat, given the opportunity.

Mel opened the back door and went into the boot room, pulling off her boots and jacket, which she hung up with the other outdoor coats. Then she slipped into the house, skirting around the kitchen and climbed the service stairs up to the second floor.

About the Author

Photo credit © Anne-Marie Bickerton

Samantha Lee Howe began her professional writing career in 2007 and has been working as a freelance writer for small, medium and large publishers ever since. She is a multi-award-winning screenwriter and a *USA Today* bestselling author.

Samantha's breakaway debut psychological thriller, *The Stranger in Our Bed*, was released in February 2020 with HarperCollins imprint, One More Chapter. The book rapidly became a *USA Today* bestseller, and has now been turned into a feature film for the USA, Canada, China, the UK and various countries in Europe. It won Best Thriller at the National Film Awards.

Samantha lives in South Yorkshire with her husband, historian, writer and publisher, David J Howe, and their cat Skye. She is the proud mother of a lovely daughter called Linzi.